ARKHAM KNIGHT

THE RIDDLER'S GAMBIT

ARKHAM KNIGHT

THE RIDDLER'S GAMBIT

ALEX IRVINE

TITAN BOOKS

BATMAN: ARKHAM KNIGHT – THE RIDDLER'S GAMBIT
Print edition ISBN: 9781783292509
E-book edition ISBN: 9781783292516

Published by Titan Books
A division of Titan Publishing Group Ltd
144 Southwark Street, London SE1 0UP

First edition: June 2015
10 9 8 7 6 5 4 3 2 1

 rocksteady™

A CIP catalogue record for this title is available from the British Library.

Printed and bound and bound by CPI Group (UK) Ltd, Croydon, CR0 4YY

Bull's Eye

by **Rafael Del Toro**, GothamGazette.com

I've never made any secret of my disdain for the so-called Batman, and I'm not going to start now.

It's been months since we saw him screeching through the streets of our fair city in his batcar, or swooping around in Arkham City attacking the TYGER agents charged with keeping the civil order, or doing any of the other things he does to take the law into his own hands. In other words, it's been months since Batman has told us—the people of Gotham City—that we're not good enough or smart enough to take care of ourselves.

Hooray!

Let's hope he's on a long, long vacation. Maybe he decided to start a new career as a baker of artisanal doughnuts. Whatever happened to him, we can only hope that all of his Bat-doodads are gathering dust in his mother's basement. After what went down in Arkham City, it would be best if Gotham City never saw a costumed freak, ever again—*any* costumed freak.

Am I the only one who's noticed that he seems to make everything worse instead of better? He shows up with his Batgear and his Bat-Attitude, and the bad guys come crawling out of the woodwork to test themselves against him. Well, on

ALEX IRVINE

behalf of the people of Gotham City, I say:

NO THANKS, BATMAN. WE'RE GOOD.

We don't need you giving the criminal lunatics another reason to improve their chops. The Joker's gone, and this whole mess with Hugo Strange took out a lot more of your year-round Halloween party, too. *Good.* If there are any more psychos out there, let them keep their costumes in their closets. Let them do something normal.

Like rob banks.

The Gotham City PD can handle that.

Take a vacation, Batman. Make it a long one. Let Gotham City see what it's like when we don't have someone out there setting himself up as the perfect bat-winged target. Enough people died at Arkham City.

You see, Batman hasn't been around for months now. Anyone else notice how quiet it's been?

Refreshing, isn't it?

So if you're reading this in your Bat-tub on your iBat, or sitting in your Bat-kitchen noshing on some Bat-toast, do us all a favor. Stay there. Stay home. Let the normal people work it out. Aren't you tired of being a vigilante?

We're tired of being collateral damage in vigilante wars.

Seriously. Stay home. We'll take it from here. We good?

Are we *Bat-good*?

Glad to hear it.

1

The Riddler waited.

He watched.

He observed, and recorded, and when he had seen enough, he began to form his observations into plans.

How to transform a joke into a riddle?

He sought the perfect spot to begin building on his previous machinations, and found it in the subterranean ruin of Wonder City. Once the city's lord and master, Rā's al Ghūl no longer factored in, since Rā's was dead, his Lazarus Pit destroyed. Talia, the daughter of the demon, had vanished, and even the Joker was gone, up in smoke—part of him mixed with the ever-present miasma of criminality that hung over Gotham City even in fair weather. The rest had been flushed, merging with the water supply system.

Thus he had become a permanent part of life's fabric—no doubt the tiny particles of him that had escaped the crematorium had settled on the streets, the buildings, and even the denizens of the metropolis. In the truest of terms, one could not conceive of Gotham City without the Joker.

That, as the Riddler saw it, was the problem.

He, Edward Nigma, would be the solution.

There was a vacuum at the very pinnacle of Gotham City's hierarchy of crime, and it was well known that nature abhorred a vacuum. So, too, did the Riddler. Therefore he would fill it.

Another man might embark on a campaign of killings, he mused, *or showy attacks on Gotham City landmarks.* But that wasn't the Riddler's style. Instead, he viewed the situation the way a chess player viewed a board. There were three stages of chess. *Funny, isn't it, how so many things are conceived of as happening in threes,* he thought.

Perhaps…

But no. *First things first.*

The opening ten moves of a chess game, when played properly, were more or less pre-programmed because all of the options were so well known. If white played pawn to king 4, black wasn't going to answer by advancing his queen's rook's pawn. Why? Because that was a sure way to lose.

No, any competent player knew the ways to direct the early part of a game along predictable paths, thus establishing a level playing field, and a reasonable probability of success.

The same principle applied to the endgame. There were defined paths there, as well. A king shepherding a pawn down the board against another king, or a rook sectioning the board to corner and defeat the enemy. Or the sacrifice that broke the castled king's line of pawns, and opened the way for the diagonal strike of a bishop.

One could see these stratagems coming several moves in advance, which was why so few *real* games ended in checkmate. The master player, recognizing the inevitable, always resigned.

At both the beginning and end, a chess game was... predictable. But what about the in between? The midgame, where possibilities multiplied faster than the human mind could follow? That was where surprises could happen, and it was where games were won or lost.

So first the Riddler framed the plan for his opening moves. They would involve building, which took time, but that was all right. The time was there. The city was still reeling from the explosive disintegration of Protocol 10 and the regime of Hugo Strange. Things were quiet. The Riddler would be quiet, too. He would work behind the scenes, and wouldn't implement his plan until it was ready.

There would be the need for allies, and there would be those who opposed him. He drew up lists of potential partners and of likely rivals. The entire roster of Gotham City's underworld would be given roles to play as pieces on the Riddler's board. He began to structure a series of puzzles, each of which would hinge on the nature of a chosen ally. But he couldn't stop there—that would be too easy! The complexities had to be maddening to the point of distraction! So he added another layer to the riddles, interweaving them into...

Oh, yes, he thought. *That will be brilliant.*

Nigma finalized his list of potential allies and began to reach out to them, designing each communication in a way that was sure to intrigue. From Wonder City, the Riddler sent out emissaries, and, as responses came back, he built his network. He recruited people he knew he could trust—and could dispose of without compunction.

He already knew how it would be done.

Some of them he brought down to Wonder City, and the sight of it amazed them—streets and buildings, many of them constructed in the nineteenth century, fallen into decay and ruin—located in the semidarkness of the underground. The remnants of a bygone era, of a singular vision, all surrounding the ruins of the Wonder Tower— once the Demon's seat of power.

Few residents of Gotham City even knew it existed.

He put his growing army to work, paid them well, and conveniently neglected to mention that they would have a little bonus coming, once this project was up and running. As for those to whom he did not reach out, they would have to be dealt with in some way. Engaged, placated, or simply removed—whichever was more conducive to the success of the plan.

Ra's al Ghūl and the Joker had cast a long shadow, but Nigma had been preparing for years to step out into a spotlight of his own making. The way was clear—this was his chance. He would not let it pass.

Of course, there was the Batman…

Too often he had crossed swords with the so-called Dark Knight, pitting his puzzles against the vigilante's wits. Not long ago he had challenged Batman using specially constructed rooms, each designed around a specific theme. His opponent had surmounted the challenges fairly easily, as Riddler had anticipated he would—but past had been prelude. His observation of Batman's tactics had led to a new generation of traps, more elaborate than before.

These would not require a human presence in order to be deadly. There would be a series of them, each self-contained but contributing an element to a larger puzzle. Each trap would be more intricate, wearing his foe down, culminating in a revelation that would destroy him—if not physically, then with the sheer knowledge of what he had lost.

The final trap would be a masterpiece.

Would Batman resign? That was the real question. Would he know he was defeated, and tip over his king? Or would he fight to the very end, proving both his valor and his stupidity?

Either would result in sweet, sweet victory.

Having gathered his resources, he had to find a location for his puzzle. He searched through both Arkham City and Wonder City, taking stock of what remained of each, and found a wealth of raw materials ripe for the picking. Hugo Strange's TYGER minions had left behind a motherlode of equipment and material. Rā's al Ghūl's robotic wonders, dubbed the mechanical guardians, still stood their silent watch, waiting for someone to return to them a sense of purpose. Nigma would use it all. He would *improve* upon it. He would recreate it all and construct the puzzle to end all puzzles... which was to say, the puzzle that would end Batman.

He would need help—he wasn't such an egomaniac that he thought he could do it on his own. If he wanted to step into the vacuum left by the Joker…

No.

For decades the face of crime in Gotham City had been insane, wearing a mad rictus and green hair. The Riddler had no desire to step into those shoes. Like all of the resources he was procuring, he would remake the role. Gone would be the lunacy, to be replaced by something a little… classier. In the way a riddle was classier than a joke. Jokes relied on a brief incongruity, a momentary collision of expectation and reality. They stimulated the low behaviors of human nature—not for nothing did they call it a belly laugh.

A good riddle demanded intellect and reasoning.

Fate had handed him the perfect opportunity. More than ever, he had the resources he needed to establish the Riddler's pre-eminence among Gotham City's criminal hierarchy, in a way that would be incontestable. The chaos he would bring would make them forget the Clown Prince of Crime, once and for all.

A delusion of grandeur?

So be it, he thought. All thoughts of grandeur were delusions… until one made them real.

The corner of the steel mill gaped in a ruin of stone and metal, evidence of the explosion that had partially destroyed the building. Like the remains of the building, the armored construct they had brought up from below was scorched, but whereas the mill was inoperable, the mechanical guardian appeared to be intact.

Looking like something out of a steampunk dream,

the tick-tock men were the perfect representatives of a technology well ahead of its time. They had been built ostensibly to protect the denizens of Rā's al Ghūl's domain, when in truth they represented his despotic control. Round eyes were dull and lifeless now, but soon they would glow green again with artificial life.

Perfect, thought Nigma. *If enough of them have survived, they'll be perfect.* Immediately he contacted the teams he had combing the abandoned streets, instructing them to find the rest.

Brutish strength combined with the elegance of the gambit—it was the mark of a true genius. Anyone could achieve power with a gun or a knife. The perfect riddle commanded its recipient to act in one way, and one way only. There was no greater mastery—and that was what the Riddler sought to achieve over Batman—absolute mastery.

Here in the ruined splendor of Arkham City.

2

Bruce Wayne mistrusted the calm.

Gotham City had been quiet in the months since the Joker's death. It wasn't in the city's nature to be calm. There was always something brewing. Everyone from the ordinary street thugs to the organized crime families seemed to be less active than usual. It was almost as if the city was mourning the madman, honoring his twisted legacy by abstaining from violence and chaos for a time.

It seemed bizarre to contemplate, given the terror the Joker had inflicted on Gotham City over the past decades, but there it was. Facts, as the saying went, were stubborn things—and the fact was that Batman hadn't seen any of the rogues' gallery of costumed opponents since the cremation. Whether they were in mourning, or waiting to see how the power vacuum would be filled, that remained to be seen.

On a more personal level, yet just as disturbingly irrational as the city's apparent grief, Bruce was grappling with the psychological effect of the Joker's death. They had been mortal enemies for so long that he couldn't help but experience a kind of loss, twisted though it might seem.

He was also dealing with the physical effects of the battles in and around Wonder City. As superbly conditioned as he was, even Bruce Wayne was getting a little older. He didn't recover as quickly as he once had.

The fortunate lull in criminal activity was giving him time to rest his battered body, and to deal with essential maintenance of his unique equipment. He was spending a lot of time in the Batcave, assisted by Robin and Alfred. They replenished supplies, repaired damaged components, and replaced any that couldn't be repaired. Regular orders for parts and tools went to Lucius Fox, CEO of Wayne Enterprises and an engineering genius in his own right.

When the lull ended—and he was certain it would—Batman would be ready.

"If I may say so, you're not your usual self, Master Bruce," Alfred said.

"How's that, Alfred?"

"Well, sir. You're never a loquacious man, but in recent days you've been positively taciturn. An inward turn of mind, it seems. I must inquire: Is all well?"

"As well as it gets," Bruce replied. "I don't trust this quiet."

"Me neither," Robin chimed in from under the Batmobile, "but we don't have to trust it to take advantage of it."

"True enough, Master Tim. True enough," Alfred said. He waited for a moment, then when the silence became awkward, he climbed the stairs and left the Batcave.

"He's right, you know," Tim Drake said.

"He usually is," Bruce responded.

"You're not yourself."

"Who else would I be, Robin?" Bruce said, trying to be flip. "It's nothing that should concern you."

Yet Robin and Alfred were right—there had been a real change in him. Other people might not have noticed it, but they knew him too well. He had to admit to himself that it was there. The Joker's death was affecting him in unexpected ways.

Was he grieving? Could that be it?

It seemed ridiculous, but when you lost someone who was a part of your life—even if that person had spent decades trying to kill you—perhaps it was natural to feel that loss.

Maybe his condition was physical. He felt strong, he felt quick, but he also felt… unwell, in a nebulous, unidentifiable way. He'd been writing it off as lingering effects of the Joker's toxins, and that still seemed the most likely cause.

Whatever the source, four months after the collapse of Protocol 10, something was wrong. Sooner or later he would shake it off. Until he did, however, it would continue to frustrate him. He wasn't comfortable with a problem he couldn't solve, didn't like a foe he couldn't fight—couldn't even identify.

"I'm fine," Bruce said. "And even if I wasn't, Gotham City doesn't care if Batman isn't feeling up to par." He hoped that would end the conversation, and got his wish when the private line from Commissioner Gordon's office pinged.

"Commissioner," he said, activating the voice-only system.

"Batman, glad I caught you," Gordon said. "I need you to come down here. We've got a… a situation, and could use your expertise."

"I'll be there," he said, than he broke off the call.

Within minutes he was suited up, and moments after that he was in the Batmobile. Before long the armored vehicle was roaring through Gotham City—past Theater Row, through Chinatown, skirting Amusement Mile and the casino. People turned to watch. Some cheered. Some cursed and made obscene gestures.

In other words, everything was normal.

Eleven minutes after leaving the Batcave he arrived at the Gotham City Police Department headquarters and left the Batmobile parked on the street. It was a conscious decision on his part. After the exposure of Hugo Strange's TYGER conspiracy, four months before, he'd determined to make himself more visible. People needed to know that someone was watching—and not just watching, but taking action.

There were still plenty of people who considered Batman a dangerous vigilante, but more of them viewed him as a warrior on the side of law and order. At times it seemed like a slim majority, but he'd spent years building it. He wasn't going to let it slip now.

It seemed to be paying off, since criminal activity was at its lowest level in years. There was still tension in the city, though. It didn't feel like a place where people went about their business freely and without fear. It felt as if there was another shoe about to drop.

Batman had long ago learned to trust his instincts, yet he also had to acknowledge that he was edgy. Was he jumping at shadows?

Something wasn't right.

Whatever it was, however, he had to relegate it to the back of his mind. He made a point of walking in the front door of GCPD headquarters. People would see that and recognize Batman as an ally of the police, one who responded when Commissioner Gordon summoned him.

Protocol 10 had shaken the civil order—almost destroyed it, in fact. Hundreds of Arkham City's inmates had died, many of them innocents who had run afoul of Hugo Strange's lunatic plan. Amidst the violence and chaos, a number of genuinely dangerous criminals had escaped. Batman had been rounding them up as fast as he could, but it had proven difficult. His adversaries had been keeping quiet. Too quiet.

Gordon was in the atrium. The commissioner looked worn and rumpled, as always. The cares of his position had aged him prematurely. So had his years of battling powerful interests who wanted the police to become their cat's-paws—personal enforcers, rather than representatives of a law that applied equally to all.

They had had their differences, Batman and Gordon, yet he knew the commissioner was one of the few people in Gotham City who would always do what he thought was right, no matter the political cost, no matter what ridicule he had to endure from the media… no matter what. In that way, Batman and Gordon were the same, and that was what bound them together in the battle against entrenched corruption and vice. Each could count on the other to be an ally, and Gordon was willing to accept the consequences of that alliance.

The commissioner reached out to shake Batman's hand.

"Glad you came," he said.

"You know you can count on me, Commissioner," Batman said. Gordon's grip was strong, and he looked slightly less worn than he had in recent months. Maybe things *were* changing.

Quincy Sharp was mayor, and that wasn't necessarily good news for Gordon. But with TYGER gone, the GCPD was no longer stuck on the sidelines. When under the influence of Hugo Strange, Sharp had replaced the police with TYGER, leaving Gordon powerless. It was a tribute to the man's character that he had continued to do his job, even with the odds stacked against him.

More remarkable still, in Batman's mind, was the fact that the commissioner continued to associate with known vigilantes. There was a certain kind of law enforcement that could not wear a badge. Gordon recognized it, even if he didn't openly endorse Batman's tactics. It was the mark of a good man, a strong man, to admit that the world didn't always operate according to his ethics.

"What is it you need me to see?" Batman asked.

Gordon left the atrium, motioning for him to follow. He walked to the back of the building and up a rear fire stairwell.

"We keep a private conference room back here," he said over his shoulder. "It seemed like a good place to... well, I'll just show you."

On the third floor, down a dimly lit corridor, Gordon unlocked a door and stood aside so Batman could enter. The room was a simple rectangle, perhaps twelve feet by twenty, with blank walls and no windows. A table and chairs occupied the center of the floor space. The table was empty except for a single envelope.

"This was inside of an unmarked package. Once I'd pulled it out, I didn't open it," Gordon said. "As soon as I saw who it was addressed to, I brought it here myself, and contacted you."

Batman approached the table and assessed the envelope from arm's length. It was addressed plainly, in block capitals.

JOKER
C/O COMMISSIONER JAMES GORDON
GOTHAM CITY POLICE DEPARTMENT

What he saw caused him to suppress a shudder that ran through his body, and he took a moment to focus. There was no return address, and no postmark. Someone had slipped this envelope into the departmental mail system without using the post office—a fact that in and of itself was disturbing.

Batman filed the fact away.

"You wore gloves?" he asked.

"No point," Gordon replied. "By the time I'd picked it up, and saw the address…" His voice trailed off, and he shrugged. "After I put it in here, I called a decontamination crew. They doused me, and they're in my office right now testing for toxins. Next they're going to survey the mail room. I've got my shipping manager interviewing everyone who works down there, to see what they might know. She's good people. I've got someone checking the security footage, too."

"Probably a good idea," Batman said, though he didn't

mention that it was probably too late. If there was a toxin on the envelope, there was no telling how many people had handled it since its entry into the building. The subtle approach wasn't exactly the Joker's style, but he hadn't been above employing it.

If, Batman thought, *the Joker had anything to do with this at all.*

He had been dead four months—Gordon had personally supervised the cremation. This envelope hadn't been sitting in the GCPD mailroom all that time. So either one of his many minions had sent it… or it was a message from another of Gotham City's villains.

"My first guess would be that one of the Joker's henchmen sent it," Batman said. "It wouldn't be unusual for him to have rigged something to be done in the event of his death. Especially given the circumstances of his death. He knew he wasn't going to live—not without the antidote."

"I was thinking along the same lines," Gordon said, peering at the package. "So what do we do?"

"Where the Joker's involved, we hedge our bets." Batman unclipped a small device from his Utility Belt and turned it on. It was a portable X-ray machine customized to detect the presence of most common explosives and toxins, and even radioactivity. He held it out over the envelope, and an image appeared on its screen.

"It's a USB drive," he said. "There doesn't appear to be anything else inside." He checked the readings. "You can call off your decontamination protocol."

"Are you sure?" Gordon asked. "I'm responsible for people's lives here."

"So am I," Batman said. "I don't see anything but an envelope. But I'll have to open it to be sure." He reached for the envelope.

Instinctively Gordon backed up a step.

The envelope had a pull tab. Batman pulled it, and the end of the envelope tore open without incident. He gave it a shake and the USB drive clattered onto the tabletop. It was plain black, with a translucent plastic cap over the end that would plug into a computer. The stores of Gotham City sold these by the thousands.

"Could someone have sent this, not knowing the Joker was gone?" Gordon said. "That doesn't make sense."

Batman nodded. "I agree. It's more likely that before he died, he arranged to have it sent," he added. "Whoever sent it, though, they wanted us to see what's on the USB drive. What better way to make sure it would get to us than to address it to that madman."

"So it's a game—we're being played." Gordon looked down at the drive. "I'll bring in some of our computer people, if you think it's safe. Have them take a look."

"I'll take it myself," Batman said. "If there are fail-safes, I'll get past them, and, if there's any sort of virus on this drive, I'll take the risk." He picked up the tiny object. "There's always the possibility that the drive can only be read once. If that's the case, my system will capture whatever's there before it can disappear."

He could see that Gordon was conflicted—as the commissioner of police, he was used to being in charge. Yet he knew this was the best way to proceed—Batman's equipment was state-of-the-art, as compared to the police systems, which had been cutting edge sometime in the last century.

"Okay," he said after a pause, "but you share everything with me. That has to be the deal."

"Understood," Batman said. He dropped the USB drive into a pocket on his Utility Belt. "I'll be in touch as soon as I know anything."

"You know the way out," Gordon said.

"I know a number of ways out, as a matter of fact," he replied wryly. "But no, you don't need to escort me. I'm sure you have better things to do." With that, he turned to leave.

"Do I ever." Gordon sighed. "But don't leave me hanging, Batman. I saw the Joker burn, watched it with my own eyes as they flushed the remains. This, though… it's got me edgy. Let me know what you find out."

"You'll be the first to know," Batman said from the doorway. Then he was gone.

It was time to touch base with Oracle.

RyderReport.com

Posted by JKB
Wednesday, 9:46 a.m.

Hot one. The Batmobile's been spotted at GCPD headquarters. Batman himself went inside. He didn't talk to anyone on his way in, and didn't appear to talk to anyone on his way out, either.

But the *Ryder Report* has its sources, friends, oh yes we do, and not all of them are chasing leads for Jack's TV show. We're hearing from inside police headquarters that Commissioner Gordon himself called the Batman in. They met for more than twenty minutes somewhere in the building. No one else was present.

When Batman came out and left in the Batmobile, he wasn't carrying anything that our sources could see. Apparently Commissioner Gordon hasn't spoken to the department about their discussion, either.

What was the topic? No one seems to know, but there were rumbles about something strange in the GCPD mail. That's unconfirmed, and for all we know the commissioner just missed having Batman around. Maybe he called him in for brioche and coffee.

Nah. Ryder's Readers know something is up, and you better believe the *Ryder Report* does, too. We'll be on this story going forward. Batman's gone back to wherever he goes, but it won't be long before we get more on this story.

Stay tuned.

Hit your refresh button.

Keep this tab open.

Jack will follow up on his show later this afternoon. By then, the odds are good that there'll be a whole lot more to talk about.

3

On the way back to the cave, Batman contacted Oracle and recounted what had occurred at GCPD headquarters. Robin and Alfred were waiting when he arrived, but he didn't say a word as he headed straight to the computer console. Without even sitting, he opened a connection to Oracle.

Batman hadn't told Gordon he was going to bring in outside resources. For one thing, Gordon didn't need to know everything about how Batman operated. More to the point, the commissioner did not know that Oracle was his daughter. It was an awkward situation, but Barbara had made it clear that she wanted it that way, and Batman was forced to honor her request.

If the life they had chosen had taught him anything, it was that barriers between public and private identities were best kept impermeable. More often than not, selective information embargoes were key to good working relationships.

He just hoped this one wouldn't come back to bite them on the ass.

"I'm knocking on your door," Oracle said. *"You going to let me in?"*

Batman keyed in a long alphanumeric string that generated permissions for Oracle to remotely access one of the Batcave's servers. That server was kept isolated from all of the other networked equipment, and reserved for work on digital files most likely to be infected with malware or other computer contaminants that might be dangerous to the cave's control systems and archives.

"I appreciate you knocking," Batman said. "It's nice that you're too polite just to let yourself in."

"For you," she said. *"Now let's see what we're looking at."*

Batman inserted the USB drive into the terminal and watched as a directory spawned. The drive's firmware folder was labeled HAHAHA. Next was DELETED. The third and final folder was called TICKTOCK.

"Let me take a look before anyone opens those folders," Oracle said. In the cave, they waited. It didn't take her long. *"The firmware is normal, boilerplate stuff. Any college kid could write it. DELETED has eight files in it, no extensions. I won't know what they are until you open them. Do you want to, or do you want me to take a look?"*

"Go ahead," Batman said.

She did, arranging the windows in a double row on the display over the Batcave's main computer terminal.

"They're all corrupt," she said. *"No known file type, no clues in the file names. TICKTOCK is an app."*

Batman scanned them himself, and at first glance he didn't see anything. Clicking on HAHAHA, he got nothing—the folder wouldn't even open.

"Let's look at TICKTOCK, then," he said.

Oracle did something remotely without opening the folder.

"It's completely self-contained," she said. *"You can run it if you want. As far as I can tell, it can't hurt anything. There's no way to be sure, though."*

He clicked on the app, and a timer display appeared in the upper right corner of the display. It read 00:02:00, then 00:01:59.

"Countdown," Robin said. "But to what?"

"Batman, you might want to get out of there," Oracle said, *"at least for the duration of the countdown."*

"I don't think so," he replied. "If there was a direct threat, one of the scans would have detected something, but we came up blank. No, given the effort they put into it, whoever sent this wants us to see what's on the drive. And if there was data being stolen, we'd be aware of it before two minutes was up."

"One minute and thirty seconds," Alfred said. "Sir."

"This is a countdown to something," Batman continued. "Worst-case scenario, the drive might be erasing itself."

"I'm not seeing any code that could do that," Oracle said. *"I still think you should be careful."*

"Robin, Alfred, go if you think it's best." Batman looked at both of them. Neither moved. "Don't put yourselves at risk, just because you're too loyal."

"I don't believe there's such a thing as 'too' loyal," Alfred said.

Robin watched the timer count down. "I think you're right, Batman." Tim was careful not to say "Bruce," and the system altered their voices enough to prevent anyone from recognizing them. Batman thought Barbara might already know his true identity, but if she hadn't figured it out, though, there was no reason to offer it up.

"It's your funeral," Oracle said.

00:00:59

Batman brought the deleted files back to the top of the stack of windows.

"Oracle," he said, "if we've got less than a minute, let's make it count. There are files referring to Wonder City here. Anything else you can piece together that goes with that? Something about TYGER... Protocol 10... maybe Hugo Strange, or the Joker himself."

"The files are pretty badly scrambled," Oracle answered. *"There's a pattern that keeps repeating itself, though. Look what happens if I put them all together."*

On the screen a new window spawned, showing a solid block of gibberish text. Highlighted throughout the block were eight separate occurrences of a nine-letter string of capital letters, one for each document.

IAMLARVAL.

"I am larval?" Robin read. "Who's larval?"

"There are no other capital letters," Oracle said. *"Quick. In the fifteen seconds you still have to live, what do you think that might mean?"*

"I think it means we have more than fifteen seconds to live," Batman said. "Otherwise there's no point in giving us the puzzle to begin with."

00:00:09

"Well, I guess we're about to find out," Robin said, tension appearing in his voice. "Oracle, you should know—"

"Hush," she said.

The counter reached zero.

Nothing happened. Then…

00:59:59

What the hell?

"Well," Batman said, "whatever the counter represented, at least we know one thing it *didn't* mean."

His fingers flew over the keyboard as he and Oracle ran simultaneous diagnostics on the sealed system he'd used to access the information on the drive. Everything there was still intact. The computer had recorded no operations other than what he had instructed, meaning that no code hidden on the drive had executed itself… unless whoever had written the code was a more skillful hacker than Batman had ever encountered.

"Was that a joke?" Robin wondered. "Or did something just go wrong? Why did it just start over, if nothing happened the first time?"

"Perhaps the countdown was a message of another sort," Alfred interjected. "Perhaps we have yet to gather all the information we require to understand it. Begging your pardon."

"That's what I'm thinking, Alfred," Batman said. "We have to be lacking some sort of critical information, though. Without the proper context, this is just a glorified stopwatch." He scanned the news feeds, to see if anything major had occurred when the timer hit zero.

Nothing.

Nothing in Gotham City, or anywhere else, for that matter. So he went back to the Wonder City document.

"Oracle, what if this isn't a corrupted text document? It could be a corrupted binary translation of an image file."

"Funny you should mention that," she said. *"I've been running four different decryption and recovery programs designed to reconstruct image files, and look what I found."* On the display, the window full of nonsense text symbols faded away and was replaced with an image. It was a diagram.

"That's the steel mill," Robin said.

"More precisely, it's the cooling tunnels," Batman added. "But they don't look the same as when I was hunting through them for the Joker."

"But the mill is decades old—this looks new. Is it a blueprint?" Oracle asked. *"I don't have any records of construction permits being issued for Wonder City, Arkham City, or the steel mill."*

"Anyone who would construct something like this wouldn't be going through the regular channels to obtain permits." Batman looked back at the string that had been repeated in the corrupt text.

IAMLARVAL.

"What could eight repetitions of that mean?" Robin wondered out loud.

"Someone wanted to get a point across, that's for sure," Oracle observed.

"There's more to it. Those strings were inserted intentionally into the corrupted file." Batman considered their options. "Robin, hit the streets. Take a look around Arkham City and see what you can find. This is an invitation, and we can't afford to ignore it."

Robin started to suit up. "What am I looking for?" he asked.

"Start in the steel mill. Observe and report any unusual

activity. That place should be deserted, and there shouldn't be any TYGER presence at all. Oracle?"

"The whole area is abandoned," she confirmed, *"at least officially. But this is Gotham City. It's a safe bet that some of Hugo Strange's old facilities are being used, if you know what I mean."* It never took long for criminals to move into abandoned places. That was true everywhere, but it seemed to happen faster in Gotham City.

"True enough," Batman said. "Robin, stay in close contact. I don't like splitting up like this, but we need to get a handle on it, and quickly. As soon as we think we know what this 'I am larval' note is about, we'll update you."

"Got it," Robin said. He gave his bō staff a spin, and headed out through a Batcave exit that led to an abandoned subway maintenance station on the river.

"I'll see what I can find out about the Joker's remaining henchmen," Oracle said. *"We've done our best to keep tabs on them, but they fall between the cracks too easily. Could be they've been absorbed into another criminal gang."*

"Good idea," Batman said. Oracle signed off, and he stood looking at the display. The repetitions of IAMLARVAL stood out from the surrounding gibberish. There was an additional meaning there…

"If I may offer a suggestion," Alfred said after a minute.

"Of course."

"This has all the earmarks of a puzzle," Alfred said. "Dare I say… a riddle?"

Batman nodded. "That's what I'm thinking, too. We have three separate parts so far. The steel mill image, the timer, and IAMLARVAL."

"It may be four, Master Bruce," Alfred said. He leaned across to the keyboard and opened a text window. With one finger, he tapped out

IAMLARVAL

Below that, he typed out

MARAVILLA

"An anagram, sir."

"You're right. I had that thought, but I was thinking in English."

"Had a bit of Spanish from youthful travels," Alfred said. "Flash of insight."

"A fortunate one," Batman said. "*Maravilla*. Wonder. Eight times."

"The Eighth Wonder of the World." Alfred chuckled. "Never thought I'd hear anyone say that about the Arkham City steel mill."

"I don't think they are, Alfred," Batman replied. "But I think you're right about there being more pieces to this puzzle... and I think you're right about who sent it." So far the material on the USB drive had all the hallmarks of the work of Edward Nigma.

The Riddler.

Nigma had left his mark all over Arkham City, and parts of Gotham City, during the TYGER takeover and the final stages of Protocol 10. Batman remembered the Riddler's traps; "death rooms," he had called them. Annoying, but hardly a world-class threat.

His train of thought was interrupted by a call on Commissioner Gordon's line. Batman answered.

"Commissioner."

"*Batman,*" Gordon replied. "*Two things. First, I'm checking in to see what you've found. The waiting is driving me crazy. Have you learned anything from that USB drive? What does it have to do with that maniac, the Joker?*"

"At the moment, I suspect it has nothing to do with the Joker," Bruce said. "That's the good news. He's dead, and we can let him stay dead." *Take your own advice,* he said to himself silently as he went on. "It's from someone else, addressed that way to get your attention, and get you to involve me." He changed the subject. "What's the other thing? You said there were two."

"*About five minutes ago, a man named Lucas Angelo was murdered in broad daylight. Shot from a rooftop with an arrow. It's an assassination.*"

"I don't mean to sound callous," Bruce said, "but you don't call me about every murder in Gotham City. Was there—?"

"*This was an assassination,*" Gordon said. "*And the reason I called you is that the word 'tick-tock' was carved into the shaft of the arrow. It's got to be some kind of message.*"

Tick-tock. Damn, that's it.

Batman swiped windows away from the corner of the display, uncovering the timer app window. It was ticking down again.

00:54:47

The timer window expanded and a line of text appeared below the countdown.

VAULT AHEAD. DON'T GET BOXED IN. YOU CAN BANK ON FINDING SOMETHING TO SINK YOUR TEETH INTO!

"Commissioner," Batman said, "I'm going to have to call you back."

4

And now, thought the Riddler, *things begin in earnest.*

So many interlocking plans, each timed to activate at just the right moment. So many moving parts, each with its own function and each depending on so many others. He had never attempted anything quite like this.

The thought thrilled him.

No one had ever done *anything* like this. There were puzzles within riddles within conundrums within enigmas, a clockwork masterpiece that depended on perfect timing—and, of course, on the indomitable will of Batman and Robin. It was the mark of genius to turn the enemy's signal virtue into his undoing. This the Riddler planned to do, and with the kind of panache that would make Gotham City stand up and take notice.

It wasn't an easy thing, standing out from the crowd of misanthropy and violence in his particular town… but he had found a way to do it.

Oh, yes he had.

The timer was ticking, and he knew *exactly* what was occurring. Gordon had called Batman and Robin. He always summoned them when he was out of his depth.

They knew, now, the seriousness of the situation. They would act quickly, and proceed to the bank.

To the vault, and what it contained.

Perfect. Parts of the magnificent puzzle were falling into place, while others already were beginning to unmake themselves. Sooner or later Batman would understand that, and when he did, the second phase of the plan would activate itself.

The Riddler watched, and resisted the urge to rub his hands together in cartoonish glee. The first bait, and they had taken it—before long the hook would be well and truly set. Question marks and fishhooks, the resemblance was uncanny, he thought, and he filed it away. There was a riddle in that, demanding to be found. Pity he hadn't thought of it for this endeavor.

Another time, he mused. *It's good to be thinking ahead, but let's not allow our attention to wander, just when it's required.* His communications were in place, as was a set of superbly calibrated challenges. His pawns were in place, the opening move was complete, and now he had to wait for Batman to catch up. By playing the only moves he could play.

The gambit was coming.

He could hardly wait.

Patience, he told himself. Would Batman interpret the signs correctly and respond to the gambit the way the Riddler had designed it? *I know you, Batman,* he thought, *far better than you know me, and that imbalance will be the difference that becomes your undoing. It's the tenth move that forces the checkmate in the fortieth.*

The real game was about to begin.

* * *

A short time later, a lackey entered the Riddler's sanctum. He reported on their progress in locating the mechanical guardians.

"We've found five of them so far," the thug said. He was heavyset, and didn't look as if he'd shaved recently.

"Excellent," the Riddler responded, smiling with undisguised glee. "What sort of condition are they in?"

"They all seem pretty much undamaged, though we won't know for sure until we can turn them on." He grinned. "It's lucky you got your hands on them when you did," he added. "If the Joker had kept control over them, no telling how much damage he'd've done. If he was calling the shots, that'd be all she wrote."

The smile disappeared from the Riddler's face. "That will be all," he said, and the man looked startled. He turned to leave, approaching the door.

Nigma shot him in the back. He collapsed without a sound.

Two other nobodies rushed into the room, reaching for their guns. For a moment they looked stunned, then they reached down and grabbed the dead man by the arms. They dragged him out without uttering a word.

5

Robin jogged along a long-abandoned tunnel once used as a turnaround for Gotham City subway cars, before the lines were moved and new facilities built on the far end of town. The overhead halogen lamps cast stark shadows. Peeling paint and mortar hung from the ceiling, and the trickle of an underground stream ran along an artificial channel sunk between the tracks.

He came to a steel door, locked by a pair of heavy deadbolts and protected by an alarm that would sound if the door was tampered with from the other side. Robin leaned in so the retinal scanner on the alarm panel could identify him. Then he put his right thumb and then his left ring finger on a pad designed to read them. Those three identifying features, presented in the correct order, would disarm the alarm—and then only for fifteen seconds.

The deadbolts shot back and Robin opened the door, easing it closed behind him. He waited and heard the deadbolts re-engage with a heavy *thunk*.

On this side the door looked as ancient as its surroundings. The only light was cast by ancient incandescent bulbs left there by a maintenance crew, and the shadows blurred in the semidarkness. Graffiti was visible on the wall under each bulb, representing someone who had tagged his personal territory.

Robin was in a maintenance tunnel paralleling the subway's existing riverside line. He listened carefully, because here he might run into crews working on tunnel improvements or signal systems. All he heard was the fading rumble of a train that had just passed by, heading downtown. Nevertheless, he kept his bō staff at the ready.

He moved quickly toward another tunnel junction where the main passage met a spur that led under the barrier between Arkham City and the rest of Gotham City. When Hugo Strange had overseen the construction of the walls around the complex, he had sealed the subway entrances, but not the tunnels. This made it easy for Robin to reach a station near the Flood Control Facility. There he would be able to climb up to the surface and get to the steel mill without being seen. Despite the violent chaos that had occurred, Arkham City wouldn't be abandoned—not completely.

Nothing in Gotham City stayed abandoned for long.

Hopping over the turnstile, he climbed the stairs, reached the surface, and found that the doors to the subway station were still chained shut from the outside. All of the station's windows were boarded up, as well. That presented him with two options. A dab of explosive gel would take the doors off their hinges, but he didn't want to make that much noise. He could break a window without much effort, but then he would have to tear off the plywood that covered the window frame. That was also more noise than he could afford.

Scanning the room, he looked up.

The station had skylights, and they weren't blocked.

Slinging his bō , he pulled out a small grappling gun and shot a hook up to the beams that supported the roof. He rewound the line and was pulled smoothly up to the ceiling, where he scissored his legs around one of the beams. Holding himself steady he cranked the skylight open, grimacing as the ancient mechanism squeaked loudly.

When it was opened enough to let him through, he paused to listen. No one seemed to have noticed his presence, so he stepped out onto the station roof.

Arkham City lay before him in ruins. What destruction its inmates hadn't committed during their imprisonment, TYGER forces and Protocol 10 had done during the final showdown that had culminated in the Joker's death. Parts of the steel mill had collapsed, as had the courthouse and the tower of the old hospital.

Burned-out cars and barricades choked the streets, here and there columns of smoke indicated fires that still smoldered, and every window was either broken or had a bullet hole in it. It would be years before the area could be rebuilt, if anyone cared to do so. A smoky pall hung over the landscape, making it impossible to tell what time of the day it was.

Sometimes it seems like there's always *a haze hanging over Gotham City,* Robin thought bleakly. *I'll bet they see the sun in Metropolis.* He held his position long enough to make certain there was no motion down in the streets. If anyone remained, they were unwilling to venture outside.

Who can blame them?

The pump house next to the Flood Control Facility

served both Arkham City and, hidden below, Wonder City. Its tunnels linked up with the cooling system that twisted and turned beneath the steel mill.

Robin sized up the approach. He scanned the parking lot in front of the pump house, empty but for a few charred hulks. A lot of dark windows gaped in the building itself—positions that could hide observers... or snipers. Arkham City was supposed to be empty, but it wasn't as if the GCPD was enforcing a curfew.

There's never a cop around when you need one.

The package, the computer files, the blueprints, all of them might have been planted to get him and Batman out into the open. A windswept expanse like the one he had to cross would make the perfect killing field.

He would have to move fast.

With a three-step running start, he launched himself off the station roof and gripped the ends of his cape, holding it out, gliding over the street in a shallow descent. If anyone was watching him, there was no sign of it. For all the evidence of his senses, he was the only person in Arkham City.

His intuition, however, told him otherwise.

Someone was here. Maybe some of Gotham City's homeless had taken up residence, hoping to disappear. Maybe the street gangs had decided to take advantage of the total lack of police. A lot of criminal bosses had set up shop here during the madness. Maybe their henchmen had decided to stay, now that Gotham City's attention had turned elsewhere after the Joker's death.

There were a lot of maybes.

He landed at the front entrance and readied his bō as

he approached. The twin glass doors were both shattered, and not recently. Robin stepped through the empty frame of the one on the right and entered a small lobby. Crossing the shadowy space, he slipped through a door next to a service window, and found the hall that led back to the pump room. Its machinery was silent. Gotham City's water authority was building a new treatment and flood control plant, and putting it in a safer neighborhood.

Dropping down to the main floor of the pump room, Robin located the outflow tunnels that channeled storm water overflow from Gotham City's sewers, sending it into the river. He opened a hatch and dropped into the nearest pipe. There was a stream of water pushing at his feet, and he moved against it until he came to the connecting pipe that had carried discharge from the steel mill's cooling tunnels. The only water in these tunnels now came from leakage. He stepped around stagnant pools and heard the skittering of rats in the darkness. Every so often he paused to make sure he wasn't hearing larger animals, particularly the dangerous two-legged kind.

Still nothing… yet he had a sense that he was being watched.

The mill's discharge pipe led to an empty holding tank. When the facility was up and running, the hot water from the operations would be cooled until its discharge could be released without killing all of the fish in the river. The discharge ports themselves were further downriver, or at least some of them were. Other wastewater was probably vented back toward the Flood Control Facility for filtration and disposal.

A ladder was built into the tank wall for inspections and maintenance. It led up to a hatch that could be opened from the inside. Sometimes safety protocols came in handy, Robin mused. No inspector wanted to be caught in here when the tank started to fill with scalding hot water. For that matter, neither did he.

He climbed the ladder. Its rungs, like the tank walls, were grimy with the accumulated impurities from decades of steelmaking. When he got to the top of the ladder, he turned the wheel to unlatch the hatch cover.

The wheel turned, but the hatch didn't open. Robin pushed as hard as he could, given the awkward position he was in. But it didn't budge. It didn't even squeak. He shone a light around the edges of the hatch, and saw the bead of a weld.

Ah, he thought. *So this is where it gets interesting.*

Hanging by one hand and holding the flashlight in the other, he turned to look out over the tank.

It was twenty feet deep, with a rounded bottom. Three openings high on one wall presumably led toward the smelting and furnace areas, where the water would be needed for cooling. On the other side, low on the wall where the tank bottom curved close to horizontal, was the discharge pipe where Robin had come in. There were no other ways in or out.

Looking back at the three cooling pipe openings, Robin saw something he hadn't noticed at first glance. Below each of them, drawn in the grime the way a child would write a message on the dirty back window of a car, was a single symbol—a question mark.

The Riddler.

It made perfect sense. This kind of cat-and-mouse puzzle was exactly his style.

Robin took another look at the ceiling. If the only way out of the tank was one of the cooling tunnels, he wouldn't be able to get at them from the floor. The ceiling was constructed of sheet metal with supporting girders. From the top of the ladder he could just reach the nearest girder. Holding the flashlight in his teeth, he got a grip on the metal support and swung to the next one, jungle-gym style, until he was dangling over the center of the tank.

Taking the flashlight into his hand again, he could use it to see into all three tunnels. The three question marks all looked identical. There was nothing to indicate which tunnel he should choose.

It crossed Robin's mind to pull out and contact the Batcave, but he didn't like the idea. It felt too cautious, and he didn't want them to think he couldn't handle himself. Batman was always reining him in, and right now Robin had the freedom to tackle this problem any way he saw fit. Was he trying to prove something? Sure. No point denying it. But he was also capable. He'd trained himself well, and he wasn't afraid of the Riddler.

He could figure this out on his own.

Again he peered into each of the tunnels. They were circular, about six feet in diameter, set in a level row with about six feet between each one. There was no signage— nothing to indicate where they came out at the other end.

He shone the light up, but the ceiling above them was no help, either.

This didn't fit Riddler's style—he never posed a riddle that didn't have an answer. That would be relying on chance, something he would never do. To rely on chance was to admit that he lacked control. Therefore, if there was no reason to distinguish between the three tunnels, any one of them would do.

Hand over hand, Robin swung along another girder until he was within a few feet of the middle tunnel. Its interior was filthy, covered in residue, but otherwise unremarkable. *Trust yourself,* he thought. He kicked back to get some momentum, and then pushed forward, letting go of the girder and landing just inside the tunnel mouth. He slid a bit, then froze in place.

No bomb went off, no electric shock stunned him, no poison gas came spewing in his direction.

So far, so good. Feeling bolder, Robin activated his comm and called Batman… but got no signal. *Okay, then,* he thought. *You wanted me to stay in touch. I tried. Moving on.* Pointing the flashlight ahead, he walked into the tunnel, the top of his hood brushing against the ceiling. Each of his steps echoed quietly. After about a hundred feet he spotted a hatch in the ceiling. This one opened without any trouble, revealing a vertical shaft with a ladder like the one in the holding tank. Stowing the flashlight, he grabbed the first rung and pulled himself up.

The shaft came out in a mechanical room that must have been located near the furnaces. As soon as he was clear of the hatch, it slammed shut. A series of clacking sounds echoed through the chamber, and lights came on from every angle, nearly blinding him after the darkness of the tunnels.

He spun in a circle, bō at the ready, anticipating an attack. None came, but the Riddler had been here. Hanging over a console of dials and gauges was a paper sign.

WELCOME!

All of the lights on the console started to blink. Robin watched them, noting a pattern. Eventually he realized that it was Morse code. The blinking paused, then repeated. *A… V…*

Aves or Mammalia

Those were classes within the animal kingdom. "Bird or mammal." *Robin or bat.* He approached the console and saw that the keyboard had been altered. All of the keys had been removed except for A and M.

Interesting, he thought. *Two different plans: one for me and one for Batman.* Lined up above the keyboard were some of the removed keys, forming a note of warning.

DONT LIE

Okay, Robin thought. *I won't.*

He pressed A.

The pattern of blinks immediately changed.

Delightful you may now exit

Every light in the room went out except for a single bulb in a far corner. Robin went in that direction and found a trapdoor with a keypad mounted on a post next to it. The display on the keypad glowed green and showed four asterisks.

A four-digit code. Ten thousand possibilities.

He flashed his light around the room, looking for any hint as to what the code might be. He searched around the edges of the keypad—it was astonishing how many people wrote down passwords and entry codes, posting them near the places where they had to be used. Then he broadened his search. He went back to the keyboard to see if its number pad had been altered in any way. All of the keys were gone, and the exposed contacts hadn't been touched.

So where was the clue?

It had to be here somewhere.

Proud and stubborn though he might be, Robin wasn't stupid. He was part of a team, and he made the call.

This time Batman answered.

EYE ON GOTHAM NEWS

Filed by **Vicki Vale**

"A murder has been reported in downtown Gotham City, not far from the West Waterfront Boulevard approach to the southern tunnel. Police are not releasing the victim's name, but sources confirm that it was an adult male, and he was killed with an arrow.

"I'll repeat that, we've got a murder in broad daylight in downtown Gotham City, and the victim appears to have been shot with an arrow.

"We are on the scene here, and as you can see, police aren't letting anyone close to the body. There has been some speculation that Batman would be present at the crime scene, since he and Commissioner Gordon are known to have met earlier this morning. But so far we haven't seen him, nor Robin. There's been nothing to indicate that they are involved in the investigation.

"Crime-scene tape has been used to cordon off the entire intersection, and if you look up where I'm pointing, over here to the north? You'll see GCPD officers and detectives on the rooftop of the old Kaplan Granary building. We're assuming that's where the assassin shot from, but as we've said, Commissioner Gordon is remaining very tight-lipped at this early stage of the investigation.

"The rooftop is a good three hundred yards from where the

body still lies, over there on the sidewalk just north of Chancey and Amidon. I'm no expert on archery, but that looks like a very long way to shoot an arrow with any accuracy. Does this mean that some of Gotham City's costumed criminals are back in action? Does it have anything to do with Batman's visit to Gotham City police headquarters this morning?

"At this point, all we have is speculation, but clearly this isn't your run-of-the-mill street crime. When we have more information—including the victim's name and an initial statement from homicide investigators—*Eye on Gotham* will bring it to you right away.

"This is Vicki Vale, reporting to you live from downtown Gotham City."

6

The Gotham Merchant's Bank stood empty, as it had for months since being badly damaged when the Joker set off an explosive in its underground vault.

The bank still operated out of several other branches, and was still owned by Roman Sionis, an organized-crime figure also known—at least to Batman—as Black Mask. Sionis's whereabouts were currently unknown. He had been incarcerated in Arkham City after tangling with Robin, but Batman suspected he had escaped during the chaos of Protocol 10's violent dissolution.

He also suspected that the cryptic note appearing under the timer was leading him to the vault. In fact, he was certain of it. The Riddler had started his gambit by invoking the Joker's name, and now he was continuing it by drawing them to the location of one of the final battles between the bat and the clown. The logic of it was inescapable. As for the rest of the riddle…

"…something to sink your teeth into!"

No doubt that solution would present itself once he'd entered the vault.

Batman approached from above, snapping a line across

Jezebel Plaza. He swung from the museum to the bank's clock face and scaled the building's facade to the roof. The steel fire door was open, the stairwell inside strewn with trash and flotsam blown in during the winter. He descended five flights to the ground floor, easing the stairwell door open and scoping out the main lobby.

It was deserted, and seemed to have been that way for some time. Everything was chaos—whatever hadn't been nailed down had been taken or destroyed by looters. The front door had been boarded up and padlocked. The vault was a floor further down, accessible via another stairway located in the middle of the room.

Voices came from the basement level. He eased the door shut, crossed the lobby, and kept going down. Two, three, four separate voices—the sounds of a group, most likely ransacking the vault.

The basement entrance was open, leading into a reception area that was similarly trashed. Across the room Batman saw the massive steel door was open, as well. Inside the vault he saw two men, armed with rifles and wearing an approximation of military uniforms. Villains had a love of outfitting their goons to look like soldiers. Underneath the trappings, however, they were all just thugs and lowlifes.

He slipped across the room and crouched next to the reception desk, keeping his full attention on the vault. The doorway compromised his view. He could see three men now, but had heard at least four different voices. He could also see that the far end of the vault was still in ruins from the explosion. Where it had once been blocked, there was now a rough opening in the rubble, as if someone had tunneled into the basement.

The subterranean reaches of Gotham City were to all intents and purposes endless—subway tunnels, underground chambers and the foundations of buildings that no longer existed and had long since been built over. Sewers, steam conduits, and even antiquated pneumatic tubes provided miles of unmonitored pathways. A thousand people could move about down here without ever being found... although some of the underworld's known residents made that an unappetizing prospect.

Solomon Grundy, among others, did not suffer intruders. Thanks to the Penguin, the undead creature had developed a taste for human flesh.

Even so, the subterranean spaces were frequently used by criminals. Staying out of sight was worth the risk to them. Why the Riddler was risking it was something Batman intended to find out... now.

Keeping three of the armed goons in view, he sidestepped out from behind the reception desk and threw three Batarangs in quick succession, aiming one at each. The first and third found their targets. One thug dropped without a sound as the Batarang hit him at the base of his skull, while the other cried out and staggered from the impact between his shoulder blades.

The second projectile whisked past its target's face and struck fragments from the concrete rubble at the far end of the vault.

While the Batarangs were still in the air, Batman charged into the vault. He zeroed in on the staggered thug, putting him down with a single punch. That left his back momentarily exposed to the one he'd missed, but that was an acceptable risk. When fighting multiple opponents, it was better to finish one off than hit two without taking either of them down.

The priority was always to even the odds.

His cape flared out behind him, masking the outline of his body and making it hard for any other thugs to target him. A burst of gunfire tore through the cloth, the bullets passing between Batman's left arm and ribcage. He pivoted and the cape struck his opponent with a *snap*, slapping the second thug's gun out of his hands.

The turn also revealed that he wasn't facing four men. He was facing six. In the corner near the wall of safe-deposit boxes, a trio of gunmen swung up their weapons.

Damn, he thought. *"Don't get boxed in!"*

The comm in his cowl chimed, but Batman ignored it. Before the thugs could draw a bead on him, he threw down a smoke pellet, swept his cape out to the right, and dodged to his left. The triple burst of gunfire shredded the edge of the cape—and also shredded the gunman Batman had missed with his Batarang. He felt a pang of guilt, but there was nothing he could have done. People in their line of business assumed the risk of collateral damage.

The smoke swirled up, obscuring the view from the corner where the three remaining gunmen continued to fire wildly. Knowing that out-of-control shooting tended to go high, rather than low, Batman dropped into a crouch and lunged through the cloud. He hit one of them low and heard the snap of a bone breaking in the man's leg. Before his target even started to scream,

Batman was already spinning to drive his right elbow into the midsection of the goon to his left, doubling him over. Continuing the spin, he caught the barrel jacket of the last thug's gun, ripped it from his hands, and smashed him across the head with the stock.

Fifteen seconds. Three unconscious, one dead, one vomiting on the floor, one down with a broken leg. A haze hung in the air from both the pellet and the gunfire. Near the hole in the collapsed wall, a draft drew the smoke away. He took note of this—it meant the tunnel definitely connected to the larger complex of passages below Gotham City.

In addition to the man-made tunnels, there was a natural cave system that had never been fully charted, and which ultimately connected to the Batcave. He had sealed the cave's entrance to it, to the best of his ability, but there could be miles of other passages and chambers used by anyone who happened to discover them.

As the smoke cleared, the thug with the broken leg continued to scream. Batman took three long steps to reach him and delivered a sharp jab to the chin.

The screaming stopped.

Then he studied the room. The walls, built from reinforced concrete as a security precaution, were relatively intact except for the immediate area where the explosion had taken place. One wall was blank, another supported the door and locking mechanisms, and the third was lined with safe-deposit boxes. That was where the thug crouched on his hands and knees, still stunned by the gut punch he had received.

Batman squatted next to him.

"Who sent you here?"

"We was just covering," the thug moaned. "Guarding. Nobody said you'd be here."

"Guarding for who?"

"Don't make me talk to you," the man pleaded. "You *know* what they'll do if they think I've ratted on them."

"All you have to say is yes or no. The Riddler?"

The thug shook his head.

"Uh-uh. Wasn't him. I never met him."

Batman leaned in close, despite the smell of vomit. "You know I don't kill people, but I'm not above using a little… persuasion." He paused to let that sink in. "Tell me again. Did the Riddler send you here?"

"No!" the thug barked, and he grimaced in pain. "I told you, I never met him."

He was telling the truth. There was a certain kind of desperation visible in low-level street thugs who knew they were in over their heads. They might lie to the police, but they were terrified of Batman. That's exactly how he wanted it.

"Then who was it?"

"I don't know," the man said. "A guy, we met once and he gave us instructions. We were doing what he told us to do. You weren't supposed to be here, like I said."

"That's because I show up when you don't expect me," Batman said, and he delivered enough of a blow to keep the thug sleeping for a while.

Tapping the controls on his gauntlet, he checked his comm. He was expecting a notification from Oracle soon. She had agreed to tell him when the timer from the USB drive reached zero again. But it was too soon—an hour hadn't yet elapsed. Close, but not quite. The call he'd received during the fight couldn't have been her.

Glancing at the cryptographic sequencer which logged all communications along his personal frequency, Batman saw that the call had come from Robin. *Good.* One call meant Robin was touching base. Multiple calls would have indicated some urgency.

So he returned his attention to the vault. The Riddler wanted him to see something here. The thugs really weren't a part of the gambit, though—they had been talking freely when he arrived. If it had been intended as an ambush, they had done a comically poor job of it. It didn't fit. Thus far, Nigma seemed to be putting far more care into his planning.

No, the goon squad was there for another purpose. Perhaps they were intended to guard something, as they seemed to think, but Batman had the sense that they had been left there as sacrificial pawns, or to make sure he stayed long enough to take a good look around. Perhaps he was being overly suspicious, but there was no such thing as too much suspicion. Not when the Riddler was up to his deadly tricks.

One of those tricks was to isolate himself from henchmen like these. He must have used an intermediary to hire and deploy them. Finding out who that intermediary was would be a job for Oracle. Batman would put her on that trail when he got back to the Batcave.

As if on cue, Oracle pinged him with a text message.

Timer has reached zero. Resetting. Now it reads fifty-nine minutes and fifty-eight... fifty-seven... you get the idea.

Batman tapped his control to stop the message from repeating. If the Riddler had simply wanted him to go through into the tunnel, he wouldn't have put the gunmen in the way. That much was clear. So the tunnel was of secondary importance, if that. Something else in the vault was the next clue. It wasn't on the blank walls, and there was nothing out of the ordinary in the open door.

That left the safe-deposit boxes. He turned to face that wall again, and saw something that hadn't been immediately evident. The boxes were all in place except one, as if the vault had never been looted. Given the condition of the rest of the bank, though, that didn't fit. And the thugs had been doing *something* to make that racket.

"Don't get boxed in."

Good advice, Batman thought. He couldn't make the mistake of assuming he knew what a riddle meant. He had to work his way through each element, step by step.

His comm chimed. Robin was calling him again. This time Batman answered, hitting the gauntlet control.

"There you are," Robin said. *"Hope I didn't rush you."*

"Is there something you want to report, or are we bantering?"

"Well, I cut through the subway tunnels into the pump house on the river by the Flood Control Facility. Then I was going to drop down into the outflow pipes and come up inside the steel mill, so whoever might still be in Arkham City wouldn't get in my way. But guess what I found?"

"I'm not going to guess."

"Remember the Riddler's challenge rooms?"

"They're pretty memorable, yes."

"Well, we've got a new one. I'm in it."

Batman frowned. Still, Robin didn't sound alarmed.

"Why aren't you *out* of it?" he asked sharply. It rankled him that he'd sent Tim into an unknown situation like that, but the clock was ticking in the truest sense. Each time it hit zero, another victim would pay with his life.

"That's why I'm calling you," Robin replied. *"There's a door here that requires a code. It's four digits. I can stand here and punch in all ten thousand possible combinations, but…"*

This was a fairly mundane puzzle for the Riddler to pose, Batman thought. Like the anagram of MARAVILLA. There had to be more to it. While he considered this, he scanned the wall of safe-deposit boxes. They were all back in their proper numerical order—4777, 4778…

Ah, he thought. "That's it."

The sounds he had thought were the gunmen ransacking the vault were actually the opposite. They had been putting the safe-deposit boxes *back* in place, leaving only the single gap to draw his attention. And that single gap would have once held a box with a particular four-digit number. Anything in that gap would not, to borrow the Riddler's phrase, be boxed in, because it wasn't contained in a box.

"What did you say?" Robin asked.

"I didn't mean to say anything," Batman responded, "but I think I might have an answer for you. Hang on—let me confirm."

"I'll wait," Robin said. *"No rush."*

Batman stepped into the center of the room so he could see straight into the empty slot. A single triangular object lay inside. Batman came closer, wary of the possibility of a booby trap. The inside walls of the slot were bare, and didn't appear to have been tampered with. He took another step closer and saw that the object lying in the box was a tooth, or something carved to resemble a tooth.

Of course.

"Something to sink your teeth into."

Looking closer, Batman examined the tooth without touching it, and inspected the shelf around it to see if he could discern any kind of mechanism that might be disturbed if he touched it. There was nothing. He shone a flashlight in to be sure. No wire, nothing gleamed in the light.

"When I said 'no rush,' I was kidding," Robin said over the comm. *"It's getting creepy in here."*

Batman looked at the box to the left of the gap—8121. To the right was 8123. It made perfect sense, by Riddler logic. The solution to one puzzle also held the beginning of the next. It still might be a trap, but they were still very early in the Riddler's scheme. His usual modus operandi was to create smaller confusions that built into a grand revelation.

"Try 8122," he said. "But just to be on the safe side, stay clear of the doorway when you do it."

"The panel is on the other side of the room," Robin said. *"And the Riddler's just showing off at this point. He's got something he wants us to see."*

"Agreed," Batman replied. "But still be careful. Go ahead. Let's see what happens."

There was a pause.

"That's it," Robin said. *"The door's open."*

"What do you see on the other side?"

"Nothing yet. Let me go through and look around."

"Good. Stay in touch."

"*I will.*" Robin clicked off and Batman took a last look around the vault to make sure he hadn't missed anything. When he was satisfied, he returned his attention to the tooth.

It was big, about as long as his hand, pointed and slightly curved. Its roots were intact and there was a small amount of tissue still attached. From the looks of it, the tooth had recently been extracted from whatever animal had once used it to eat.

A clue, then. An animal tooth, set in a specific place. There would be no solving this part of the riddle, however, without knowing what animal.

Batman picked up the tooth and held it in the palm of his hand.

There was a click from the empty space that had held box 8122, and a slow hiss. The bottom of the box rose slightly, and there was another click.

A pressure plate.

Batman was three long steps from the vault door. He had covered two of them when the bomb hidden in the wall of safe-deposit boxes went off.

He lost some time, but not much.

When he came to his senses, he lay crumpled against the base of the stone staircase, singed and smoking. The shrapnel from the metal boxes had shredded part of his cape and nicked him through his suit in several places. The fire raging in the vault was sucking air down the stairs. It had already spread into the reception area. Batman's ears rang, and the impact of the blast wave had left him feeling like there was something in his lungs he couldn't quite cough up.

The Riddler's adapting his style, he mused. *It may be time to pull out the armored suit.*

The interior of the vault looked like the inside of a blast furnace. Fire burned so intensely there that it was swirling out through the door—and up, as if the explosion had knocked down an exterior wall and exposed the vault to open air. There was no way any of the Riddler's thugs had survived.

Creaking sounds from the ceiling over the reception desk got him moving again. He went up the stairs, limping at a sharp pain in his right heel. Other than that he seemed intact, for the most part, though as he reached the main floor, he noticed his nose was bleeding.

The lobby was filled with smoke, making it impossible to see. He pulled a re-breather from his belt and clamped it over his mouth, taking a deep breath of filtered air. Not trusting the structural integrity of the floor so close to the explosion, he moved to the stairwell and climbed as quickly as he could to the roof of the bank.

When he got out onto the roof again, he could see just how much damage the building had suffered. The explosion had collapsed part of the outside wall of the bank on the far side from the stairwell's roof access, advancing the work the Joker had begun months before. Flames were spreading in the rubble and licking up the sides of the building.

The bank was old, with quite a bit of woodwork, and filled with old furniture. It would burn itself to ruins, and the fire could easily jump to other neighboring buildings. Batman called Gotham City's emergency number and reported the fire. Then he crossed the roof to the clock face and zip-lined his way back across Jezebel Square to where he'd first perched to survey the situation.

He paused long enough to scan for survivors. Even the Riddler's gunmen didn't deserve to die like that.

In the distance he heard sirens, and saw lights on the freeway. This would be a multiple-alarm blaze. As if to punctuate the thought, another part of the wall collapsed, and Batman stepped back from the fresh upwelling blast of heat.

Strange, he thought. *Twice I've been brought to the Gotham Merchant's Bank, and twice someone has tried to blow it up.* The Riddler wasn't usually interested in copying other villains, and in the past he'd chafed at the very suggestion that he was a poor-man's Joker. Was this just a coincidence?

Possibly. More likely, the Riddler had cleaned up his own mess and left no chance that any of the goon squad would yield useful information. Cold-blooded, but effective.

This level of ruthlessness is something new.

When it became clear that nothing would be gained by staying, Batman started moving again. The Batmobile was several blocks away—far enough to avoid alerting anyone in the bank to his approach. As he eased into the driver's seat, he activated the comm to let the GCPD know about the bodies in the vault.

Then he paused to consider his next move.

Traditionally the best way to defeat the Riddler was to

figure out what manner of game he was playing, and then subvert the rules. Batman didn't yet know those rules, but time was his ally. The longer he acted in accordance with the Riddler's manipulations, the more overconfident the man would become. It irritated Batman to be led by the nose, but he had to accept it for the time being.

His comm chimed again. This time it was Commissioner Gordon. Batman tapped the control.

"Let me guess," he said. "There's been another murder."

Taking Them to Trask

Duane Trask, Gotham Globe Radio

"Looks like Gotham City's long nightmare of peace and quiet might finally be coming to an end. My fellow observer of all things Gothamesque, Rafael Del Toro, is once again clamoring for Batman to hang up his pointy ears and leave us all alone.

"I disagree.

"Batman's got his problems—and we've itemized them here in great detail at other times—but on the whole he's good for this city. We need someone like him around to... well, I was about to say 'keep us honest,' but, after all, this is Gotham City. I'm not sure the Pope himself, patrolling the streets in his Popemobile, could do that.

"Apparently the latest outbreak of random violence in our fair city is a sniper roaming the streets. About an hour ago, he—or she—claimed his—or her—first victim.

"And about a minute ago, yet another.

"Maybe I'm jumping the gun, so to speak, by connecting these murders, but it can't be a coincidence that we've got two murders exactly an hour apart... can it?

"Not in Gotham City, it can't. Something's going on. I'm sure the police are doing their best to figure out what it is, and who's responsible, but in the meantime, people, stay inside if you don't have to go anywhere. I'm serious. Treat this like a hurricane. Stay away from windows, pull your curtains... we're the people of Gotham City, and criminal loons breed here like mosquitoes in a swamp. Take it seriously.

"Please.

"Now who could it be, and what could they be after? You will have noticed, as I mentioned, that things have been pretty quiet around here lately. The occasional mob hit, the regular brutality and mayhem of the human species, but nothing too unusual. Especially not when you consider just how unusual they got when Hugo Strange and his band of jackbooted thugs—to, ahem, coin a phrase—were running Arkham City a few months ago. Their little Protocol 10 plan was classic Gotham City. Grandiose ambition married to a high body count and widespread destruction. Batman was there to prevent it from getting worse than it already was, for which we here at Globe Radio salute him.

"Do you salute him? Do you think Batman is good for this city? Or do you think, as Rafael Del Toro seems to think, that Gotham City would be better off without his help?

"We've got lines open.

"Let's hear what's on your minds. And seriously, people, if you see anything that looks sniper-ish, call the cops right away.

"Avery's in the car. What's on your mind, Avery?"

> *"Duane, thanks for taking my call. I was just coming over the bridge headed downtown and there's a huge fire in Arkham City. Like something just blew up over there..."*

7

The trapdoor opened automatically, revealing a vertical passage. A blinking arrow appeared, pointing down—as if there was any doubt about where Robin had to go next.

The Riddler loved his atmospherics, that was for sure.

The shaft itself was decorated with question marks all the way down to a landing where a maintenance hallway extended as far as Robin could see. At intervals along its length were light fixtures, also in the shape of question marks.

Really? It occurred to Robin that somewhere in Gotham City there was a small manufacturer of light fixtures who had recently filled a large special order. He wondered if that was something Oracle could track down... although it was just as likely that the Riddler had his own shop somewhere and oversaw their manufacture himself. If he'd used someone else, a regular Joe who made lights, the poor schmuck was probably at the bottom of the river.

He moved cautiously down the hall, keeping an eye out for traps. Every crack in the concrete floor, every seam in the wall, even the question marks themselves might explode or leak poison gas or shoot out a lethal electrical shock. But nothing happened, and the longer nothing happened, the more Robin tensed in anticipation. The lack of a real threat was starting to make him jumpy—it was tough on the nerves.

He wondered if this was part of the plan, to smother him in constant menace so that eventually he was dulled to the possibility of danger—and that was when the trap would spring.

Robin almost wished it would, but it didn't happen. At the end of the hall was a large square room. Unlike the rest of the building, it was pristine and appeared to be newly built. Its floor was divided into a grid, with crisscrossing rows of squares each about three inches wide. He counted the squares: eight by eight.

Like a chessboard.

Looking into the seams, Robin saw steel. Then he studied his surroundings. There were seven doors in the walls of the room, each with a large question mark painted on it in bright green, and one open doorway. Each door was numbered, except for the last. It was one of the few things Robin had seen recently that didn't sport a green question mark.

Standing inside the main room were three men wearing costumes. One had a horse's head, the second a tall pointed hat, and the third a crenellated helmet. Chess pieces: knight, bishop, rook. Each of them wore bright green coveralls bearing a single letter and number. The knight's read N4, the bishop's B3, the rook's R2. Robin wondered where the pawns were, or the king and queen.

What was the puzzle?

He took a single step into the main room. The costumed

goons didn't make a move to attack him. In fact they didn't make any move at all.

Suddenly the question mark over door number one started blinking furiously. That was his first goal, and he figured he'd have to get there using some kind of chess moves. Yet if he started the game, would the knight, bishop, and rook move when he did? Would they retaliate?

What piece was he supposed to be?

That question cracked it for him. There was a classic technique of teaching chess—it involved setting up puzzles. The student was given a position and a goal: checkmate in three moves, or force a draw. Here the goal was clear.

Get to door number one.

The goons themselves were clues. N4, R2, B3. Those were his choices. Robin could take four knight moves, two rook moves, or three bishop moves.

Looking at door number one, he saw that the square in front of it was black. The square he stood on was white. That ruled out the bishop, since bishops could only move on diagonals of the same color. R2 wasn't possible because the Riddler's goons were blocking the two files between him and his goal, meaning it would take him three rook moves to go past them, move laterally, and then approach the first door.

That left the knight—N4. Robin plotted it out in his head. The first knight move would take him forward two squares and one to the right. The next, forward two more and another to the right. Then...

"Knight," he said, and made the first move.

The Riddler's goons stayed where they were. He was

standing directly in front of the one wearing R2. Robin moved again, brushing past R2, who did not react. N4 and B3 also held their positions. Because of their masks, Robin couldn't even tell whether they were watching him.

His third move, up two squares and again one to the right, put him one square out and two to the right of the target square in front of door number one. He glanced over his shoulder. The goons hadn't even turned to look at him. Whatever confrontation the Riddler had planned, it wasn't going to happen in this room.

At least not right away.

Before he went any further, he buzzed Batman. When the connection went through, in his earpiece he could hear the rumble of the Batmobile's engine.

"Careful about talking on the phone while you're driving," he said, but the joke was wasted.

"What's your status?"

"I'm in a room designed to look like a chessboard," Robin said. "It has seven doors, numbered one through seven, and there are three of the Riddler's goons standing on the board dressed like a knight, bishop, and rook."

"They aren't doing anything?"

"It's a puzzle. I already figured it out. The way they were standing, the only way I could get to the first door without one of them blocking me was to move like a knight. I did that and now I'm in front of the door." He looked at door number one, assessing whether there was anything about it he should describe. "I'm guessing that at some point I'll have to go through all seven."

"Or you'll be forced to make a choice about which door to

choose. Remember that old riddle."

"The one about the door to paradise and the door to hell? Yeah," Robin said. Batman had made a study of riddles, and Robin had learned them along the way.

"Keep it in mind," Batman said. *"I've received instructions, too. I found a tooth in the bank vault. Either the Riddler or someone in his employ left it there."*

"What kind of a tooth?"

"That's what I'm going to find out. Not human, that's for sure. The next step comes from that answer, and the clock is ticking. There's been another murder, and the counter is reset."

"Crap. Any connection between the two victims?"

"Gordon is investigating. One, Lucas Angelo, was a software engineer and the other, Brian Isaacson, built the Ace Chemical works." Robin heard the Batmobile downshift, and the chirp of its tires as they went over the steel housing of the barrier at the cave's vehicle gate. *"Time to get back to work,"* Batman said. *"I'll find out where this tooth came from, and you move forward as you can. Don't take chances."*

"I already did. I moved."

"You know what I mean."

Keeping the comm link open, Robin studied the barrier in front of him. It was nothing remarkable—a standard-issue steel door, the kind used on factory floors and stairwells all over the country, or found next to warehouse loading docks. The knob was stainless steel, and looked new. Robin took off one glove and pushed a finger against the lock's cylinder. It didn't move. Old locks always did, at least a little.

He looked more closely. The cut edge of the keyhole

was still sharp. No key had ever been turned in the lock. Conclusion: This door was new, and had been put here when the room was created. Corollary: Whatever was behind it, Nigma had built that, too.

Time to get on the same page with Batman. So far their best results came from working in tandem.

"The Riddler's passed up dozens of opportunities to kill me already," he said. "His goons could have jumped me on the way here, or his three chess pieces could've come after me the minute I stepped through the door. But they didn't even move—still haven't. It's kind of creepy, actually.

"So there must be a plan, like in a regular chess game," he continued. "This is the opening gambit, right? He wouldn't go to so much trouble if all he wanted to do was kill me."

"You're thinking like a rational person," Batman countered. *"The Riddler operates on different principles. He's not a complete lunatic like the Joker or Zsasz, but not the most balanced individual we've fought, and he seems to be more vicious than usual. Worse, he's controlling the game, and that puts us at a disadvantage."*

This was true, Robin reflected, but the Riddler wasn't completely off the deep end. He was meticulous, and everything he did tended to make perfect sense, in a twisted sort of way.

"I still think I'm right," Robin said. "Don't you?"

"Not necessarily, but I hope you're right because you're already in there. Explore and get through. The minute you run into something you can't handle, shoot me your location." Batman paused, and then added, *"For the moment we'll work in parallel, and keep it that way as long as we can."*

There was the familiar sound as the Batmobile's engine shut off and the hatch opened, then closed again with a solid *thunk*. He thought he heard Alfred's voice in the background.

"I think keeping us apart is in the Riddler's plan, too," Robin said, putting his glove back on. As satisfied as he could be that there wasn't a booby trap, he reached out for the doorknob. It turned smoothly, but he didn't open it yet. He listened for any faint clicks or other sounds that might signal the presence of a nasty surprise.

"Agreed," Batman replied, *"and I don't like it. He's got the initiative, and we're reacting. We need to reverse that as soon as possible. The Riddler always outsmarts himself in the end, but we have to be careful that we don't get careless before that happens."*

"You know me, Batman. I'm all about careful."

With that, Robin cut the comm link.

He took a deep breath and opened door number one.

Taking Them to Trask

Duane Trask, Gotham Globe Radio

"Joey from Midtown, you're on the air."

"Yeah, um, thanks for taking my call. Listen, I just heard that Batman was over in Arkham City, in the old bank. You know the one with the clock on it? Yeah, he was over there. I don't know what he was doing, but—"

"You saw him there?"

"No, uh-uh, I didn't see him. Someone told me they—"

"Who? Who told you?"

"Well, I can't really say. Someone who wasn't exactly supposed to be where they were, doing what they were doing, y'know what I mean?"

"Maybe. I guess. Not really. You're saying your friend is one of Arkham City's squatter population? Or just a guy who was doing something illegal?"

"No, nothin' like that, no. Just, you know, he wasn't supposed to be there, is all."

"Joey, I'm starting to think you're not telling me the whole story."

"I can't, man, you gotta understand. Look, you wanna hear about the Batman or not?"

"Sure. Tell me about Batman."

"He was in Arkham City, y'see, and he climbed up on

the roof of the bank. Then not too long after that he came out the front door. He was talking to somebody. You wanna know what he said?"

"I'm all ears, Joey. Tell me what he said."

"He said, 'Let me guess. There's been another murder.'"

"Joey. Can you repeat that?"

"Let me guess. There's been another murder."

"I'm going to quote that back to you, just so I'm sure I have it right. Batman was walking around the old Gotham Merchant's Bank, talking to someone. Who was he talking to?"

"Nobody. It was like he had a walkie-talkie in his costume or something. Headphones. You know."

"Okay. He walked out of the Gotham Merchant's Bank, talking to someone on headphones or a walkie-talkie. And he said... give it to me one more time, Joey."

"He said, 'Let me guess. There's been another murder.'"

"'Let me guess, there's been another murder.' Joey, can you hang on just one second? I'm going to have my producer take your information so we can speak off the air."

"No, man, I said what I had to say."

"Just a second, Joey. We'd like to confirm—Joey? Joey? Well. He's gone, folks. If that's true—people, if what we've just heard is true, then what's going on in Gotham City this morning is even stranger than we could have expected. So far, we know that a man was murdered downtown, with an arrow that was apparently shot from as much as three hundred yards away.

"There are reports that Batman met with Gotham City Police Commissioner James Gordon this morning, and then went to Arkham City. This is where it gets tricky because we can't verify it, but if you were listening just now you heard Joey from Midtown say that Batman was inside the old Gotham Merchant's Bank, and when he came out he was talking to someone—who, we don't know—and they were talking about another murder.

"Not *a* murder. *Another* murder, as in, related to the arrow murder downtown. So Batman knows something we don't, people. He knows there's a connection between those murders, and so does whoever he was talking to.

"You want my guess about who that was? Commissioner... James... Gordon.

"We'll be back after this."

8

Typical headstrong Robin—ready–fire–aim. Batman hoped it didn't get them into trouble, and hoped he'd read the chess puzzle correctly. They wouldn't know until Tim got back to the central room and assessed his next move.

This troubled him, the way it always troubled him when Robin seized on the first course of action and plunged ahead. Even worse, if the Riddler *had* expected Robin, he would also be expecting Robin's aggressive approach. More than likely he had built that anticipation into his planning.

Either way, there was nothing to be done about it now. *Damn it.* Pulling the tooth he'd recovered from a compartment in his Utility Belt, he approached Alfred, who greeted him with an expression of concern.

"If you don't mind my saying so, Master Bruce, you look a bit seared and blackened." He studied the damage Batman had sustained. "I trust all goes according to plan?"

"Depends on whose plan you mean, Alfred," Batman replied. He took off his cowl, and was Bruce again. "Someone left a welcoming committee for me in the bank vault. It definitely appears to be the Riddler, and he has Robin dancing to his tune, as well. He's keeping both of us occupied, leaving him free to commit whatever crime he has in mind."

"And what might that be, sir?"

"That's what I'm hoping to find out," Bruce said. He held up the tooth. "This is our latest clue, such as it is." He moved to a lab table he kept reserved for chemical analysis, and set the tooth down. He didn't do much of that sort of study, but maintained facilities necessary for just about any conceivable path of investigation. In this case, however, there might be a simpler way to proceed.

The most straightforward way to identify the tooth would be to place it in a three-dimensional imaging array, get a good picture of it, and run that picture through a database of teeth from all of the recognized animal species. The imager only took seconds to capture a good likeness, and then Bruce connected to the database at Gotham University's biology program. That, in turn, linked to every major educational database, from Ohio State to Oxford. He entered a matching query and waited while the program compared the tooth to the thousands of different tooth types encountered across the animal kingdom.

"If I may say so, sir," Alfred commented. "This is a bit of an unusual prologue for the Riddler, is it not? It seems we have three separate paths along which to follow him."

"That we do, Alfred," Bruce said. "The trick is figuring out how they're related, and then figuring out where he's made a mistake."

"If he has made a mistake, Master Bruce," Alfred countered. "What if he has not?"

"He always does sooner or later, Alfred. If he didn't, he'd

be perfect and I'd have been dead a long time ago."

Suddenly the computer chimed.

NO MATCH

"Curiouser and curiouser," Alfred said.

Bruce broadened the search to include similar features. The tooth he was working with was about six inches long and an inch and a half thick at its base, slightly curved, with deep quadruple roots and slight serration on the convex side of its curve. It looked like it might have come from any kind of large predatory animal, yet there weren't too many animals with six-inch teeth.

The new search came back with more than a thousand matches. Apparently this tooth had certain qualities that existed in just about every large predatory animal on Earth.

"It must be a mutant of some kind," Bruce said. "Bred from a known species, but different enough to dodge identification." He looked again at the roots, and saw that there was plenty of tissue there for them to recover usable DNA.

Working together, he and Alfred scraped a tissue sample off the root, chopped it into a fine paste, and mixed the paste into a glue medium for electrophoresis. This process separated the organic material based on the size of its molecules, isolating the DNA. When he had a viable sample, Bruce keyed a short sequence into a computer terminal.

Then he powered up the DNA sequencer built into his bioresearch station. It was based on commercial SMRT models that read DNA base pairs in real time, by tracking the frequencies of light they emitted when they were exposed to nucleotides stained with fluorescent dyes. He inserted the sample into the sequencer and started the process. The sequencer hummed and clicked. It would take several minutes to isolate enough base pairs to get a reliable species identification.

"Where is Master Tim now?" Alfred asked.

"He's exploring Arkham City," Bruce said. "The Riddler has been busy under the steel mill, and Robin's taking a look around." He neglected to mention the likelihood of traps.

"I trust he will remain in close contact," Alfred said. "One can only imagine what mischief the Riddler will have planned."

"You know Robin," Bruce said. "Always trying to prove himself. I told him to stay in touch, but it's a safe bet that I'll need to take the initiative."

"As always, sir, yes," Alfred said.

Another *ping*, and the DNA sequencer completed the first stage of its analysis. A long string of base pairs scrolled across the terminal screen. What appeared on the screen was a greater surprise than the explosion at the bank.

SPECIES: HUMAN

"Surely a mistake?" Alfred wondered.

Bruce didn't answer, but he didn't think so. As soon as he saw those words, he had a feeling he knew what was going to come next.

Based on the sequencer's confirmation, he linked the

device to DNA databases used to track known individuals—particularly those who had committed major crimes anywhere in the world. Here again the links were impressive, from the Department of Homeland Security to Interpol.

It wasn't long before a new window popped up on the screen.

IDENTITY CONFIRMED: WAYLON JONES

Killer Croc. There was no question about it.

Batman ran the check again to be sure. Because of his access to Gotham City Police Department records, he had extensive DNA records from Jones, dating all the way back to Croc's first brush with the law, and his first tour inside Blackgate Penitentiary. The database software recovered and displayed old mug shots demonstrating Jones's gradual transformation over the years from a brutal human with a skin disfigurement to the mutated monster he had become.

Prison records and police reports appeared behind the images, telling a decades-long story of violence. It started with assaults, escalated to murders, and then reached new heights with reports of cannibalism. Current whereabouts were said to be unknown, but Batman had a few places he knew to look. Pretty soon, he thought, he might have to start looking there.

This information raised more questions than it answered. How was Killer Croc involved with the Riddler? He was a homicidal maniac, pure and simple, living only for mayhem. Not at all the kind of associate the Riddler would want involved in a plan if he had to depend on a choreographed execution.

An even greater question was the one Alfred was first to articulate.

"Who on Earth could pull one of Killer Croc's teeth?"

The answer was simple.

"Nobody, Alfred—not if Croc was in a position to stop them." It was possible that someone might have tranquilized Croc, but that was much easier said than done, and would have yielded serious collateral damage.

His mind raced. Why go to so much trouble? And why involve so volatile an element as Jones? What role could he play that another meta-human—a more reliable one—could not? No answer suggested itself, and that sense of frustration escalated. He would have to get the information straight from the Croc's mouth, so to speak.

That meant finding a monster that made a habit of hiding out in the subterranean wilderness beneath the streets of Gotham City. *Once more unto the breach.* And Croc wouldn't be the only threat down there—there was Solomon Grundy, as well. Gotham City's underground was vast, however, and even though Bruce knew some of Croc's preferred hidey-holes, he couldn't just expect to take a quick trip down into a subway spur or sewer pipe—especially not if Croc didn't want to be found.

Ironically, his best bet was the Riddler.

He would provide the answer, or at least a clue. He had let Batman know who his target would be. Now Bruce had to figure out what clue the Riddler had left that would lead him in the right direction.

Was one of the murders a clue?

Bruce glanced over at the app timer. 00:22:31.

The victims had been a software engineer and the contractor who had built the Ace Chemical factory, later adapted by the Joker into one of his favorite hideouts. Killer Croc wasn't much of a computer user, to say the least, and Ace Chemical wasn't a place he was likely to go—*especially* when the Clown Prince was still alive. No, his preferred methods were limited to pure physical brutality.

On the other hand, the Joker's absence had sent shock waves through the whole Gotham City underworld. They had operated for years with the Joker as the lead architect of their schemes, and they might well be carrying on as if the Joker were still alive and in control. It wasn't easy to shrug off years of status quo. In a strange way, the Joker's death had probably affected Gotham City more profoundly than any other single death could have.

None of that, however, got him any closer to figuring out where Croc might be. Maybe a fresh perspective…

"What's your guess, Alfred?" he asked. "Is Killer Croc hiding out in the Ace Chemical plant?"

"I shouldn't think so," Alfred said. "What would he do there?"

"Nothing that makes any sense," he replied, glad of the confirmation. "If nothing else, Edward Nigma is all about making sense. So where, then?"

"Dare I suggest that Master Tim might be able to shed some light?"

Bruce nodded, and pinged Robin, but got no answer. With a deep frown, he hoped it was Tim's independent streak causing him not to respond—that Tim was right, and Riddler wasn't prepared to kill him and be done with it.

He started to shrug out of the shredded and singed suit he was wearing.

"I'm going to get a change of clothes, and then go find out."

EYE ON GOTHAM NEWS

Filed by **Vicki Vale**

"We're starting to learn more about the identities of the two men killed this morning—exactly one hour apart—on the streets of Gotham City.

"One, Lucas Angelo, was a software engineer with no known criminal record or associations. He was murdered by an arrow fired from the top of a nearby building. Gotham City police have that arrow and it is being analyzed at their crime lab at this moment. They have issued no statement, but unconfirmed reports suggest that a message of some kind was written on the shaft of the arrow. One witness at the scene said the word was 'Tick-Tock.' As in a clock, as in time ticking down.

"Normally we wouldn't run with a single source on a bit of information like that, but the next murder—of Brian Isaacson, a contractor who engineered extensive renovations on the Ace Chemical plant—occurred exactly one hour later. Tick, tock.

"Isaacson was reported to have been shot with a rifle. The source of the shot and the position of the killer have not been determined. Police are scouring nearby rooftops and the upper floors of abandoned buildings in the area, and believe they're narrowing down the possible locations the sniper could have chosen.

"It is not known at this point whether the same person is

responsible for both killings. Nor is it known whether they have any relation to the sighting of Batman at Gotham City police headquarters, earlier this morning.

"We've had reports that Batman was at the Gotham Merchant's Bank building—not the new one in Middleton, but the old landmark in Arkham City. It was partially destroyed by the Joker during the riots that led to the downfall of Hugo Strange, and if Batman was indeed there, you have to wonder if that means some organized criminal activity is occurring. Since Batman's visit, there have been reports of a four-alarm fire, with four engine companies and two ladder companies responding. We're staying on that story, as well as new developments in the sniper case.

"These have been pretty quiet months in Gotham City, since the Joker died, but it looks like things might start to get lively again. From the corner of Broadway and Hamm Alley, this is Vicki Vale, *Eye on Gotham*."

9

On the other side of door number one, a stairway led down to a junction room with two hallways feeding out of it at right angles. As Robin understood the layout of the steel mill, one of them would travel under the length of the building, and the other would cut across the corner closest to the furnace, potentially leading to another part of Arkham City.

Or, he thought, *Wonder City*. The old ruin underlaid much of Arkham City, and it seemed like a natural place for the Riddler to concoct his schemes.

He chose the one on the left, running perpendicular to the long axis of the steel mill.

Question marks lit his way as he continued to the end of the passage. He estimated he'd gone a hundred yards or so, at a noticeable downward angle. He was probably forty or fifty feet below street level at this point, and somewhere to the west-northwest of the steel mill. If he kept going this way, he would run into either the Bowery subway station and terminal, or the sewer infrastructure underneath it. Something to keep in mind as he tried to anticipate what the Riddler had in store.

The hallway ended on a catwalk overlooking a giant

cistern, lit by a few bare bulbs. The sockets looked old, but the bulbs were new.

There were dozens of these in Gotham City, designed originally to hold drinking water and later repurposed for storm water overflow. They were huge cylinders with pumping machinery built into the walls near the bottom. The catwalk ran around the entire circumference of the cistern, about eight feet below its ceiling. He didn't see a door other than the one he'd used to enter.

As Robin paused on the catwalk to take this all in, the door clanged shut behind him. He didn't bother checking to see if he could open it. Whatever the Riddler had in store for him, it had begun. Looking back would just waste time.

Below the catwalk, inflow tunnels ringed the cistern wall. He counted six of them, and a blank video screen had been placed over each one. While the cistern itself was old stone, covered in stains and slime, the screens were brand new. At the bottom of the cistern, thirty feet or so below the catwalk, lay a drain ringed with brick. Seeing it set off the first alarm bell in Robin's head. Usually they were kept closed to hold water. This one was open.

He heard a roar, and water burst out of one of the inflow pipes. The flow arced down into the cistern, forming a small whirlpool over the drain. A moment later, a second pipe started discharging water. Then the next four, at even intervals, until the cistern was filling faster than the drain opening could evacuate the water. The small whirlpool became a maelstrom, thundering in the closed space as the water level rose toward the catwalk.

Not good.

Robin looked up. The ceiling was steel and concrete, with a few empty light fixtures and a single question mark hanging from a short cable. There was no emergency exit. There were no vents large enough to accommodate his size.

In short, there was no way out.

Moving at a trot, Robin made a circuit of the catwalk to make sure he wasn't missing anything. Along the way he tapped at the walls sharply with his bō, listening over the roar of the water for any change in the resonance. A hidden exit wasn't impossible… but it didn't turn out to exist. Robin got all the way around the catwalk, back to the door, and this time he did try to open it. He couldn't put it past the Riddler to resort to the obvious.

The knob didn't turn.

He'd been right. There was no way out.

No, he corrected himself. *In a Riddler puzzle, there's always a way out.* He was still certain of his analysis—his death wouldn't come until later. That lunatic wouldn't have set everything up the way he had just to have him walk into a room and drown. He *loved* drama, and was a big believer in letting the tension build.

So the problem wasn't with the room, it was with Robin. He was missing the key needed to understand the puzzle… yet he didn't have any information. The Riddler had left no clue.

Again he corrected himself. The Riddler *always* left a clue. Otherwise it wouldn't be a riddle. And by definition, riddles could be solved. *Great* riddles had solutions that looked obvious in hindsight. The trick was to see—but to see what?

The water. Without the water, there was no threat. With no way to go up, and no way to go through the door, so the solution had to be in the whirlpool. It was holding its shape as the water rose and the noise grew louder in the smaller volume of air.

That had to be it.

By timing the discharge from each pipe in a certain pattern, the Riddler had created the whirlpool. *Detect the intentionality,* Batman always said. *Learn to distinguish it from the random.* And here, the intentionality was in the maelstrom.

The water level was within six feet or so of where he stood. If he was still on the catwalk when the water submerged it, the force of the whirlpool would sweep him around, turning every railing and post into a lethal weapon. He wouldn't survive that. It left one option, and only one: to get out through the drain. And that meant jumping into the heart of the beast.

The water roared and rose.

The catwalk began shaking. If it fell apart, the pieces of it would spin uncontrollably, killing him in the water. He had to be out of the chamber before that happened.

I've done a lot of crazy things in my life, Robin thought, *but this might just be the craziest.* No sense in trying the re-breather—it would just be snatched away by the force of the water.

He jumped.

While he was still in the air, the screens lit up over each

tunnel. He caught sight of two of them before he hit the surface.

FORWARD STEP

Then Robin hit the water and was instantly tumbling in the vortex of the current. It was freezing cold, so cold that his heart skipped a beat at the moment of contact. He couldn't fight the current, but he had to know what those words had been. For the Riddler, the clues were *everything*. If he couldn't read them, he was certain he would die.

The whirlpool dragged him toward the funnel at its center, and Robin tried to angle his body around so he could break the surface just once more before he spun down the drain. His cape lashed around him in the torrent, once nearly wrapping around his head, but just as he reached the wall of the funnel he detected an upward current, and forced himself into it. His head briefly broke the surface. He was spinning around fast now, so fast that he couldn't tell what order the words were in as they registered in his mind.

BACK STEP FORWARD STEPS ONE TWO STEP BACK FORWARD TWO ONE STEPS STEP BACK FORWARD STEP TWO BACK STEPS ONE.

Then the funnel closed around him and he was corkscrewing feet-first down into the drain. The pressure popped his ears and he could hear the groan in his head as it squeezed his sinuses. He held his breath and tried to keep his legs straight and his arms folded across his chest.

It felt like he was encased in ice. The urge to breathe was nearly irresistible, but Robin held out as he hit the wall twice in quick succession. The second time he felt something gash the back of his leg.

Arrrr! he thought, but he kept his mouth clamped shut.

A moment later he was in free fall, and before he could react he landed in a deep pool. The water had found the next chamber, but the drain in this one was much smaller. Without a whirlpool, the pull was much less—it must not have been constructed to accommodate all six of the inflow tunnels at once.

It was pitch black in the chamber.

Robin swam to the surface and kicked away from the torrent pouring down from above. He found a wall in the dark and grabbed something that offered him a good grip, treading water as best he could, trying to get his breath. Already his fingers and toes were getting numb. Soon hypothermia would set in, and before that happened, his brain would get foggy. The real riddle here wasn't how to swim—it was how to keep himself warm long enough to figure out what he had seen up above.

The words had come so fast that he couldn't tell whether any of them had occurred twice. No, they couldn't have. There were six tunnels and Robin knew he'd seen six words.

The solution fell into place.

One step forward, two steps back.

The water level continued to rise. He had no way of seeing if there was any way out. Then, gradually, the sound of the water started to change…

That was it. He'd taken one step forward when he jumped off the catwalk. The only way out was to take two steps back.

Something hit him in the leg and he realized it must be a piece of the catwalk. He swam to the far side of the chamber, hearing the muffled clangs of other debris hitting the drainpipe walls on their way down. Reaching up, Robin found he could touch the ceiling. Soon this chamber would be full.

When that happened, water would no longer be able to flow down from above—it would begin to back up. Then it would be time to take his two steps back… if he could hold his breath long enough and not pass out from the cold. He reached for his re-breather now, only to find that it had been swept away by the current.

Damn.

He started hyperventilating, trying to get as much oxygen into his blood as possible before the water reached the ceiling. As he did so, he worked his way around the edge of the chamber until he could feel the flow from the drainpipe without it dragging him out and down.

The top of his cowl touched the ceiling. Robin kept breathing. The rushing of the water grew louder in the confined space. It reached his mouth, and he tipped his head to keep breathing. Every gulp of oxygen mattered.

It reached his nose.

He filled his lungs one last time and sank down as the last few inches of air were forced out of the chamber. The sudden muffling, together with the absolute darkness, was disorienting. Robin felt along the wall looking for the drainpipe. He couldn't afford to go past it. He tapped on the wall as he went, and when he heard an echo he felt with his feet. There was the mouth of the drainpipe.

He doubled over and pulled himself in, then kicked his way up, pulling with his hands when his fingers found small ribs or ridges on the pipe's interior. He'd been moving so fast on his way down that he had no idea how long the pipe was. Paradoxically he was relying on the Riddler's hatred of chance to save him. The man wouldn't design a trap that couldn't be escaped. He'd save that for the big finale, when people were watching.

God, I hope that's the case, he thought fervently. It seemed like a lot of faith to put in a homicidal maniac. At the moment, though, faith was all he had. Faith in his ability to hold his breath, faith that the tunnel wouldn't be blocked with pieces of the catwalk, faith that the cistern wouldn't be full to the ceiling…

Faith in the Riddler. He needed the Riddler, and as the cold started to fog his mind it seemed to Robin that Batman had needed the Joker, too.

Then he was out of the drainpipe, in open water. Now that the cistern was nearly full, the whirlpool had all but abated. He pushed up, lungs burning and heart hammering against his sternum. Looking up he saw the wavering pinpoints of the lights spaced along the cistern's ceiling. He couldn't feel his legs, but he kept telling them to move.

When Robin's head broke the surface, at first he didn't notice, he was so lost in his own mind. But the change in sounds registered, and he exhaled with a grunt that echoed in the few feet of air left in the container. He was so exhausted that the weight of his cloak almost dragged him right back down again, but he thrashed over toward the wall and banged his hand against a catwalk strut that had survived the whirlpool.

How long had he been in the water? Three minutes? Four?

He didn't have much left in him. Where was the door? He held onto the strut and looked around, trying to get his bearings.

In the dim light Robin could see that the water had receded a little, exposing the ruined remains of the catwalk and the door through which he had come in. He climbed out of the water and worked his way along the wall until he got to the door. The immediate cold faded, but he was still numb. Stretching from the nearest broken piece of the catwalk, he could just barely reach the latch.

It wouldn't turn... but when he tried to turn it, he heard a mechanical *thunk* from somewhere nearby. A moment later, water started to fall into the cistern from the ceiling.

In the water, one of the Riddler's signs lit up again, blinking rapidly.

TWO... TWO... TWO... TWO...

So there was still a second step, but he didn't know what that could be. And his mind was so muddled, it was all he could do to think. There was no other way out, and if the cistern filled to the top...

"I already took one step back, you bastard," he said out loud, trying to clear his head by talking. "I can't take another without going through that door."

TWO... TWO... TWO... TWO...

What could it be? Robin wondered. But what if it didn't refer to the second step? What if he was trying to get Robin to...

The hell with it, he decided. *Even if that's not what he means, I'm gonna call.*

Batman answered immediately.

"Robin. The tooth came from Killer Croc."

"Killer Croc?" Robin replied. That shocked him into greater clarity. "Someone pulled one of Killer Croc's teeth? No way. You'd have to kill him first."

"That was my first reaction, too, but the facts are the facts. It's Croc's tooth. He's involved in the Riddler's plan somehow. What's your status?"

Robin glanced around the cistern, suddenly aware of what might be lurking beneath those dark waters.

"I'm trapped in a room somewhere near the Sionis mill. It's flooding. That's the Riddler's plan for me." He gave Batman a quick update. "One step forward, two steps back. Funny, right? Also, the 'two' kept blinking. I'm pretty sure he means that it's going to take the two of us to solve this puzzle. For some bizarre reason, he wants us to stay in touch. So, you know. Water's rising here. Maybe you can pitch in."

"The Riddler loves thematic consistency," Batman said. *"The solution will be somewhere in the Flood Control Facility."*

"That's what I was thinking, too," Robin agreed. His teeth were chattering, but the numbness was beginning to subside.

"I'm on my way. How fast is the water rising?" asked Batman.

"Not too fast," Robin said, "but don't stop to smell the flowers, if you know what I mean?"

"I do." Batman clicked off, and then all Robin could do was wait and shiver. The water rose, but slowly.

He had a little time.

RyderReport.com

Posted by JKB

Wednesday, 12:37 p.m.

For the lunch crowd

You've already heard that Batman is flitting about our fair city today, after a period of inactivity that some Gothamites no doubt found calming. The fact that he's back in… action?… means that something bad is happening, and here at the *Ryder Report* we're starting to piece together what that bad thing might be.

Sources indicate that the Gotham City Police Department received a suspicious package this morning. That was the reason for Batman's visit to police HQ. What was in the package? That we don't know, but our little birdie tells us that Batman met with the commissioner in a secure room, and left immediately after the meeting.

About an hour after that, some nut shot an arrow through the thorax of Lucas Angelo, a software developer specializing in robotics and control systems. He's the guy who wrote the programs that keep airplanes over Gotham City from crashing. Most of the time, anyway.

Then an hour later a sniper's bullet cleans out Brian Isaacson's brainpan and decorates a nearby wall with its contents. Gross! Chilling! We like our murders in Gotham City to be up close and personal, not random and far away.

Who was Brian Isaacson? He was a contractor who left his mark on quite a few buildings around town, specializing in refurbishing and redeveloping old factories. When the old Ace Chemical plant got a facelift a few years back, that was Brian Isaacson running the project. It was also probably the Joker writing the checks for it, but nobody knew that at the time.

As we learn more about those two unfortunates—and the police investigation into their murders, we'll pass that information on to you. Is there some kind of clock ticking? What's Batman up to? We're on this story, don't you worry. If the next hour brings another murder, we'll let you know.

Jack himself will have a full report on his show. You won't want to miss it.

10

Batman gunned the engine, his suit creaking a little at the elbows from the newness of the material. He hadn't had the time to don an armored uniform, so this would have to do.

As he drove, the timer reached zero. He had its window feeding out to a heads-up display on the inside of the windshield. When he saw 00:00:00, he started a countdown in his head, until…

A chirp from the dashboard let him know that Commissioner Gordon was calling.

"Batman."

"Who was it this time?"

"Her name was Rosalyn Mateosian. She was a specialist in the miniaturization of electronics."

"What killed her?"

"Don't you mean who?"

"If I know what, it helps me figure out the who."

"Another bullet. The last time it was an ordinary nine-millimeter. We have the slug and it's in for analysis now. This one was a steel-jacketed round. It went right through her head, and we dug it out of a flowerpot in the window of a coffee shop, more or less intact. It has two letters

carved on it—a D and an S."

DS. Deadshot, also known as Floyd Lawton. The Riddler had given them a clue… or maybe Deadshot had just wanted to leave a calling card. That was typical of him. He often seemed to want to get caught, but not before he'd indulged his bottomless appetite for killing.

In their last encounter, Batman had stopped Deadshot in an attempt to assassinate Jack Ryder. He'd secured the assassin in an abandoned train car, and alerted the police. As far as he had known, Deadshot was in Blackgate Penitentiary.

Apparently not.

"Thank you for the update, Commissioner," Batman said as he approached the main gate leading into Arkham City. The Batmobile jounced over small craters in the street, made by TYGER helicopter armaments in the final Protocol 10 showdown.

"You going to tell me what DS means?" Gordon asked, sounding vaguely irritated. *"I can tell from your voice that you know."*

"I don't know, but I suspect," Batman corrected him. "I'll let you know when I know. We'll talk soon." He cut the link and steered the Batmobile to the Flood Control Facility. Part of it had burned down during Hugo Strange's last desperate attempt to retain power, but the main offices were intact.

The hatch opened and Batman vaulted out. As it sealed again with a pneumatic *thump*, he dashed in through the front door. There was no time for subtlety. Moving quickly through the offices and into the core of the facility, he followed signs that pointed toward the control room and found the door locked.

Taking a step back, he sprayed explosive gel on the doorknob and jamb. Then he took another step back and set the gel off. The small explosion blew the door loose, flinging it open to slam against the interior wall. He stepped through the doorway and onto a steel-grate landing at the top of a short stairway that dropped down to the control-room floor.

The room was dark save for emergency lights powered by an on-site generator. Batman vaulted over the railing down to the floor and approached the control console near the bottom of the stairs. To left and right, the room extended into shadows. The only sound was the faint hum of an unseen generator... and from the right, the burble of running water. Clouds of steam lazily rolled out from that direction, as well.

A number of the dials and gauges on the control console were lit up, and as Batman's eyes adjusted to the dimness he saw that certain areas of the console were painted green. Good. The Riddler had been here. Now to figure out what puzzle-within-a-puzzle the control console held.

"A little birdie told me you might stop by." The voice rumbled from the shadows to his left.

He spun and saw a mountainous humanoid form emerging from the darkness, its head malformed and skin glistening in the stark emergency lighting. At about the same time the smell hit him—rotting meat and the rank scent of sewer scum. Killer Croc. Another part of the Riddler's plan revealed itself.

"What a surprise," Batman said.

"Surprises aren't my style," Croc said.

"But they're the Riddler's style, aren't they?"

"That guy?" Croc growled. "Next time I see him, I plan to eat his face while he's still alive to feel it."

Interesting, Batman thought. He circled away from his opponent, waiting for him to make the first move. There was no time for casual conversation—Robin wouldn't be alive at the end of it. But to rush Killer Croc was to invite maiming at best, and more likely a bloody death.

"Who was it, then?" he asked.

Croc's mouth split open into a fearsome grin, baring dozens of teeth. Batman saw the gap where one had recently been pulled.

"I don't kiss and tell," Croc said.

"Let's be real," Batman said. "You didn't kiss anybody." That was when Croc rushed him.

Batman had run through the scenarios and expected a bull's rush, because Croc could never stop himself for long. His bloodlust pushed him beyond any rational control. Now that it was happening, Batman was ready. He jumped straight up, kicked himself into a backflip, and landed with both feet squarely on the top of Croc's head.

The impact jarred Batman's bones straight up into the small of his back, but it also dropped Croc to his knees. The creature lashed out with a backhand sweep of his right arm, and Batman leapt to the left, avoiding it neatly. He caught the arm and torqued it into a hammerlock, planting a foot in the middle of Croc's back and driving him forward headfirst into one of the steel girders that supported the stairway.

The girder snapped off at floor level, and the whole

staircase sagged. Batman dodged back before his own momentum could thrust his face into the frame, but that cost him his hold on Killer Croc's arm. He skipped back and Croc reared up, tearing loose the entire stairway and landing. The popping rivets and welds sounded like a fusillade. The beams hung over Croc's shoulders, and he lifted the structure up with a roar.

Batman tensed in preparation to duck, anticipating that Killer Croc would come at him swinging the stairway like a club—but he'd guessed wrong. With both hands Croc threw the stairway at him, and Batman just had time to duck his head and take the impact on his shoulders instead of his face. His left arm went numb and he was knocked over, landing in a tangle of broken beams and bent sheets of steel grating.

With one arm he tried to push himself up, but he didn't have time to avoid Croc's follow-up. Leaping into the air, Croc landed on the grating with both feet. Beneath it, Batman was pounded into the floor.

"You want to stomp?" Croc roared. "I can stomp, too!"

Heaving himself to the right so he could keep his good arm under him, Batman shifted the heap of metal and unbalanced his assailant. The creature toppled off and smashed into an edge of the control console, as the force of his own shifting weight slid the remains of the staircase across the floor.

Batman threw it off and scrambled free. He was starting to get some feeling back in the fingers of his left hand, and he was going to need it.

The console looked undamaged, and that was a good

thing. He didn't want to risk damaging it in the course of their combat, so he ran toward the far end of the control room, away from where Croc had appeared. There was a railing there, and beyond it a ten-foot drop to four exposed water pipes, each perhaps five feet in diameter. One of them was broken open, with a steady stream of water pouring through the break onto the floor below.

A thick cluster of cables ran down from the ceiling. Some of them ran to the console, and others to an electrical closet with the familiar warning sign of a human figure reeling away from a lightning bolt. If the generator was still providing power…

"Nowhere to go, Batman," Killer Croc growled from behind him.

Batman turned. "I was about to say the same thing to you," he said.

Croc charged him again, and this time Batman let him come. Reaching out with an insulated glove, he chose one of the cables and ripped it out of the junction box set into the floor. A shower of sparks burst from the end of the cable and some of the emergency lights went out… but not all of them, and the lights on the control panel still glowed.

Croc tried to cut his momentum, but it was too late for him to stop. Batman jumped up and back, bracing himself on the railing. He held out the spitting end of the cable as the juggernaut came within arm's reach. It jabbed into Croc's chest as he smashed into Batman and through the railing, sending them both over the edge toward the pipes below. A blinding flare of light burst from the cable end as thousands of volts of electricity crackled through his body.

Batman held the cable steady as they fell, insulated from the current by his suit. Croc roared, trying to say something, but the muscles in his jaw spasmed so violently that the sound became a long *uh-uh-uh-uh* that ended when both of them crashed onto one of the pipes, and then slid off to splash into the puddle that had collected beneath them.

As they reached the floor, the cable was jerked out of Batman's hand. Its live end hung halfway between the floor above and the surface of the water.

Killer Croc lay face down in the water, and ceased to move. Despite his incredible bulk, Batman turned him over and heaved him around so he would be looking up at the cable when he came to his senses. He reached up and pulled it closer. As he did so, several metal mounts broke loose with a *pop-pop-pop* sound, then landed with a clatter on the concrete.

He didn't have to wait for long.

Croc's eyelids fluttered, and his hands balled into fists.

"Easy," Batman said. He was standing over Croc holding the cable high.

Croc kept still. His slitted reptilian eyes focused on Batman, full of violence.

"I'll make you a deal," Batman said. "You tell me what I want to know, I'll let you slither back down into the sewers, and we'll forget all about this little dance."

Croc's eyes narrowed.

"The Dark Knight letting a bad guy go?" A hint of a smile played across his face, looking more like a sneer. "You got something else you need to do, huh?"

Batman leaned in close, braving the rotting-meat stink

of Killer Croc's breath. "Do I need to convince you?" he growled. As he did, he pulled the sparking cable even closer.

"Lighten up, already," Croc said. "You got a deal."

"How did you lose the tooth?" Batman asked. "I found it in a bank vault." Croc looked surprised at that, but the sneer quickly returned.

"Mad Hatter found me, asked if he could have a tooth. I thought about asking him why, but have you ever tried to get a straight answer out of him?"

He had a point, Batman thought. "So you just let him pull one of your teeth?"

"No big deal," Croc said. He grinned again and stuck his tongue through the gap. "I got plenty of teeth. Plus the money was right."

It always came down to money. Batman wondered how his life would have been different if he had grown up having to worry about money. He also wondered how a creature like Croc managed to spend it.

"And who was the little birdie who told you I'd be here?"

"Oh, her. You know. Joker's little girlfriend, whatsher-name."

"Harley Quinn."

"That's her. I seen a lot of crazy people in this town, but she's right up at the top of the list."

Batman considered this. Harley Quinn had been in love with the Joker, and no doubt blamed him for the Joker's death. Also, Killer Croc was right. She was deranged, and probably had been unbalanced even further by thinking she was pregnant, back before the Joker had died. He could only imagine the life such a child would have had.

He was glad the pregnancy had turned out to be false, even if the shock of it had prepared Quinn for becoming one of the Riddler's allies.

"That it?" Killer Croc rumbled. "You said we had a deal."

Batman let him up and stepped back. He would keep his word, especially since any further fighting would take more time than he could afford. And the outcome would be uncertain.

"Go," he said. He reached into his belt and held up the tooth, which he'd brought along in case Killer Croc harbored a sentimental attachment to it. It was impossible to know what might be meaningful, or what might provide an advantage in a negotiation.

"Nah," Croc said, hauling his massive bulk upright and shambling into the shadows the way he'd come without looking back. "Keep it. Make a Christmas ornament out of it or something. Don't matter to me. I'll grow another one."

Batman didn't answer. He stowed the tooth in a compartment on his Utility Belt.

"Hey, Batman," Killer Croc said from the darkness. "You still got that stink on you. I didn't think you'd live this long."

It took him a moment to figure out what Croc was talking about. Then he remembered when they'd tangled in the steel mill, after Batman had first fought Rā's al Ghūl. *I smell death on you,* Croc had said. Apparently he still smelled it—or he was saying that to get into Batman's head. Usually Killer Croc wasn't that subtle, though. If he was serious, what could that scent be?

"I'll take that into account, considering the scent you give off," Batman responded. Killer Croc just chuckled, a sound like rocks being ground into dust. After a moment he was gone, and Batman was alone again in the Flood Control Facility.

Stink of death, he thought. *It's almost as if Killer Croc can smell the way the ghost of the Joker hangs over everything.* That was getting a bit metaphysical, and he quickly dismissed the idea from his thoughts. He had more pressing demands on his time.

Specifically, saving Robin's life. When he was satisfied that Croc was indeed gone, he climbed back up to the main control-room floor and returned his attention to the central panel.

"Robin," he said, touching the control on his gauntlet.

"There you are," Robin answered. *"Hope you didn't hurry."*

"I ran into Killer Croc. How much time do you have?"

"Not too much," Robin said, an edge to his voice.

"Please be precise."

"The water's rising about two inches a minute, my head's touching the ceiling, and the surface is just under my chin. So, what, four minutes or so? Is that precise enough?"

"Yes." Batman surveyed the control panel. The Riddler would have left some sign of how he wanted them to proceed.

"Did Croc want his tooth back?"

"No, he didn't seem to care about it," Batman said.

"Figures. He's got plenty."

"That's more or less what he said." He paused, then added, "Tell me exactly what you see."

Robin started describing the cistern and what he had seen so far. Batman looked more closely at some of the gauges on the area of the console that had been painted bright green.

Finally he saw what he needed. Each of the gauges measured flow, in cubic feet per second—ft^3/s—through the huge array of pipes that ran through and around the Flood Control Facility. But on some of them, the "f" of "ft" was replaced by a question mark—six of them, to be precise. Only one was vertical—the others pointed at different angles.

"You said there were six pipes coming into the cistern?" he asked.

"Oh, good—you were listening."

"Do you remember in what order they started flowing?"

There was a pause.

"Yeah."

That was half of the answer. The other half was which gauges corresponded with which pipes. Batman doubted the Riddler would be so lenient as to permit him to shut them down in any order.

The six angles of the question marks each had to correspond to an orientation, Batman thought. But was it a directional orientation, or were they keyed to the location of the door?

"Robin," he said. "Can you point north from where you are?"

"Seriously?"

That answered the question. As far as their opponent knew, Robin wouldn't possess an instinctive sense of direction. So the question marks had to have been keyed to the location of the door.

"Never mind," he said. "I need you to do exactly as I say. Face the door and use it as your twelve o'clock. Then tell me in order which pipes started flowing."

Batman heard Robin shifting himself around. From the sounds he was making, it was taking more effort than he would have expected. Robin had to get out of there before he had no reserves left to call upon.

"*Okay,*" Robin said. "*Here's the order as I remember it. They went ten o'clock, two o'clock, six o'clock, then four o'clock, eight o'clock, midnight.*"

"Are you sure?" Batman heard the slap of water, and then the unmistakable swirling sound of the mic going underwater.

"*Doesn't matter,*" Robin said, his voice distorted. "*The water's almost to my nose.*"

Batman dialed the first five pipes down. Nothing happened. This was it. If they had figured the puzzle wrong…

"Hold on," he said. "Here comes number six."

Robin didn't answer.

THIRD MURDER IN THREE HOURS
GOTHAMITES WARNED TO STAY INDOORS, "NO DISCERNABLE PATTERN"

Globe staff

GOTHAM CITY: For the third time in as many hours, a citizen of Gotham City has been shot down by an unknown sniper. The most recent victim was Rosalyn Mateosian, an electronics engineer at Remsburg Research Laboratories.

Eyewitness accounts indicate that Mateosian was walking to a food truck for lunch when a single impact to the head felled her. None of the witnesses reported seeing an assailant or hearing a gunshot. According to a source at the Gotham City Police Department who asked to remain anonymous, this has led to speculation that the killer of Mateosian—as well as Brian Isaacson and Lucas Angelo before her—is using silenced weaponry or specialized subsonic ammunition.

GCPD detectives are still processing the scene. When asked if there was a pattern, the detective on the scene referred all queries to the department's public affairs liaison officer, Kathy Molinari. She in turn had no comment beyond a written statement saying as of yet there was "no pattern detectable" in the killings. Molinari also pointed out that dissimilar weapons used in the first two killings in fact suggested two different killers, since most professional killers chose a single weapon.

Conspiracy theories are already beginning to proliferate. Many Gothamites are speculating that this morning's appearance of Batman, after a long hiatus, is related to the outbreak of murders. Gotham City, in recent months a more quiet place than usual, is again becoming frightened and edgy. On the North Side, a young man carrying a paintball gun was assaulted by several persons claiming they had located the assassin. He remains hospitalized, in a stable condition.

Despite the department's official denials of a pattern, the reaction of detectives in the field suggests they have their own view. When a spectator at the scene of the latest incident called out to one of the detectives, asking what people should do as the next hour on the clock ticked down, a detective glanced up at the sky and said, "If I was you, I'd stay inside."

Correction: *The first version of this article misspelled Mateosian's name.* The Globe *regrets the error.*

11

"Here comes number six."

Robin heard a muffled *clunk* coming through the water. He was holding his breath and his feet were completely numb. A moment after the sound died away, he felt the currents begin to move more aggressively, and heard the renewed rush of water below him in the drain opening.

He stubbornly held onto the broken catwalk strut, and felt the meniscus of the water's surface creep down the sides of his head. Nearly a minute after he had pulled in his last breath, the water level had dropped enough that he could take another. He did so with a gulp.

Batman was talking in his earpiece but it took Robin a moment to get his breath enough to respond.

"I'm here," he said.

"But not by much," Batman said, an angry sound to his voice. *"The Riddler managed the timing of these traps very carefully."*

"I could stand a little more care," Robin answered. "Or maybe a little less. I'm not sure which is better." He braced his feet as the water dropped, and he sucked in breath after breath, his muscles starting to tremble and his head going foggy again. He'd never been this cold, at least not since the last time he'd tangled with Victor Fries.

The water level dropped below his feet and Robin heard a series of clicks from just above him. He looked up and a bright green question mark lit up over the door... which lay wide open.

"The Riddler's opened a way out," he said. His teeth started chattering and he realized that before that moment he'd been too cold for it to happen. Batman must have heard it over the comm link.

"You need to get warm," he said. *"And dry, if you can. Before you go any further."*

"Let me get back to you," Robin said.

He swung up into the doorway and stripped off his cloak. Then he opened his tunic, letting the warmer air get at his skin. He squeezed as much water as possible out of his costume and his boots. What he really wanted was to lie down and sleep, and his fingers were still so cold he could barely work the clasp holding the cloak on. But Robin knew he wasn't out of the woods yet. There were still six more doors.

If each of them led to a trap like this...

He put the thought out of his mind. Without a doubt the Riddler meant to kill him, at least ultimately, but he wanted it to happen on *his* schedule, and no other. He would take much greater satisfaction in eliminating a strong adversary, instead of a half-dead hypothermia case.

To get his blood moving and generate heat, he did a quick set of calisthenics and exercises with the bō. His mind started to clear, and it hit home again just how close he'd been to dying. The Riddler had definitely started playing for higher stakes. The USB drive had been an invitation to a lethal game, and now they would have to play it through as best they could.

When he had warmed up a little, he put his cloak on again and looked back out into the holding tank. The drain at the bottom was closed. That, together with the question mark over the door told Robin that the only way out was back up the passage.

Jogging as best he could, he returned to the junction room at the bottom of the stairs leading down from door number one. He could return the way he had come, or follow the second passage leading out of the junction room at a right angle.

Given his manic attention to detail, the Riddler wasn't likely to abide by any deviation from the game. To do so would likely invite instant retaliation, and Robin would likely be dead in an instant. So he climbed the stairs back toward the door, pausing on the steel landing to look around and see if anything had changed since the last time he'd passed through. Nothing seemed different. The same bits of debris were in the same corners, and there were no visible signs that anyone else had passed this way.

Before attempting to open it, he looked the door up and down as best he could in the incandescent light. It, too, seemed the same as it had before, although he hadn't taken a close look at this side of it in his earlier transit. He chided himself for that bit of amateurism.

Then he rattled the latch and found that it was locked from the other side. It was too heavy to blow with explosive gel, and there were no visible hinges that could be broken.

I guess it's the other direction after all, he mused as he descended again. Moving cautiously down the hall that would cut across the corner closest to the furnace, he found that it hooked around to another short stairwell, this one also leading to a door. He climbed the stairs and when he touched the latch, he heard a staccato clang of machinery from somewhere else in the complex.

The knob turned easily. He opened the door and stepped into the room. As it closed behind him, he saw that it was door number two.

Aha, he thought. *Out through odd numbers, in through even?* But there were seven doors. That suggested the Riddler had built in an actual exit… or that whatever lay behind door number seven was intended to be inescapably fatal.

The latter seemed infinitely more likely.

He found himself standing on a white square. Door number three faced a white square. The three costumed chessmen were in different places on the board, still wearing their same numbers. He had already used N4, and the knight was standing on the black square one space out in front of number three.

The other options were B3 and R2.

With N4 standing where he was, there was no viable sequence of rook moves that would put Robin in front of his goal. That left the bishop, so Robin stepped out into the room, keeping his feet on white squares in a left diagonal until he was past R2. Then he zigzagged to the right, cutting across the board until he was next to N4. As before, none of the chessmen reacted to his presence. Robin took the third bishop move, stepping one square diagonally to his left and facing door number three.

Before he went through it, he considered blowing up the Riddler's plan by attacking the chessmen and trying to force a different door. Would it work? Robin didn't think he would have trouble with the chessmen—he could take two of them down before the third knew the attack was happening. But he had a feeling none of the other doors would open without heavy explosives, which he didn't have.

And again, Nigma wouldn't take well to the rules being broken. Especially since they were *his* rules. So while it irritated him, Robin knew the best way forward was to follow the Riddler's format until a better alternative presented itself.

Standing at arm's length from number three, he contacted Batman again.

"I'm back on the chessboard. I leave through odd-numbered doors and come back through even-numbered ones. Number one led down to the cistern. When I came back, number two was the only way back into the room. Now the chessmen are in a different pattern, and I'm looking at number three."

"If you exit through odd-numbered doors, that means there are four stages," Batman said. *"But you're only looking at three chessmen, correct?"*

"Yeah, I was wondering about that too. The fourth time through is likely to be different."

"Without a doubt. Keep that in mind when you come through next time. The Riddler might tip his hand."

"Roger that," Robin said, and he was secretly pleased

to know that Batman expected him to succeed. "Opening door number three."

"Keep moving. The clock is ticking," Batman answered. *"Literally. Every time that timer reaches zero, there's another murder. Soon enough we'll start to see a pattern in those, but the faster you can get through that labyrinth, the more lives we'll save."*

"Who's been killed so far?"

"A software engineer, a building contractor, and an electronics designer. There's no known relationship between the three of them, or at least not one Gordon has uncovered. But I'm beginning to see a pattern that makes a nasty sort of sense. What's more, it's likely that Deadshot is behind all three murders."

"Great, one of our favorite people," Robin replied. "So I can look forward to seeing him at some point. It's all I need to make this a perfect day."

"That's possible, but I certainly hope not," Batman said. *"Bear in mind how the Riddler has arranged events so far. He's keeping us working in tandem, but not together,"* he added. *"That's becoming clearer all the time. He constructed this trap so I'd have to come here in order to release you. There must be a reason for him wanting me in Arkham City instead of working from the Batcave. I'm going to follow that angle."*

"Well, while you do that, I'm going to take the plunge again," Robin said. "So to speak."

"Good plan," Batman said. This time he didn't add, "Be careful."

Door number three opened easily. Robin felt a soft breeze hit his back as air from the room moved into the space on the other side of the door, and a draft around his feet as colder air from that dark space rolled into the room.

Terrific. I was just starting to remember what warm felt like.

He entered the space and saw that it was a cargo elevator, old and well used. There was only one button on its control panel. Robin pushed it and door number three closed. The rusty elevator doors slid shut, and the elevator dropped. Robin counted the seconds. Freight elevators rarely traveled at more than a hundred feet per minute.

He was between twenty-nine and thirty when the elevator car stopped and the doors opened again. That put Robin fifty feet or less below the floor level of the chessboard. Fifty feet was plenty of space for an elaborate trap, and it also put him somewhere near the depth of the subway tunnels that led under this part of the city. He stepped out into a large open space with a grime-covered concrete floor and rusted steel beams holding up the ceiling.

The first thing he noticed was the cold. He could see his breath against the semidarkness, and the air bit at the inside of his nose with every inhalation. It was going to be a theme, then. Pulling a halogen light out of a waterproof pocket on his belt, he shone it out into the space. There he saw several arrangements of spheres, seemingly suspended in midair. Each sphere was about the size of a beach ball. From where he stood, he couldn't tell how many individual arrangements there were, though it might be three.

The rectangular room looked to be somewhere in the neighborhood of two hundred feet long, and its width about half of that. The elevator was located in a corner, set into one of the shorter walls. Robin thought the long wall to his right—the closer one—must run parallel to the passage that led from the junction room to the holding tank. That would put the lower discharge tunnel under the floor.

He stepped carefully out of the car, not touching any of the spheres and stopping just a few feet from the elevator. This offered him a slightly different angle on the room, and he scanned for a door. After a moment he found it, all the way at the opposite corner. As his light fell on it, a bright green question mark lit up on the door.

Okay then, he thought. *No question where I'm supposed to go. So what's going to stop me from getting there?* He studied the floor underneath the nearest of the sphere arrangements, and didn't see anything unusual. The hanging globes didn't look different from one another.

Robin started to shiver again. His uniform had dried. Nevertheless, his nose and ears stung from the cold, and the cloth of his cloak crackled when he took a step. The flood puzzle had set the stage for this one, making him more vulnerable to the temperature.

Taking a chance and wanting to get this over with, he walked straight across the room on a diagonal, leaning out of the way of the hanging spheres and reaching the far door without incident. There was no knob or latch, no keypad or control panel on the wall near it. The question mark, a little less than a foot tall, glowed a steady green.

The solution is in these globes, he decided. *And I'd better find it fast.* He could already feel the cold seeping into him. So he walked around the room, viewing the arrangements from different perspectives before he dared touch any of them. They hung at about waist height, and he could tell that they would look decidedly different if viewed from above or below them.

Pursuing that track, he lay on his back. Ignoring the shock of the cold concrete, he slid himself under one of the formations, scooting along the floor until he had moved along its entire length. Something about it tugged at his memory, but the cold was slowing his mind again. He wasn't shivering anymore, and a distant alarm bell went off in his head.

Wasn't that a bad thing?

He drifted a little, and nearly fell asleep—

No!

Robin jerked, like someone snapping out of a dream. Frost crackled on the parts of his cloak that were touching the frigid surface.

Hypothermia. That's what it means when you stop shivering, he recalled. *Your body is losing the ability to regulate its temperature.* He had to move, had to try to generate some heat somehow. He rolled over and got to his feet, shook his head, and out of the fog that had nearly put his mind into a lethal drift, a memory loomed.

School.

Science class.

Circles and lines…

They were chemical models. He was looking at chemical compounds represented in three-dimensional space.

But what compounds?

Robin looked up and saw that the cables holding the spheres were hung from tracks built into the ceiling, along the girders. The girders looked dull and old, but the tracks were new and shiny in the flashlight's beam. The nature of the puzzle became clear. He had to rearrange them somehow. Also, now that he was looking at the tracks, he could tell that there were two groups of spheres, and not three as he had first thought in the gloom.

But that realization didn't bring him any closer to answering the questions he had. What were the compounds? Which one should he reconfigure first, and how? What would the consequences be if he did them in the wrong order?

It was time to bring Batman in. He activated the comm and, forming his words carefully because his face was so cold, he described the room.

"What do they look like when you lie underneath them?" Batman asked immediately.

"I just did that," Robin said, "and I almost didn't get up."

"I'm afraid you need to do it again," Batman said. *"Keep talking and keep moving. A quick look is all you should need."*

"If you say so." Robin lay on his back and scooted under the formation closest to the door. "It's… well, there are seven globes in this one. They are arranged in… wait a minute." He stood up, noticing something he hadn't seen before. "Some of the globes have the numeral '2' on them."

"Any other distinguishing marks? Numbers?"

Robin ran a light over all of the other globes and realized that several of were marked '2,' but that was the only thing to indicate any difference. They were the same size, the same color…

"Do you think all of the twos go together?"

"*I doubt it,*" Batman said. "*That's too straightforward for the Riddler.*"

"Well, there are two distinct arrangements," Robin said. "Each of them is some kind of chemical compound. That's what it looks like they're meant to be, anyway. The globes are hanging on tracks so I can move them, but I don't want to just shove them around."

"*No, we need to know what we're trying to do before we do something.*"

What do you mean, "we"? Robin thought abstractly. Batman said something else Robin didn't hear. The globes shone softly in the beam of his flashlight, and he started to relax. It didn't seem as cold as it had been a minute ago…

"*Robin!*"

He jerked again, catching himself as he was just about to sit down. That hypothermia-induced calm was dangerous. He started moving around, trying to stamp some feeling back into his feet.

"Sorry," he said. "My mind wandered a little. It's—" He tried not to let any of the fear he felt show through in the tone of his voice. "It's really cold in here."

"*Stay focused,*" Batman said firmly. "*You know the cold is part of the puzzle. The Riddler got you soaked, almost killed you, and now he's testing you again. Testing both of us.*"

"Your part of the test seems a little easier than mine," Robin commented.

"*Tell that to Killer Croc,*" Batman said. "*And speaking of old friends, I think I know where I need to go next.*"

"Go fast," Robin said. "I'm not sure how long jumping jacks are going to keep me awake."

Taking Them to Trask

Duane Trask, Gotham Globe Radio

"And we're back.

"As we were saying before the commercial break, the Gotham Merchant's Bank building in Arkham City is on fire and an assassin is roaming the streets of our fair hamlet. What are you seeing, people of Gotham City? We want to know. Cecil. You're on."

"Yeah, um, hi. First time in a long time."

"Welcome."

"Uh, yeah. So sometimes I go into Arkham City on, you know..."

"Business."

"Right, yeah. Business. And today I was there and I saw Batman. He was in the Flood Control Facility. In and out in maybe ten, fifteen minutes. But you could hear stuff going on in there. Like when the big outflow pipes get turned on, there's this long moan, has something to do with the pressure—"

"Are you an employee of Gotham City Public Works?"

"No, I just... I've been around there a little bit."

"Okay. I just wanted to establish that you're not an expert, or find out if you were."

"I'm not. Not at that, anyway."

"What are you an expert at, Cecil?"

"I probably shouldn't say."

"I'm sure you shouldn't. Okay. Moving on. So you saw Batman."

"Yeah, I saw him go in and come out. Then he sounded like he was talking to himself, but I think he was on some kind of walkie-talkie thing in his, um, what do you call it… not his hat, but you know."

"I believe the correct term is 'cowl.'"

"Okay, right. Cowl. Well, he was talking to someone and this is why I called, because he mentioned Deadshot."

"Deadshot. Are you sure?"

"Yeah, I'm sure. I heard him. Plain as day. You remember Deadshot?"

"Listeners, Cecil is asking me if I remember Deadshot. Thanks for the call, Cecil. My producer's going to get your number before you go so we can follow up for the paper. Now, do we remember Deadshot? I'll tell you what I remember about Deadshot.

"A few months back, Hugo Strange sent him on a little killing spree and one of the people he was after happened to be my old friend and colleague Jack Ryder. Batman saved Jack, but he wasn't able to save three other victims. Strange, it turns out, was using Deadshot to tie up loose ends.

"Does anyone think it's a little… well, strange that we've got these assassinations of seemingly random people again, just when Batman happens to be overheard mentioning Deadshot?

"Whoa! The phone lines just blew up. Apparently a *lot* of you remember Deadshot! We're up against a break here, but as soon as we come back we'll have ourselves a little conversation about Deadshot, and maybe some other costumed crackpots, too.

"Before we go to the break, remember this one thing: If there's anything we know about Deadshot, it's that he is a deadly marksman with a variety of weapons. Our three murder victims today were killed with three different weapons, or so it is being reported. That fits Deadshot's M.O. Am I all-the-way convinced? No. Not yet. But I wouldn't be surprised to find out that Cecil is right.

"There's more to this story. We're on it. Back after this— wait, I just got a very interesting note from my producer. Donna, is this legit? You're sure? You're not sure. Well, let's find out. Listeners, we're about to talk to one Edward Nigma. Edward, you're on."

"Greetings, Mr. Trask. I don't often listen to your show, I confess, but today I am following events with some interest."

"I'm sure. Our listeners may or may not know that Edward Nigma is an alias for the Riddler. Is that who you are, sir?"

"It is."

"How do we know that?"

"Well, you don't. But you will receive confirmation soon. What if I were to tell you that before the end of the day, Batman will be trying to stop not one clock, but two?"

"Let me guess. That's a riddle."

"Very astute. And you will witness its solution in a matter of a few hours. Keep up the good work, Mr. Trask. The people must be informed about what is going on."

"Edward... Edward... Well, listeners, that was someone claiming to be the Riddler. He left us a little puzzle to chew on. We know about one clock, it seems; my guess is that he was referring to the killings. They've been happening an hour apart. But what's the other clock? Is he talking about an actual clock—like the one on the Gotham Merchant's Bank building? That one's already stopped for good, it looks like.

"What else could it be?

"Stay tuned. We've got a hell of a story unfolding here."

12

Killer Croc's tooth had led to Killer Croc. Now the combination of a chemical puzzle and the frigid trap suggested to Batman that the Riddler had involved Victor Fries, better known as Mr. Freeze. Further, he reasoned that since one of the murder victims had been involved with the Ace Chemical factory, that was likely where they'd find Mr. Freeze—and hopefully the clue that would help Robin.

He had to act quickly.

Batman scaled the smokestack that vented the Flood Control Facility's generator. Ace Chemical was visible in the distance, at the edge of the former Restricted Area… which, now that there was no authority to enforce those restrictions, was just another abandoned block of streets and decaying buildings.

Originally built just before World War II, the factory had been well on its way to ruin even before the walling off of Arkham City, and it was a thorough wreck now. Batman swung and glided from rooftop to rooftop, passing the fire still burning in the Gotham Merchant's Bank building. The streets around the bank were clogged with fire trucks, and a coroner's van was on the scene. It looked like the firefighters were getting the blaze under control, though.

Just another bomb in Gotham City.

He skirted around to the south to avoid going near the Monarch Theater that still stood just to the northeast of the factory. Behind that theater was the place where Batman had been born, known as Crime Alley. He preferred not to get close to it, if he didn't have to.

Everything in Gotham City was full of echoes, and there were times when he found it difficult to sort out the present from his memories. He was beginning to suspect that some of his more ambitious enemies were taking advantage of that fact. Deadshot had been one of Hugo Strange's pawns in the buildup to Protocol 10, and now he was active again.

Killer Croc was still hanging around in the same part of the sewers where he'd been before, near the steel mill... and he was still talking about that damned "scent" he'd detected.

Now here was Mr. Freeze, who had been both enemy and ally during the brutal days of TYGER. Freeze had been dragooned into the Joker's scramble to find a cure for the Titan toxin in his blood. Yet unlike many of Gotham City's pre-eminent villains, Fries wasn't a psychopath. He was a man driven to extremes by love, but he had spent so long in extreme emotional states that he was less and less able to come back to anything resembling normal.

Which, Batman knew, was something people said about him.

He wondered if he was going to encounter the Penguin, Clayface—any number of Gotham City's rogues' gallery might be drafted into the Riddler's grand plan. Except for those who were no longer among the living.

Rā's al Ghūl, Scarecrow, the Joker himself…

Too many others were resurfacing, and all at once, for it to be coincidence. Echoes of the past, echoes of the future. Were they part of another riddle?

Batman paused on a rooftop between the factory and the Jezebel Theater, holding a surveillance position in a destroyed TYGER sniper nest less than a hundred yards from the Ace Chemical lot. He didn't see any people, or any sign of a human presence in the building, for that matter—except for steam pouring from one smokestack near the far side of the works.

And that was enough.

That part of the factory housed a series of vats and tanks where raw materials were mixed under carefully controlled conditions. The temperature controls there required the venting of a lot of waste heat, which would account for the steam. That is, if someone was manufacturing chemicals, or doing something else that required precise control.

Mr. Freeze was there. He'd bet his cowl on it.

Staying in the shadows, Batman skirted the fenced perimeter until he reached the railroad spur where tank cars had once delivered raw materials. The fence had been beaten down in several places, and he had no problem getting across the parking lot on foot, sprinting to the loading docks. He entered through an open bay and crossed the receiving area to a door with a sign that read:

> **EMPLOYEES ONLY!**
> **PROTECTIVE GEAR MANDATORY!**

The distant sound of pumps echoed from deep in the building's interior. Touching the door, he felt a slight vibration. He went through it and into a short hallway. An open door on his right revealed a changing area with old protective suits hanging on pegs. Ahead was another door with the same warnings as the last. This one had a narrow window made of reinforced glass. Looking through it, Batman could see part of the factory floor.

The far end of the cavernous area was obscured by roiling steam, but he thought he saw motion there. Preparing himself, Batman slipped through the door and dropped down to the factory floor. Some of the machinery had recently been repaired. Shiny new parts gleamed in the dimness, standing out from the grime coating the rest of the works. Ace Chemical was up and running again, at least partially.

The Joker had been created here, and later made use of the plant to produce some of his more deadly toxins. Now he was gone, and someone else had stepped into his place.

It never ends, Batman thought. Gotham City was a bottomless wellspring of criminality. It was as if the Joker's absence had created a space that demanded filling by other forms of evil. Briefly he wondered who would step in for him, once he was gone. Robin would try, certainly. Perhaps Catwoman would make the choice to abandon her love of theft. But even those two would be standing against a seemingly endless roster of the depraved.

That was as good a reason as any to stay alive.

He moved across the factory to a large assembly of pumps and pressurized tanks. The floor in this area was littered with heavy plastic shipping totes, broken open and emptied out. Labels on their lids read CONUNDRUM SOLUTIONS, INC.

He radioed Oracle and spoke quietly.

"No time for a long conversation. Run down a company called Conundrum Solutions."

"Where should I send what I find?" she asked.

"I'll be in touch." Batman clicked off and took another step toward the roiling steam. He could feel the air getting colder. The vapor itself wasn't hot—it was more like the sea smoke that sometimes hung over Gotham City's harbor when the temperature dropped below zero. The temperature drop had to be due to whatever process was underway, and perhaps—

"Ah, Batman," a tinny voice said. "A mutual acquaintance alerted me that you would be paying this facility a visit."

The timbre of the voice gave the speaker away even before Batman saw the tall, thin figure coming out of the steam, body encased in a frosty blue and gray outfit that looked like a cross between a hazmat suit, a spacesuit, and a suit of armor. A transparent helmet like a bell jar covered his head. Elements of his equipment glowed a soft cyan, while hoses conducting supercooled gases to the suit's temperature-control system snaked around its torso. Freezing mist pooled around the figure's feet, swirling as he walked.

The face within the helmet was unnaturally pale and masked by glowing red-tinted goggles. His head was clean-shaven.

Mr. Freeze.

EYE ON GOTHAM NEWS

Filed by **Vicki Vale**

"This is Vicki Vale, en route to Arkham City. It's not often that a reporter gets a call from a source and that source turns out to be none other than the Riddler himself. But that's what just happened to me—Phil, find me, will you?

"Dammit. Let's start over.

"Find me in three... two...

"This is Vicki Vale, en route to Arkham City. It's not often that a reporter gets a call from a source and that source turns out to be none other than the Riddler himself. But that's what just happened, and that's why I'm standing here just inside the gates of the notorious former prison area. Over my shoulder you can see the Ace Chemical factory, and in the other direction you can probably see the subway station and the old steel mill.

"All of these were critical sites during the uprising that took place a few months ago. Hugo Strange and Quincy Sharp and TYGER commandos were on one side, and on the other... well, accounts differ. People are still sorting it all out. We know Batman was involved, and we know he was there when the Joker died. Some villains turned on Strange and helped Batman, while others tried to kill him—and each other, and in the end Hugo Strange, as well.

"The death toll numbered in the hundreds, and likely will

never be confirmed. What's certain is that it included the Joker. There are rumors that Scarecrow was actually *eaten* by Killer Croc, but those remain unconfirmed.

"We bring up that gruesome story because the Riddler reached out to this reporter this morning and asked to meet at the edge of Arkham City. He's got a story he wants to tell, and guess who's going to be right there to listen?

"You guessed right.

"I'm moving toward an abandoned entrance to the subway system below Arkham City. This entrance is located between the Flood Control Facility and the steel mill. It looks... are you getting that, Phil? It looks like someone else has been through here recently. There are footprints in the dust—sorry if it's dark here, folks, we're going down into a part of the station where the power hasn't been on in, oh, I'd say months.

"Let's hold right here for a moment. You can see the footprints there, looking like they came up from under the station. Then there are broken windows high up in the ceiling, where it arches over the landing. This is where the Riddler said he wanted to meet. What story he wants to tell, I'm not sure, but it's sure to be interesting. The only thing I know for sure is that it involves both Batman and Robin.

"Part of the conditions for our meeting is that we turn off the cameras, so we're going to... there. You're only hearing my voice now, but this is still *Eye on Gotham*. Stay tuned. I'll be keeping our loyal viewers posted as often as I can. This is Vicki Vale, reporting to you live from the edge of Arkham City...

"You got that, Phil?

"Phil?

"Phil, where did you go?"

13

"Doing some work for the Riddler here, Fries?"

"No, far from it. This is a project of my own. Now that the Joker has shuffled off this mortal coil, I have this facility entirely to myself. It's marvelous what one can do with the proper tools and equipment."

It was an eerie effect as his electronically enhanced voice came simultaneously from his suit and some speakers mounted in the rafters overhead. A half-dozen goons appeared out of the freezing mist, wearing containment suits with designs that echoed his unique ensemble, and bearing weapons with barrels that glowed with the same pale blue that shone from the freeze gun mounted on their boss's right arm.

"The Riddler did suggest you would be dropping in, and I took steps to ensure that both his plans and mine would continue, despite your interference." Mr. Freeze took a step back and was wreathed in the mist again. "Please excuse me," he said. "My work calls. It is nearly finished."

The tactical situation wasn't complicated. Whatever Mr. Freeze was doing, Batman suspected it wasn't designed to enhance the well-being of Gotham City's citizenry. He didn't have to wait long for that suspicion to be confirmed, as the singular voice came over the speakers again.

"While you fight for your life, I will entertain you," Mr. Freeze said. "I am in the process of supercooling the natural gas held in tanks along the river by Gotham Power and Light. When I have achieved the desired temperature, I will reset the containment and distribution systems so that supercooled gas enters the power-generating station, where it will encounter the normal ambient temperature. You are an educated man, Batman. You know what will happen next."

He did. The supercooled gas, colliding with the sudden higher temperature, would expand violently. The force of the expansion would be enough to shatter many of the pipes and valves channeling the gas supply, causing a huge eruption of volatile natural gas… which would then ignite the moment it encountered an open flame, or even a spark from a live wire torn loose in the initial expansion.

The entire storage and generation works would go up in a fireball powerful enough to level everything within hundreds of yards. That blast radius included several apartment buildings and at least one police precinct. Casualties would be in the hundreds, at the very least, and Gotham City would be without electricity until power could be rerouted from elsewhere.

"Your silence is telling, Batman," Mr. Freeze said. The mists began to clear, and Batman saw that he was standing on a platform over a shining tangle of valves and pumps. "Already the cooling agents are circulating. Liquid nitrogen is quite effective. Soon the gas will be too cold to return to normal temperature without a quite spectacular explosion." He cast a brief look over his shoulder. "Fight well, and you will live long enough to see it. Gentlemen?"

Mr. Freeze's goons raised their weapons. *Six of them,* Batman thought. Just as there had been six in the Gotham Merchant's Bank vault.

Another echo.

Mr. Freeze needed them to buy him time so he could finish circulating the liquid nitrogen across the river to the GP&L facility. Most likely he was using the existing gas mains, reversing their flow to send cooling elements back up the pipes. Even if the explosive expansion of the liquid nitrogen didn't itself destroy the works, the reversed flow would over-pressurize the natural-gas storage chambers.

Boyle's law would do the rest.

The plan had one weakness, however. Whereas another man might not know what needed to be done, Batman had been in the Ace Chemical plant before—and often enough to know it well. He knew where the gas mains were, and he had seen the pumping and mixing feeder mechanisms in operation. He could stop the process.

That was why Freeze was depending on his goons.

Make it two weaknesses.

It was time to do something unexpected.

He dropped into a crouch, swept his cape up to cover himself, and smashed a smoke pellet onto the floor about six feet in front of him. Mixing with the mist, the smoke exploded outward into a hemisphere, covering all of Mr. Freeze's goons. They started firing wildly. A freeze beam crackled as it made contact with Batman's cape. He shrugged the cape out into its full spread and shot a grapnel line up to the rafters over the main mixing mechanism.

He pulled the trigger and began to ascend.

A quick tap activated his radio.

"Commissioner Gordon," he said. The voice-recognition software called Gordon.

As he reached the rafters, Batman swung his legs up to lock his feet through the angle created by the roof girders and the crossbeams that supported the light fixtures. With one hand he held his cape out for protection against the barrage of freeze beams. With the other he picked two Batarangs off his Utility Belt.

A bolt holding one of the crossbeams snapped off from the extreme cold, and the beam swung down to clang off the top of a tank housing.

"Batman," Gordon said. *"What is it?"*

"Tell Gotham Power and Light to shut down operations at the waterfront tanks. Immediately." Hanging upside down, he located the junction valve where the supercooled holding tank vented into the feeder pipes. He wasn't going to have long to do this right. Mr. Freeze's goons were already swinging around to get a better shot at him, and with the Batarangs in one hand he couldn't shift his cape to shield himself.

"What the hell for?"

"No time to explain," Batman said. He arched out of the way of a freeze beam that shattered the bulb and fixture of an emergency light. Glass tinkled down to the concrete floor. Pain from his heel made it difficult to keep steady hanging upside down.

He had to move.

Two quick Batarangs broke off the stem of the control valve on the holding tank, and then punched a hole into one of the feeder pipes. Made highly brittle by the temperature of the liquid nitrogen flowing through it, the pipe cracked open.

Gordon was shouting questions.

"Just do it, Commissioner," Batman snapped. "I'll be in touch."

The moment the liquid nitrogen came in contact with room-temperature air, it evaporated.

Explosively.

A twenty-foot section of pipework disintegrated in a detonation that peppered the area with fragments of frozen metal. The goons screamed as they were caught in the blast, and Mr. Freeze crouched down behind the console on the control platform. More liquid nitrogen poured from the broken end of the pipe where it met the holding tank. As it vaporized, the factory floor was covered in a freezing fog.

With the supply interrupted and the feeder pipe vented to the open air, the existing liquid nitrogen would quickly evaporate. Batman hoped it would be quick enough to avoid supercooling the gas in Gotham Power and Light's tanks. He guessed from Mr. Freeze's fury that it would.

"Kill him!" Mr. Freeze screamed over the speakers.

The unexpected had yielded success. Freeze thought he had everything under control, but Batman had demonstrated that he wasn't bound by those rules. Instantly his opponents began to doubt themselves, and that gave him the upper hand.

This was what he and Robin needed to do with the Riddler, but as yet they hadn't found an opportunity. Thus far Nigma's gambit was airtight, but the moment would come when they could break open his carefully constructed belief in his own invulnerability. First, however, Batman had to get Robin out of the death room under the mill, and to do that he needed Victor Fries.

The blast had dissipated the smoke, which meant the three remaining combat-ready goons could see Batman again. They started firing just as he let go of the girder and scissored into a glide, aimed for the command platform.

A blast from one of the freeze guns hit his legs just as he was shifting to come in for a landing, encasing them in ice. Instead of dropping into a fighting posture on the platform next to Mr. Freeze, Batman hit hard and collapsed into a roll, crashing into the railing on the far side. He couldn't stand, and Mr. Freeze turned to bring his own weapon to bear.

But Batman still had the use of his upper body. He threw a Batarang that struck Freeze's arm, deflecting his aim. The freeze gun laid a layer of frost over a bank of gauges.

Batman thrust his legs against the railing, breaking off some of the ice. Freeze fired again, and Batman heaved himself up and out of the way. The steel railing crackled as the freeze beam instantly dropped its temperature by two hundred degrees.

His next kick shattered it entirely, and freed one of his legs. He planted that foot and shoved himself into a lunge, tackling his opponent. As they both slammed down to the floor, the remaining goons were shouting and coming closer. Yet they couldn't fire without hitting both Batman and their boss.

Freeze's voice boomed over the speakers.

"Fire, fools! You can't hurt me!"

Batman knew that if they were caught in the field of fire, he would be frozen solid and Mr. Freeze would be largely unaffected. His containment suit was designed to handle extreme cold. Yet there was one thing Batman could do, inspired by Mr. Freeze's own plan. He freed one arm and found his explosive gel, then sprayed a thick coat directly over Mr. Freeze's helmet. As the gel coated the face mask, a look of fearful understanding appeared on his opponent's face.

If struck by a beam, the gel would be supercooled, and what would happen as it warmed? Exactly the same thing that would happen to the natural gas in Gotham Power and Light's holding tanks. The explosion might not kill Freeze, but exposure to ambient temperatures would.

A beam hit both of them at waist level.

"Stop! Don't fire!" Mr. Freeze screamed—so loudly that some of the speakers overloaded and spat electronic noise. Another freeze beam crackled across his shoulders and the back of his helmet before the goons got the message.

Batman flexed his legs, cracking off the rest of the ice coating. His heel was killing him. Then he braced his hands on Mr. Freeze's shoulders and pushed, breaking himself free from the grip of the refrigeration suit. Cautiously the henchmen began to climb the stairs, weapons leveled but silent.

"Let's talk, Victor," he said. "You tell me what you've

been doing for the Riddler, and your climate control stays intact."

"Stay back! Weapons down!" Mr. Freeze waved at his minions.

They backed down the stairs.

"I do this all for Nora. Only for Nora."

Victor Fries peered through his helmet, looking defeated. The gel was still there, as an insurance policy. The goons had discarded their weapons, though they didn't look happy about it. Batman didn't care.

"You were going to blow up part of the riverfront for Nora? Spare me," he said. "And your deal with the Riddler had a clause in it you didn't know about. He may have told you I was coming, but he was the one who led me to you in the first place. He's killing the people who helped him build his death rooms, and he's pointing me toward the ones he doesn't think he can kill himself."

"Mr. Nigma and I have an arrangement," Mr. Freeze said, regaining some of his dignity. "Haven't you and I worked out a mutually beneficial arrangement in the past? That should be considered a valid precedent."

There was truth in that. Mr. Freeze had helped find a serum that would counteract the blood toxins that eventually killed the Joker. It hadn't stopped him, however, from betraying their "arrangement," and Batman wasn't in a mood to re-establish diplomatic relations.

He didn't have time.

"Conundrum Solutions—that's what the two of you

built," he said. "But what were you producing for him?"

"Part of our arrangement is secrecy," Freeze replied smoothly. "Surely you understand, Batman. Having been party to a similar agreement in the past, how can you expect me to violate my contract with Mr. Nigma?"

Instead of responding, Batman brandished a Batarang. "Other than a violent temperature change, you know what else sets off that explosive gel?" he asked, but he didn't wait for an answer. "A sharp impact."

"No! There's no need for that," Freeze said quickly. "In exchange for the use of this facility, Mr. Nigma asked me to redesign a certain type of battery. Two batteries."

"For what purpose?"

"He wished them to function both as power supply and explosive. All batteries are capable of exploding. What I did was demonstrate to him how two kinds of batteries could be used together to create a *controlled* detonation."

"Why does he want exploding batteries?"

"How should I know?" Mr. Freeze said. "And more to the point, why should I care? There are samples in the crate there." He pointed.

"Have one of your men bring them here," Batman said.

Mr. Freeze nodded and one of his henchmen brought over two objects. One was a rectangular brick, similar to a laptop battery, but larger. The other was also rectangular, but featured terminals more like the standard nine-volt battery commonly used in small electronics. It, too, was larger than normal, and neither bore any manufacturer's mark.

"I discovered a method of creating a chain reaction using a linkage between the lithium-ion type and the lead-acid variety. Overcharging one leads to excessive heat. Overcharging the other leads to the off-gassing of hydrogen and oxygen."

Excess heat in a confined space, combined with free hydrogen and oxygen, created the near certainty of an explosion—especially if whoever controlled the process introduced a spark or a flame into the interaction.

"You disappoint me, Fries," Batman muttered. "I thought you were better than the average villain, but you're little more than a paid weapons master."

"You are in no position to judge me, Batman," Freeze responded, his expression as unreadable as ever. "I have Nora to consider."

Batman looked around. "I don't see Nora."

"And you will not see her," Freeze said. "She is safe... as long as my arrangement with Mr. Nigma continues."

"You might want to reconsider that deal," Batman said. "Like I said, the Riddler's been eliminating the people he worked with on his project under the steel mill. He led me to Killer Croc. Now he led me to you. Your loyalty might prove to have been misplaced."

"I have only my own intuition to rely upon, Batman." Freeze drew himself up and spoke in a sober and proud tone. "My own motivations. You have reasons for doing what you do, and so do I."

"Don't compare yourself to me, Freeze," Batman said. "Nora's condition is tragic, and I sympathize, but you could conduct your research without getting your hands dirty."

"And you could remove your mask, reveal your true identity to all of Gotham City, yet you do not. You like being the feared stranger, the Dark Knight who spreads terror. You are hardly in a position to judge."

"Psychoanalyze someone else, Freeze." The clock was ticking. "What happened after you developed those batteries for the Riddler?"

"I sent him the designs and got to work on my own project. A superb show it would have been, Batman. Fire born from cold. If only you had minded your own business…"

"That *is* my business, Victor—ruining yours," Batman said. "Now you're going to give me a chemistry lesson. Fast."

Minutes later Batman was on his way back across the floor. Behind him, on the control platform, Mr. Freeze and his men were securely bound with electrical cables Batman had ripped out of the consoles. He called Commissioner Gordon to see how the investigation into the murder victims was progressing.

"Your friend Oracle is something else," Gordon said. *"He tracked down a connection we hadn't seen."*

"Yes, he's very good," Batman agreed without correcting the commissioner. What Gordon didn't know wouldn't hurt Barbara. "What did he find?"

"A company called Conundrum Solutions," Gordon said. *"All of the victims made multiple calls to a number traceable to that company, and they made them all within the space of the same few days, just last week."*

"Another clue," Batman said.

"And a pretty big one," Gordon said. *"We're working with the major cellular carriers to find out who else was in contact*

with Conundrum during the same time frame. So far we have two more numbers, and we're tracking down the people who own them. They have to be warned."

"Yes, and quickly," Batman agreed. "Commissioner, when you find out who those people are, bring them in, but don't tell them why. There's too much about this trail of breadcrumbs we don't know yet. They may be able to shed some light, as long as we can keep them alive."

"Understood," Gordon replied. *"Gotham Power and Light want to know when they can power up again."*

Behind Batman, liquid nitrogen was still evaporating out of the broken pipe, but slowly now, in trails of vapor that curled lazily out over the floor. Automatic shutoff valves had sealed all the circulating systems and feeder pipes that led out of the factory, which meant that the power company's mains would be able to equalize their pressure again without the threat of a disaster.

"It should be all right now," he said, then added, "You should send officers to Ace Chemical. Mr. Freeze needs a ride."

CHEMICAL DISASTER AVERTED ON WEST RIVER WATERFRONT

Globe staff

GOTHAM CITY: A massive explosion and fire has been averted on the West River waterfront. Acting on an anonymous tip, the Gotham City Police Department had Gotham Power and Light suspend its operations at the waterfront storage tanks, where the city's reserves of natural gas and heating oil are stored. The result was an immediate emergency lockdown.

GP&L is still investigating the incident, but their preliminary determination is that someone attempted to damage the pipelines running under the West River and into the riverfront generating station. According to a company spokesman, initial reports indicate the attack on the pipelines used supercooling chemicals to freeze them, and render them vulnerable to cracking and rupture. The resulting leaks could have had catastrophic effects, including a chain reaction that could have blown up the entire gas reserve.

In an official statement, a GP&L spokesman said, "This is the perfect example of emergency measures kicking in and saving lives. Such an explosion would have leveled much of the waterfront and spread fires for several blocks in all directions. The death toll would have likely been in the thousands." In addition, much of Gotham City would have been without electrical power for days, until sources could be routed around the destroyed transformers.

Victor Fries, better known as Mr. Freeze, was apprehended at the Ace Chemical factory and is currently being transported to Blackgate Penitentiary to await arraignment. Several loud explosions were heard at the plant prior to his apprehension. Gotham City Police trucks and emergency response vehicles were visible around the supposedly deserted facility. A GCPD official who did not wish to be named said that Batman was involved in the operation, and that it was his action that prevented the destruction. Fries is well known to be searching for a cure for his wife Nora's debilitating medical issues, though it is unknown whether or not that played a part in today's incident.

One of the victims, Brian Isaacson, appears to have been a builder and construction engineer whose company was the lead contractor in the renovation and retrofitting of Ace Chemical approximately ten years ago. It remains unclear whether there is any connection between Isaacson or his company and today's events.

The anonymous GCPD source also indicated that Batman was at Ace Chemical due to "some kind of contact with the Riddler." The source was unable to characterize that contact, or add any further detail. This link, speculative as it may be, lends credence to other alleged connections between Batman's recent return to action and possible criminal conspiracies.

A man purporting to be the Riddler, who is also known by the names Edward Nashton and Edward Nigma, called Gotham Globe Radio's *Taking Them to Trask* program a short time ago, but his identity has not been verified, and the caller apparently mentioned Batman only in the context of a riddle given during the call.

14

Robin was doing push-ups to stay warm when Batman's voice growled in his ear mic.

"I have your answer. I think."

"Let's hear it."

"You said there are two patterns of spheres, right?"

"Right."

"Each of them represents the basic chemical action of a kind of battery. I'll explain more about it later, but right now we need to get you out of there."

"That we do," Robin said. "I'm... well, let's just say it's been a long time since I could feel my feet. And I started singin' to m'self to keep m'self company. I'm—"

"Robin! Stay focused!"

He bristled at that.

"You stay foc'sed when you're thrown into a room at twenny below."

"I'm not saying it's easy," Batman said. *"I'm saying it has to be done. Now listen. One of these is a lithium-ion battery structure, and the other is a lead-acid structure. The problem is that the Riddler hired Mr. Freeze to design batteries that could double as controlled explosives; that's possible through*

the interaction between the heat generated by the lithium-ion reaction and the free hydrogen and oxygen created when a lead-acid battery is overcharged."

Robin tried to follow, but he was losing track.

"'Kay," he said.

"Do you understand?" Batman pressed. *"If you end this puzzle incorrectly, the best bet is that whole room is going to go off like a bomb."*

"If I don' start doing it, pretty soon I'm not gonna be able to lif' my arms."

"You're slurring your speech."

"Uh-huh," Robin said. "Cold. Lips are numb. Whish… which one do I do first?"

"If you shift the lead-acid one first, the room will fill with free hydrogen and oxygen. Not a good idea. The lithium-ion one will begin to generate excess heat via a process called thermal runaway. That's the process the Riddler wanted Mr. Freeze to manage, and we can expect it to be part of the puzzle here. You'll have to do the lithium-ion one first, then the lead-acid one. Then—"

"—Hope the door opens before ever'thing goes boom."

"Precisely."

"Soun's like a plan."

"Timing is everything. First you'll have to figure out which of them represents the lead-acid combination and which represents the lithium-ion," Batman said.

"Ion isn't too specific," Robin said. "What's a lithium-ion battery run on? What's the compound?"

"In the batteries the Riddler gave Mr. Freeze, it's lithium cobalt oxide."

"Lithium cobalt ox-oxide," Robin said. "That's LiCoO$_2$. Four atoms, right?"

"Yes, but that's the positive electrode. The negative electrode will probably be graphite."

"That's jus' carbon."

"A specific arrangement of six carbon atoms."

"Okay. Okay. So the lithium-ion side should have ten spheres. No, nine, 'cause here's one with a number two on it. Tha's two of the same atom. Got it. One side should be six carbon atoms."

"In a hexagon."

"Right." Robin looked up and started dragging the spheres into place. The chains rattled along the tracks and fine black dust sifted down from the ceiling. He couldn't help himself. He laughed.

"What's the joke?"

"A little encouragement from the Riddler. He lubricated these tracks with graphite." Robin got six of the spheres hanging in a hexagonal shape. Then he went to the other three. "What does lithium cobalt oxide look like?"

"That one's tricky. In batteries, the lithium is laid in layers between the cobalt oxide structures. So you'll need a triangle and—"

"I only have three sp'eres left."

"Can you arrange them so the lithium is separated from the cobalt and the O^2?"

Robin looked up at the tracks. "I think so."

"Then do it."

He did. The spheres started to glow.

"Something's hap'ning," Robin said. "The spheres are…"

ouch. They're gettin' hot." It was alarming and a relief, both at the same time.

"*Thermal runaway,*" Batman said. "*That's as we predicted. Now do the lead-acid combination, but be ready to run.*"

"What if I do it, and the door doesn't open?"

Batman paused. "*How many doors are in the room you went through to get there?*"

"Seven."

"*How many have you been through?*"

The spheres were giving off so much heat that the room was filling with fog, and Robin couldn't stand close to them. The heat scalded his frozen skin and awakening nerves were screaming in his fingers and toes and ears.

"Three," he said. "If I get out of here, four."

"*So there are at least one and probably two challenges left,*" Batman said. "*The Riddler won't cheat on his own riddles. At least not yet.*"

"That's a lot of trust to put in him," Robin commented.

"*If you've got a better idea, I'm listening.*"

The room was like a sauna now. If he stayed here too much longer, Robin was going to evade the threat of freezing only to be faced with heatstroke. So he went to the other pattern of hanging spheres.

"What's the lead-acid combination?"

"*Both lead oxide and lead, kept separately, interact with sulfuric acid. Ions move around and the result is lead sulfate on both sides, with water in the middle. The charging action is to break up that lead sulfate and rebuild the sulfuric acid, but overcharging breaks different chemical bonds and causes the outgassing of hydrogen and oxygen.*"

"Lead oxide," Robin said. "Pb_3O_4. Two spheres, one of them with a two on it. Okay. Got that."

Then on the other side, a lone lead atom. In between, sulfuric acid and water.

"H_2SO_4 and H_2O, roger that. Hang on." Robin found a track that extended a little away from the rest of them. He pulled a sphere out to hang at the far end of that track. That was the lone lead atom. Then he went to the other side of the arrangement and found a sphere with a two on it. He pulled that one away from the center of the arrangement, and then pulled an unlabeled sphere out next to it on a parallel track.

"I've got the lead and lead oxide in place."

The room had grown hot enough that he was drenched in his own sweat. It was uncomfortable to the point of scorching whenever he moved toward the center of the room, closer to the growing heat coming from the lithium-ion pattern.

"Are we sure we did this in the right order?" Robin asked, wiping the sweat from his eyes. It was gathering in the bottoms of the eye slots on his mask.

"Your guess is as good as mine," Batman said. *"When you get the sulfuric acid in place, you'd better run."*

Robin placed himself in the center of the lead-acid arrangement. He had six spheres left. Four of them were marked with the number 2.

Oh, crap.

"There's a problem," he said. "I need four of the spheres for H_2SO_4, but I have six. Once I make the sulfuric acid, I'll have an unmarked sphere and one marked with a leftover two."

"Water," Batman said. *"The Riddler is nothing if not meticulous."*

"Very funny," Robin said. "Okay. Water. I'll do that one first. Then I'll put the sulfuric acid together, because that's what breaks everything apart, right?"

"I would think so," Batman said. *"But whichever one you do first, do the other one fast."*

"Got it," Robin said. It was so hot in the room now that convection currents were visible in the air. The tracks and the ceiling wavered in his vision. He dragged two of the spheres to positions near each other on the side nearer the lead-oxide pairing. Then he started pulling the last four spheres into place.

"H_2," he said. There was a little shower of graphite as that one locked into place. "S," he said. Another *clink*. "Sure would be nice if the door would open. Okay…

"First O_2."

Clink.

The floor started to burn his feet through the boot soles.

"Second O_2," he said, and locked it into place.

Suddenly electricity crackled down the chains from the ceiling, spitting and arcing from chain to chain. An arc jumped to Robin's hands where they still touched the chain, and the jolt knocked him off his feet. He rolled on the floor, stunned, but the floor burned him and he tucked his cape around himself and kept the roll going, aiming toward the door. His cloak smoldered where it came into contact with the floor.

An hour ago he'd been dying of hypothermia. Now he was being roasted alive. The electricity continued to spit and sizzle on the chains. The spheres in the lead-acid configuration started to heat up from the current—

and perhaps ten seconds after Robin had locked in the combination of atoms, all seven spheres shattered.

At that moment, the door opened.

Robin ran though it like a bat out of hell. The passage ahead of him was dead straight and inclined slightly up. He could see a branch ahead.

If he could just reach it…

There was a sharp crack from behind him, and a split second later a thunderous explosion. As the sound reached him, so did the blast wave. He was just at the intersection in the passage and he threw himself to the right, wrapping himself in his cape and diving into the side hall as the rolling fireball from the explosion scoured the main passage just behind him. The heat was unbearable. He kept rolling, slapping out whatever fires ignited on his cape.

The fires dissipated and Robin came to a halt, breathing heavily and smelling smoke, including that from the charred bits of his suit and cape. He sat up and leaned against the wall, looking back down to the main passage. Bits of trash and debris burned on the floor back that way. If he'd still been out there when the fire passed, he wouldn't be breathing now.

How much longer could he keep doing this?

He shut the question down and canceled that entire train of thought. Doubt would kill him just as dead as the Riddler's puzzles. Reactivating his comm, he pinged Batman.

"I'm out," he said. "Warmed up, too—or I guess I should say I'm kind of charred on the outside and still frozen on the inside. My homeostasis is pretty shot."

"Alfred will make you some tea when you get home," Batman said. *"What's next?"*

"I'm headed back to the chessboard," Robin said. "At least I think so. I'll let you know." In truth, he wasn't sure which branch of the hall to take. He could see what looked like a dead end down the side spur, but the main passage was still littered with burning wreckage. From the sound of it, there was a lively fire burning in there, past the intersection.

Robin went up the side spur as far as he could go, and realized quickly that it was the wrong call. Smoke from the fire below was thick here, and he couldn't see or feel a way out. He doubled back to the main passage, turned right—away from the source of the explosion—and discovered that the Riddler had left him another message.

Beyond the intersection, the hall broadened into a room, and in the center of the room stood a wooden framework in the shape of a question mark. Ignited by the fire from the explosion, the question mark burned brightly, illuminating the entire chamber. On the far side of it was a stairwell.

"Okay," Robin said. "I've gotta admit, that's pretty slick." He didn't know if the Riddler was listening or not, but it never hurt to stroke a megalomaniac's ego. It was often the best way to disarm him, or get him to show a weakness. And it *had* been pretty slick, setting up a flammable sculpture so that it would be lit by the explosion.

It gave new meaning to "burning question."

It encouraged him to know the Riddler wouldn't have bothered to build it if he didn't intend someone to see it. So he was still setting up puzzles with the expectation that Robin could survive them.

I guess stroking the ego works both ways, Robin thought. *But I've still got doors five and seven ahead of me.* And number seven was the outlier. If the pattern held, he would re-enter the chessboard through door number four, confront another puzzle on the other side of number five, and then—assuming he lived that long—come back through door number six.

So seven was… what? The lucky number? For who?

Maybe *that* was the burning question.

A powerful breeze blew down the stairs from somewhere above, pushing the smoke away from him, offering momentary relief. Robin got to the top stair and followed a short hallway that angled away at ten o'clock. That would lead to…

Sure enough. He reached a door, opened it, and found that the chessmen had shifted their positions again. Just to be sure he wasn't missing something, Robin gamed out the possibilities for the knight and bishop, even though he had already used them. The bishop was out, since he was on a black square and door number five was next to a white one. There was no way to execute four knight moves without landing on one of the chessmen.

That left the rook. The lack of a fourth option bothered Robin more now—the puzzle behind door number seven was becoming maddening. Yet there was nothing he could do, so there was no sense in dwelling on it.

First he had to make it back through number six. So he marched out into the room four squares, faced right, and walked straight up to door number five.

Two rook moves.

No sense putting it off.

As Batman had said, the clock was ticking. So Robin opened the door and walked through.

RyderReport.com

Posted by JKB
Wednesday, 1:55 p.m.

Tick, tock, tick, tock…

Unless Batman has caught the sniper terrorizing the streets of Gotham City, there will be a fourth murder in about five minutes from the time this report will be posted—not the time I'm actually writing the words. You guys know how it works, right? None of this happens in real time.

There's been lots of speculation about who the sniper is. A caller on Duane Trask's show claimed to have heard Batman talking about Deadshot, or at least that's what Duane said happened. We don't know for sure, because we don't listen to Duane's show.

As far as we know, nobody else does either.

Deadshot, you'll remember, went on a murderous rampage after smuggling himself *into* (you read that right) Arkham City. He was about to go after our pal Jack Ryder when Batman stepped in, which is the single best thing Batman's ever done in his life. Although for all we know, Jack could have handled Deadshot on his own.

Anyway, we bring it up because if Deadshot's on another murderous rampage, then that seems a little like… well, you know when a band goes on one tour too many? Yeah. That.

Oh, and Duane also seems to think the Riddler called him, too. Apparently he's the go-to guy for deranged killers. Way to go, Duane! Unless the Riddler was a prank, in which case, *Wah wah wah*, Duane!

Tick, tock, tick, tock.

Time passes for all of us. Deadshot might be on a "greatest hits" tour, but for us it's the same old song and dance. This city is besieged by wackos, and we're relying on another wacko to protect us against them. No wonder we're all crazy.

Speaking of crazy, Vicki Vale—remember her? Desperate to make herself part of every story? Well, she's convinced herself that she's talking to the Riddler, and last we knew she was headed down under Arkham City. We're all for professional rivalries, but we hope nothing bad happens to Vicki down there. Who knows, maybe she'll come out with a story we haven't already broken…

Jack's going to have a full rundown on the whole Arkham situation in about an hour, on *Midday Gotham*.

UPDATE UPDATE UPDATE: Right before I hit "Post" on this post, word came that there was a huge underground explosion in Arkham City. Nothing too specific, but it looks to have been somewhere under the old steel mill. There are conflicting reports.

The one thing everyone agrees on is that there was a hell of a boom. Smoke is visible over Arkham City, apparently coming from the sewer grates. Killer Croc isn't going to like this.

Be sure to watch Jack on *Midday Gotham* for more details.

15

As soon as Batman finished talking to Robin, an automated message from Oracle pinged in his ear.

"Five minutes left in the current countdown."

As he approached the Batmobile he arranged the pieces of the puzzle in his head. In truth, there were far too few of them. Factor one—the death rooms, each themed and each somehow connected to a villain the Riddler had brought in as a partner. Factor two—the murders of people who appeared to have been brought in to provide technical expertise in the construction of the traps. Factor three...

The rogues' gallery?

The old steel mill?

Maravilla?

That was the problem. There really *wasn't* a factor three—or if there was, it was maddeningly elusive. The death rooms were leading to something. They had to be. That was the Riddler's modus operandi, to use an old, worn phrase. He had a grand, insidious plan of some sort, and still he dangled it out of reach.

He was dragging them through several of the same locales where they had pursued the Joker and his associates during the culminating violence of Protocol 10. That much, at least, seemed clear. But why? How did it relate to his endgame, his ultimate goal?

Is it possible the Joker is alive? That would explain the deliberate echoes of previous events. But it was unthinkable. Batman had seen the Joker's body. Gordon had watched it burn, and helped dispose of the ashes.

He was gone.

Unless he'd employed a disguise, or a body double…

No, Batman thought. *Not this time. There was too much evidence.* They had confirmed it every way possible. *Then why am I still clinging to the chance that he might have survived?* He had fought the Joker for years, and come close to death on more occasions than he could count. He should be joyous that it had ended, yet it seemed as if he had lost someone terribly close.

Perhaps he had. That was what Alfred and Robin had been hinting at, before the arrival of the package. As bizarre as it seemed, as much as he hated to admit it, Batman knew that in some twisted way, the Joker was still a part of him.

A man's greatness can be measured by his enemies. They had defined each other for so long. So much of Batman's identity, his history, was tied up in the seemingly endless battle against his opposite number. Batman stood for order, the Joker for chaos, but it was more than that. They were worthy adversaries. Their minds were evenly matched, and through all of the horrors he had perpetrated over the years, the Joker had forced Batman to be *better*.

If the Joker really was gone, might it be that Batman's finest days were behind him?

No, not "if," he thought. *The Joker is gone, and I was Batman before he ever appeared, and I'm still Batman without him. Gotham City is what defines me, not the homicidal lunatics who plague it.*

From his vantage point parked near Ace Chemical, Batman watched a pair of Gotham City Police Department cruisers navigate the rubble-strewn streets, followed by a Special Operations van designed to handle Mr. Freeze. The first car pulled up next to the Batmobile, and Gordon himself got out of the passenger side.

"How are they doing with that fire?" Gordon asked, looking past Batman at the plume of smoke stretching from the Gotham Merchant's Bank downstream over the West River.

"I haven't been keeping track," Batman replied. "Too many other things to do." He gestured toward the factory. "Mr. Freeze and six of his men are inside. Some of them will need medical attention."

"We'll see to it," Gordon said.

"What did you find out about other phone numbers linked to Conundrum Solutions?"

"There are two. One belongs to a man called Pierre Ouellette, who runs a chemical supply company. We've got him at a safe house. We haven't been able to trace the other one. It's a burner phone, probably already in the river. We're trying to identify what other numbers it might have called, but that kind of a trace takes a little more time."

"Where is the safe house?" Batman asked.

"I shouldn't tell you," Gordon said. "You're—"

Batman's comm pinged.

"One minute," Oracle said.

"Commissioner, wherever you took Pierre Ouellette, the Riddler will have someone watching. We can be certain of that. He's been controlling the playing field ever since this little game began. If you don't give me the location, you'll have another body on your hands."

"On my hands?" Gordon shot back. "They're not coming after me, Batman. They're coming after you."

This was true. The Riddler and others like him didn't spend their time concocting schemes to entrap police officers. To them, the ordinary cop on the beat was little more than collateral damage.

"Forty-five seconds."

"Fair enough," Batman said, "but if you withhold this information from me, there's nothing I can do to protect Ouellette."

"What if you're wrong?" Gordon shot back. "Or what if his next target is the other number?"

"Consider how this has worked so far," Batman said. "The Riddler has guided our every step. He's got each of us slavishly following a pre-arranged pattern, and we've done nothing to break free from the pattern. He doesn't want me running around Gotham City, hunting for a missing person—that doesn't fit with his scheme."

"Thirty seconds."

He saw Gordon wrestling with contradictory impulses. He wanted to save lives, wanted to trust Batman, but he also needed to follow the procedures by which he lived and breathed, and show faith in the abilities of his own department to protect the citizens of Gotham City.

"This is the opportunity to break the pattern, and force the Riddler to relinquish control," Batman said, pressing the point. "Unless we do so, we keep dancing to his tune."

"Fifteen seconds."

"I'm not giving you the safe house location," Gordon said. "I can't. You couldn't get there in time anyway. You're not the only one watching the countdown."

"Then someone is going to die."

"I'm telling you, you can't get there in time!" Gordon snapped. "We're doing everything we can. You're chasing a lunatic in a green suit, Robin is off God-knows-where, and I'm the one dealing with an assassin loose in my city. You handle your part of the problem and I'll handle mine."

"Zero," Oracle said.

"All right," Batman said. He felt weary. He was chasing, always chasing, with the Riddler and his cronies always one step ahead… and now another person was dead. All they could do was wait for the report.

"Commissioner!" one of the officers in the nearest car shouted. Gordon turned. "There's been another one." The officer listened to his radio, then repeated what he had just heard. "It was Theresa Gray."

Gordon looked shocked.

"Who is Theresa Gray?" Batman asked.

A strange combination of shame, anger, and sadness twisted Gordon's face.

"She manages shipping and receiving at Gotham City police headquarters," he said. He took off his glasses and rubbed the bridge of his nose. "Or did. She was—when I talked to you this morning and told you I had the manager interviewing staff, that was her. That was Theresa.

"Now we know how the Riddler's package got there, don't we?" he added bitterly.

We know something else, too, Batman thought. *We know the Riddler has an hour to plan how to get at Pierre Ouellette inside the safe house.* He didn't say it, though. He had to give Gordon a few minutes to adjust to the loss, and to the thought that the Riddler had infiltrated the Gotham City police.

"*She's good people,*" Gordon had said that morning. This would be a personal betrayal, and the murder of a colleague. Gordon would take it hard… but there was no time to grieve, or indulge in self-doubt.

They had one hour. One hour for the Riddler to scheme, but it was also an hour for Batman to plan, to figure out the inner workings of the Riddler's gambit, and understand how it all fit together.

"You were right, Batman," Gordon said. "This one's on me. I trusted her."

"No, Commissioner. You were right. It was the other number. Even if I'd gone to the safe house, Ouellette wasn't the target this time."

"That means he will be next time," Gordon said.

Batman nodded. "We have an hour. I have some things to do. I'm sure you do, too."

<click>

"This is Vicki Vale. I'm in some kind of labyrinth underneath Arkham City. There are question marks everywhere, and I mean everywhere. Like the Riddler wants you to know at every single moment who's running this.

"Phil's gone and I don't have video other than my phone. Saving it for an actual interview with the Riddler. I'll toggle the camera view back and forth and it'll look like *60 Minutes* or something.

"Talking to myself, *lalalala*.

"Wasting my battery."

<click>

"This is Vicki Vale. I've reached the place where I'm supposed to meet the Riddler. I went down into the subway station, then along the tracks, then ducked into what looked like a maintenance tunnel. Bright green question marks showed the way to what looks like some kind of control room.

"There are monitors showing different rooms. One of them looks like some kind of underground water tank, another like a checkerboard, while another's like... a parlor? Dining room? Then there's... I can't tell what that one is.

"There's Robin. That's him. He is in one of those rooms.

"Is that Wonder City?

"I hope Phil's okay.

"I think that's Wonder City. Does that mean the Riddler is down there? Is that the nerve center for his whole plan? Is that... has he built something down there? Sure looks like it.

"Pictures. Need to get pictures.

"Stupid Phil."

<click>

"This is Vicki Vale. I'm down a side tunnel, it's curving down, and it's cold. I was supposed to meet the Riddler in that control room, but I couldn't stay there. I heard a noise coming from down the hallway and it wasn't the Riddler. It was… well, it didn't sound human.

"Killer Croc lives down here. Who knows what other monsters might? The Penguin might—"

Noise—possibly a human voice.

"Vicki Vale. Who are you?

"I thought you were… how do I put this? With the Joker?

Noise—possibly a human voice.

"Hold on a minute, I had an *appointment*—"

<click>

16

Door number five opened into a long, curving hallway, lit with the now-familiar question marks all the way to the end. There, instead of hitting a stairwell or doorway, the hall started spiraling downward in a curve that got tighter and tighter until it turned into a chute.

Robin stopped at the point where the tunnel was barely four feet wide, and the floor sloped so steeply that he had to lean against a wall and keep his center of gravity low to avoid sliding forward. He could see light coming up from below, but there was no noise. Bracing himself against both walls, he leaned out over the chute.

There was a room, warmly lit and carpeted with what looked like an expensive patterned rug. The floor underneath it was polished wood. Leaning a little further out to shift his angle of view, Robin saw a mirror hanging on a wall that was covered in fleur-de-lis wallpaper. After the concrete and steel of the past few hours, the room was mighty easy on the eyes.

Curious, he leaned back and let himself slide the rest of the way down. When he landed on the rug he dropped into a crouch, and heard clinking from nearby, simultaneous with his impact. He pulled out his bō staff and turned in a complete circle, ready for an opponent even though he didn't think the Riddler was especially interested in seeing him fight.

Looking up through the circular hole in the ceiling, he could see the tight spiral of the chute. It hadn't changed on his entry, and the hole hadn't closed. That might mean that he'd have to figure out some way to climb back up there, once he had passed whatever test this room held.

Returning his attention to the room around him, he saw that the clinking had come from an oak table that took up the middle of the room, which must have shook when he'd landed. He had a sinking feeling he knew what was in store.

The table was set for tea.

Steam curled from the spout of a fine china teapot. Next to that was a loaf of fresh bread with three slices already cut. The bread knife lay on a serving plate next to the loaf. A butter dish with a spreading knife sat between the teapot and the bread, and sticking out from under the bread plate was an envelope.

Robin approached the table and looked it over. Nothing appeared out of the ordinary, within the context of a Victorian-style tea setting in a chamber carved out of the bedrock beneath Arkham City. On the envelope was a picture of a bird. He looked more closely.

It was a robin.

The envelope was made of good paper, heavy and textured in his hands. It was sealed with wax, and pressed into the wax was a question mark. Robin broke the seal and unfolded the letter within.

I wouldn't want you to weaken too soon!
Nothing like a refreshing tea to energize and focus
one's thoughts. Shake off the chill (or no, silly me! you
must have warmed up already!), have a little snack, take
a moment to relax...
But not too long.
Time is of the essence!

The Riddler was offering him a snack. *Cute,* Robin thought. He could only imagine what kind of weird hallucinogens or toxins the food might contain. He was thirsty, though—he didn't want tea, but even after nearly drowning, he craved a drink of water. Being nearly roasted had that effect on a person.

The chute spiraling down into the room made more sense now, as well—it must have been meant to evoke the rabbit hole. As much as he wanted to, however, he didn't touch anything. More than likely, that was the first test in the room.

Eat me, he mused. *Drink me.* Should he? Did he have to eat and drink to move through? What would happen if he did? How did this relate to what the Riddler wanted Batman to do up on the surface? The tea set seemed like an obvious nod to *Alice in Wonderland*, which in turn meant the Riddler was involved with yet another member of their criminal rogues' gallery. Robin knew the book—Batman had made it an essential part of his training, but he didn't have it memorized.

He could easily be missing something. Robin tried to remember the details. Alice grew at one point, shrunk at another... there was a rabbit with a clock, and the Red

Queen cutting off everyone's heads…

Damn! He shook his head in frustration. He wasn't seeing whatever it was he was supposed to see. Irritated with himself, he reopened the comm link to Batman.

"I'm through door number five, and if you could see this room you'd think I was time-traveling, too," he said. "Victorian all the way, right down to the tea set and fancy wallpaper."

"The Mad Hatter," Batman said without hesitation.

"Right," Robin agreed, although he hadn't yet seen any sign of the man. "But that's too easy, isn't it? It took some effort to connect the dots with Killer Croc and Mr. Freeze. This seems like a no-brainer."

"Good point. So what else do you see? Face one wall and start describing. Give me everything. If I'm going to need to find the Mad Hatter, I need to arrive with more than a bunch of pithy quotes from the book."

"Okay, give me a second." Robin turned away from the table, and looked at the back wall. "There's wallpaper—a pattern of green fleurs-de-lis on a gold background. A fancy sideboard with candlesticks and an empty serving bowl. This is the wall closest to the chute I dropped through. There's a rectangular framed mirror on the wall, with gold leaf on the frame." He stepped to the side. "It's warped, like a funhouse mirror."

"Anything else?"

"No, I'm turning now. This wall is all paneling, some kind of dark-stained wood. There's a picture rail about eight inches from the top of the wall, and a baseboard at the bottom. The paneling looks like it might be pine, if that matters."

"Everything might matter."

"There's no art or furniture on this wall except an overstuffed chair in the corner. The chair is upholstered in a dark green paisley." Robin looked closer. "Scratch that. It's not paisley. It's a pattern of interlocking question marks. That's all for this wall."

"Turn again," Batman said. Robin did, so that he was looking across the table to the far wall.

"The wall is papered, with the same pattern. Fleurs-de-lis. Two sconces with lit candles in them. No art or pictures. There's a... what do you call those couches that only have one arm?"

"A chaise longue?"

"Something like that. Close enough. A chaise longue. It matches the chair in the other corner. In the middle of the room there's a pedestal round table, about sixty inches in diameter, with six chairs. The tablecloth is white, probably linen? There's a teapot with hot tea on the table and a plate of fresh bread and butter next to it. There was a note for me on the table." Robin read it to Batman and then added, "There are a lot more cups at the table than there are chairs."

"That fits in with the story," Batman said. *"When Alice has tea with the Dormouse and the rest of them, doesn't she say the table is set for more people than there are?"*

"You tell me," Robin said, even though it sounded right. "You know the book better than I do." He turned so that he was standing with the table at his left. "Last wall. More wallpaper. A picture of a caterpillar and a butterfly—realistic, not like the illustrations in the book. Some kind of daguerreotype of a family, five people, each wearing a suit coat with question marks all over it just like the Riddler. And a grandfather clock."

"The caterpillar is from Lewis Carroll. It smokes a hookah. Butterfly... is there a butterfly in Alice in Wonderland?"

"I don't remember. But caterpillars turn into butterflies. Might be some kind of clue."

"Hmm," Batman said. *"What time does the clock say?"*

"Four forty-four," Robin said. "There's a manufacturer's logo in place of the six on the clock face. Hroll Gem, and a serial number."

"Hroll Gem," Batman repeated. *"No 'and company' or any other business identification?"*

"Nope," Robin said. "That's it."

"The answer is there somewhere," Batman said. *"I've never heard the surname Hroll, but it's not uncommon for gem merchants and jewelers to be in the clock business. You're the one seeing the room. How does it all fit together? If this chamber follows the pattern of the others, we're counting down toward a threat to your life."*

"Yeah, I'm curious about when we get to that part myself," Robin said. "And how do we use this information to find the Mad Hatter?"

"Lewis Carroll loved math puzzles..." Batman said, and something about fours and twelve, or four times four times four being sixty-four; but Robin was distracted by a piece of paper that fluttered down from the ceiling into his field of vision. He picked it up and saw two words.

EAT ME.

Then part of the blank paneled wall recessed, with a grating sound, causing him to turn and freeze in place, still gripping the bō. The size of a doorway, the opening exposed a hidden room large enough for a block of wood, a blond woman resting her head on it, facing away... and another figure standing over her dressed in the unmistakable costume of Lewis Carroll's Red Queen.

"Hi there!"

No.

Yes. It was Harley Quinn dressed as the Red Queen. Her normal jester's motley was modified into a bodysuit covered in hearts—except that all of them were anatomically correct, and the costume looked like it was soaked with real blood. *So there's the queen*, Robin thought. That left only the king, unless the Riddler was going to fill the chessboard with pawns.

"Off with her heeaaaadd!" Harley Quinn squealed, making up in volume what she lacked in gravitas. To further scramble the air of menace with her bobby-soxer schtick, she tossed her pigtails back and kicked a heel up in the air, looking much like a World War II-era pinup.

The woman with her head on the block of wood turned it toward Robin, and he recognized the reporter Vicki Vale. Her hands were bound behind her back with zip ties, and one of Harley Quinn's feet rested across her legs just below the knees.

"Robin," Batman said. *"Who is that?"*

"You were right. There's more to it. Gotta go," Robin said. "I'll catch you up in a minute."

He killed the comm link.

Midday Gotham

with Jack Ryder

GNN CABLE NEWS NETWORK

WGTU Gotham City Radio

> *<Jack Ryder enters to rock and roll theme music resembling a famous song, but not quite closely enough for him to be sued.>*

"Hellllooooooooo, Gotham City! This is Midday Gotham and we are rolling on a story that is developing hot and heavy all over town. Batman is back!"

> *<Mixed applause and boos. Ryder sits at a radio microphone set up in front of a live audience. He puts on the headphones. The music cuts out.>*

"Do I hear some mixed opinions about Batman? I think I do! Listen, I have mixed opinions about the guy myself. We all know he stepped up big a few months back when Deadshot had me in his crosshairs... or do we? The more I think about it, the more I start to wonder if Batman set the whole thing up.

"You know, he's got the resources. He's got the connections. Who's to say he wouldn't do that, just to put the most powerful voice in Gotham City in debt to him?"

> *<Gasps and murmurs from crowd.>*

"That's right. Otherwise... I mean, in the middle of everything else that's going on in Arkham City, with the Joker and the Penguin and Hugo Strange and everyone under the sun on their own personal vision quest to rack up a body count, Batman just happens to be at the right place at the right time to stop

Deadshot from killing me?"

<Boos and angry shouting from the crowd.>

"That's right. But that's also what brings us to today... because today, my friends, Batman is back in action, and wouldn't you know it, so too are some of the costumed freaks he's always making such a big show of apprehending. If you're listening on the radio, you didn't see the air quotes around 'apprehending,' or around 'killing me' earlier. You should all come in and check out my show.

"Tickets are free!"

<Wild cheering.>

"Every day, free! First come, first served! Line up early and get the straight scoop about what's happening in this city, from the only man fearless enough to tell it like it is.

"And who is that?"

<"JACK RYDER!">

"You got that right. I'm the one who's going to tell you that something is going on between Commissioner Gordon and Batman. You think it's an accident that we've got a string of murders that starts right after Batman pays a visit to police HQ? No? I don't either.

"They know something they're not telling us. From other sources, including my colleague Vicki Vale, we know the Riddler is out there up to something. Why isn't Commissioner Gordon leveling with the people of Gotham City? We're right here. We're listening. We're waiting, Commissioner. We want to know what kind of arrangement you have with Batman, and why this city seems to descend into chaos every time the Batmobile starts roaring around town.

"Is Batman fighting crime, or does he bring it with him? We

had some nice peace and quiet before he reappeared. For all we know the whole thing, Batman's whole career, is a setup— just like it was a setup when he 'saved my life.'

"My web site, the *Ryder Report*—check it out on all the social media sites via the links you'll see on your screen, and if you're listening to the radio I'll tell you to head to RyderReport-dot-com and check out all the social stuff there. You want the latest on the Riddler? Deadshot? Mr. Freeze? We've got 'em all, and also we're keeping a close eye on our hero in black, Batman himself.

"The *Ryder Report* will be right on top of this developing story on a minute-to-minute basis. I can only do one show a day, but the Internet never stops, and neither does the *Ryder Report*'s team of crack investigators.

"We'll be right back."

17

Batman heard the soft click as Robin ended the call. A woman had been shouting in the background, and the voice grated on him like a thousand fingernails dragging across a chalkboard—it sounded like Harley Quinn, and that couldn't be good.

He reflexively started to call Robin back, but stopped. If Tim had broken off the call, it meant he had felt the need to focus. Calling him back wouldn't help, and it might just get him killed. Batman's time was better spent figuring out how to find the Mad Hatter.

Four forty-four. A caterpillar. A family portrait. Candlesticks. He shuffled the various items around in his head, hoping they would fall into a discernable pattern of some sort. But if there was one, it continued to elude him.

Hroll Gem.

There was nothing unusual about the gem part—that fit the history of grandfather clocks, some of which had been sold by the likes of Tiffany & Company and Bailey Banks and Biddle. But Hroll...

Wait. He was looking for the Mad Hatter. Lewis Carroll had created the character from a Victorian stereotype, because so many haberdashers were made ill and even driven insane by the chemicals used in the manufacture of hats. The primary culprit was mercury in the form of mercuric nitrate, which accelerated the felting process. The dangers of mercury had been known as early as the seventeenth century, and the saying "mad as a hatter" appeared not very long after that.

In fact, American hatters had used mercury processes until World War II, when mercury was needed for detonators instead. The actual symptoms included emotional volatility, pathological shyness, and physical tremors. Of those, the Mad Hatter of Gotham City specialized in the volatility.

Batman stopped before he went too far down the tangent. His mind floated like that sometimes when he was getting close to an intuitive jump—and more recently, though he hadn't told Alfred or Robin, it drifted for no reason he could discern. Mercury… the chemical symbol of mercury on the periodic table was Hg. The same as the initial letters of the clock's manufacturer. But what happened if the H and the G were removed? What remained?

ROLL EM.

Roll 'Em. The casino.

That was where Batman would find the Mad Hatter.

Robin took two steps toward Harley Quinn before she stopped him by holding up a double-bladed axe—a far cry from the customized baseball bat she usually carried.

"Don't be all in a rush to come in," she said, wagging a finger on her free hand. "I might get too excited and drop this axe and then"—she giggled loudly—"off with her head!"

Robin stopped.

Vicki Vale was looking at him. "You know," she said, "I've done a lot of things for a scoop, but this is my first time being threatened with decapitation." Despite the situation, her voice was firm.

"Isn't she something?" Quinn said. "I'm about to cut off her head, and she's just as cool as can be." She leaned her upper body down while still holding the axe out, reminding Robin how physically strong she was. It was easy to forget that, when you were watching her flirty-jester act. "Vicki, you got moxie, you know that! No wonder you couldn't resist a little tip that brought you into big bad old Arkham City."

Quinn looked back over at Robin.

"Put down your stick," she said. "It's making me kind of nervous. When I'm nervous, my palms get sweaty and I lose my grip on things like axe handles."

"You're wearing gloves," Robin pointed out.

For just a fraction of a second, her mask slipped and he saw cold fury. Then it was back in place as Harley Quinn grinned and giggled again.

"So literal!" she said. "We're not in a literal room. This is a crazy room! *Anything* can happen here."

"Let's start over," Robin said.

"Okay… hi there!" she said brightly, still keeping the axe in place. Then her expression turned serious. "I know, I know, don't worry—you think I'm still mad about my puddin' getting sick… but you didn't do it. I know you didn't. Batman did. And that's why you have to die."

"I'm not following you," Robin said, even though he

was. He had to buy some time.

"Batman took my Mista J. away from me," Quinn said. "We were going to have… a f-f-family…" She took a moment to master her emotions. "But that'll never happen now. Just like you're never going to get out of here alive, and then, yeah. That's when Batman will know what it's like to lose someone he loves."

"He already has," Robin said.

She cocked her head and smiled at him. "Tell me more."

"No."

She pouted, and then smiled broadly.

"Oh, it's a secret? I love secrets."

"So do I," Vale said. "Harley, you and the Joker were—?"

"Yes, yes we were." Quinn sniffled. "It was going to be so beautiful. We were going to be together forever. He was mean sometimes, kinda, but he never really meant it. He loved me. A child, a little bouncing bundle of joy—that would have settled him down. Then we could have been the First Family of Gotham City… except… he got sick."

"That's terrible," Vale said. She cut a glance at Robin as she said it, and he gave her back a tiny nod.

Keep her going. He leaned his bō against the table and held up his hands, palms out. "See?" he said aloud. "We're just talking."

"No, we're not!" Quinn shrieked. "We're cutting people's heads off, starting with hers!"

"We don't have to do that," Vale said. Robin was amazed at her calm. He dropped his hands to his sides and saw her eyes track the motion. *Good,* he thought. He wiggled the fingers of his right hand. Her gaze locked there.

"Harley," he said as evenly as he could. "We're in a crazy room, right? So we can do crazy things."

"You got that right," she answered with a coquettish smile. "It's going to get super crazy in here."

Robin extended the last three fingers of his right hand, keeping it low at his side. Vale was still watching. He curled his middle finger into his palm.

"If you cut her head off, that's pretty crazy, right?" he said.

"Super crazy. Bonkers. Ultra loony," she agreed. Robin curled his ring finger in. Vale held perfectly still and watched.

"But if you cut her head off first, Harley, like right now, how are you going to get more crazy than that?" he asked.

She paused. Robin curled his pinky into the palm of his hand, completing the countdown.

Vale flung herself to the left off the block of wood. With incredible speed, Quinn brought the axe down, barely missing her head and burying the blade inches deep in the wood. A thick lock of Vale's blond hair lay sheared off on the block. The motion of her body pulled Quinn's foot to one side, unbalancing her for a critical second. That was all Robin needed to plant his feet and leap at her.

She was trying to pull the axe out of the wood block, but it was sunk too far into the grain. So instead she lifted the whole block of wood and swung it with a feral screech. He just got his left arm up to parry. It hit him hard enough to knock him sideways into the armchair. His arm went numb from the elbow down.

The axe snapped off just below the head, broken by the incredible torque of Quinn's swing and the impact on his arm and shoulder. He sprang out of the armchair toward his bō as she came after him wielding the broken axe handle like a spear. Just as he got the bō in his grasp, her thrust punched through his cape and she jerked him off balance. He sprawled on the floor and rolled, pulling the broken handle out of her hands.

In the same motion he swept the bō around to crack into her ankles. She hit the ground and Robin went after her, pinning her down with the staff across her collarbones and scissoring his legs around hers.

Behind him, in the execution chamber, Vale struggled to stand up.

One of Robin's feet hit the wood block as he struggled to hold Quinn down. She was strong, but so was he, and when he rammed the bō up under her chin and started pressing down on her neck, she choked out a surrender.

"Okay, pretty boy," she said, her voice strangled. "You got me dead to rights. I give up." He felt her body relax under his, but he only lightened the pressure on her neck enough for her to breathe and speak clearly. He kept her legs pinned.

"Talk," he said. "What's the game with our reporter friend?"

"Oh, her? Mister Question Mark is feeling a little neglected. He's got this swell plan and nobody knows about it, so he thought maybe somebody should, you know, do a little PR. Get the word out."

With her hands still tied behind her back, Vale walked over to Robin.

"And how exactly was I supposed to do that without my head?"

"I told you, this is a crazy room!" Quinn giggled.

"Besides, then you would have been a real talking head!" At that, she laughed herself into a coughing fit. Under the smeared black-and-white makeup her face turned bright red, and tears caused the makeup around her eyes to smear. She looked grotesque.

Robin didn't let her up. For all he knew, she was faking it. He did turn his head slightly so she wasn't coughing right in his face.

That was all she needed.

The next thing he knew he was flat on his back, seeing stars brought on by an elbow to the chin. By the time he got back to his feet, Quinn had his bō pinned against Vicki Vale's throat.

"Don't make any sudden moves, Boy Wonder," she said. "I can kill this Lois Lane wannabe just as dead with a stick as I can with an axe."

"Seriously?" Vale said. "I get off the chopping block, you ruin my haircut, and now we're going to do this all over again?"

Harley pecked her on the cheek.

"As many times as we need to, sweet pea."

"We don't need to," Robin said. "You want to kill me, kill me. All you get from killing her is another notch on your belt, or however you keep track."

"Sounds like reason enough to me," Quinn said. "But you're right, smarty-pants. I don't need to. Mister Question Mark has something he wants you to do. If you do it, I'll let her go and you can go on your merry way."

"What is it?"

"Remember that piece of paper that distracted you from

your big important conversation with… that bastard who killed my puddin'?" Harley Quinn scanned the floor. "It's right there. Pick it up."

Robin did. It was still just a piece of paper with the words EAT ME printed on it.

"Do what it says," she ordered.

Robin looked over at the table. He tried to game out what the Riddler was up to. The bread could be poisoned, certainly. That would start another clock, while the toxin ran its course and killed him slowly while Batman was pressed to find an antidote. It would also fit with the *Alice in Wonderland* theme, since Alice was always drinking and eating things that changed her.

At least he didn't *think* the poison would kill him right away, but that was relying on the Riddler's self-restraint. Was the third death room the charm—the one where the Riddler proved he really meant business?

Robin didn't think so. The Riddler would want Batman to be on hand to witness the final act, and even though Vicki Vale would run straight back to her paper with a breathless exclusive, that wouldn't provide enough satisfaction.

The real finale was still ahead.

"Okay," he said, and stepped over to the table to pick up a slice of bread, reaching for the butter knife.

"No, dummy!" Quinn said scornfully. "God, how do you idiots ever solve any crime at all? You're so… argh! Eat the paper! Eat the damned paper!"

"Eat the paper," Robin repeated.

"Yes! That's what I said," she continued. "Can't you tell? The tea and bread are just there for looking at.

"Eat. The. Paper!"

"Okay," Robin said. He tore off a piece of the paper, put it in his mouth, and started to chew. It dissolved quickly—much more so than paper should have. It reminded him of the edible rice paper made in Asia from dried starch.

"Okay, I did it," he said, continuing to chew on his impromptu snack. "So now you can tell me what it really was. Poison? A hallucinogenic drug?"

"You have secrets, I have secrets," she said. "You know who else has secrets? The Riddler. He lets people in on them little by little, just how he wants… and then right when you think you know everything, you know what you really know? That you're going to die.

"You know what a jester is?" she said.

"Why don't you tell me?"

"The old jesters used to ride with the king and whisper into his ear—things like, "You're just a man, you're going to die." They were the only ones who could talk to the king like he was an ordinary man, an ordinary mortal. That's what I'm saying to you, Mr. Robin, and I know you'll tell Batman, too. You're ordinary men, you're going to die. You're no different than anyone else. That's called a memento mori, and that's what I am. Now that Mista J. is gone, I'm making sure you know that before long, you'll be gone, too."

She brightened up, and her voice changed into a chirp.

"Mmmkay? Good! Now chew that up or the Riddler's going to—"

"Almost done," Robin said. As he swallowed the last of the paper, or whatever it really was, he mused that if there were any two people in Gotham City who didn't need a memento mori, those two people were him and Batman.

"Then I guess we're all set." She eased her grip on Vale's neck and let Robin's bō drop to the floor. "That's my speech. You like it?"

"I've heard better," Robin said.

She pouted. Then, just as quickly, she brightened again. "Oh, wait, jiminy! I forgot part of it!" she said.

As she spoke, she drew a gun and fired.

BREAKING

EYE ON GOTHAM
CAMERAMAN FOUND DEAD

Globe staff

GOTHAM CITY: *Gotham Globe* freelance cameraman and editor Philip Chester has been found dead near the southern end of the Bowery in Arkham City. Cause of death is under investigation, but reports from the scene indicate that the body was discovered cut into several parts. The Gotham City Police Department is treating it as a homicide.

Chester was working on a story with *Eye on Gotham* reporter Vicki Vale, whose whereabouts are currently unknown. GCPD detectives and uniformed officers are searching the area where Chester's body was found for Vale, who reported being contacted by the Riddler shortly before her disappearance.

The victim was last seen in a video dispatch from near the Sionis steel mill, where he filmed Vale reporting on her planned meeting with the criminal leader. Chester's camera and other equipment were not with his body, and have not been recovered. Detectives are searching for them, and believe the camera will contain footage that will shed light on both Vale's location and the events leading up to the murder.

The search area has been expanded to include most of Arkham City. An *Eye on Gotham* helicopter has joined GCPD aircraft, but police ask that citizens do not form search parties, due to the dangerous environment.

"We can't keep an eye on civilian volunteers while we're trying to conduct a search and keep our own personnel safe," a police spokesperson said. "Everyone needs to have a little patience while we process the scene."

Before joining the *Eye on Gotham* team, Philip Chester was a videographer for a number of small television production studios in Gotham City. He is a veteran of the United States Navy, where he wrote and directed short documentaries on shipboard life during long deployments. He leaves behind a wife and three children, ages nine, seven, and four.

18

It took Batman approximately two minutes to get from the Ace Chemical factory, through Park Row and across the barricaded part of the Old Gotham Freeway, to Amusement Mile, where the Gotham Casino stood near the old police headquarters, which had been abandoned since early in Commissioner Gillian B. Loeb's tenure.

Once the casino had been Oswald Cobblepot's showplace, but Batman had seen and heard nothing from the Penguin since the end of Protocol 10. Was he now in league with the Mad Hatter—and by extension the Riddler? It wasn't out of the question.

Perched on the small water tower near the once-lavish building, Batman looked down at the street side. Its grand facade was shabby and neglected now, much of the neon shattered. The only cars on the street were abandoned— he had left the Batmobile on the freeway access road near the southwest corner of the Gotham City Olympus. No light was visible through any of the casino's windows, but that didn't mean anything. Like all of its kind, the Gotham Casino's gaming area was sequestered from the rest of the world. Management liked to keep its gamblers away from windows and clocks, so it was easier for them to get lost in chasing that ever-elusive big score.

He dropped to the street and approached the front door. Easily bypassing the lock, he entered the casino, passing through a huge dark lobby hung with chandeliers. Their dangling crystals picked up light from an open doorway across the way, giving the lobby ceiling the effect of a starry sky. Batman heard the ratchet and jingle of slot machines. He crossed to the door and looked through.

The floor was alive with activity, all of it confined to a single area. A long row of people, all dressed in frock coats and silk suits, formal right down to the white spats on their shoes, moved from slot machine to slot machine, each pulling the lever once and then moving on after seeing the result. Behind them came others, wearing rabbit ears and uniforms decorated with the four suits of a deck of cards. They wrote with quill pens on long, dragging sheets of paper, recording the results of each spin and scurrying to keep up with their formally dressed partners.

Some of them looked up and saw Batman, but his presence didn't affect their activity. They looked at him, looked over their shoulders as if someone must be watching, and then hurried on.

"Jervis Tetch!"

Batman's voice carried over the clangor of the machines, yet everyone on the casino floor continued to ignore him. He walked along the rows of slot machines, scanning the room for the Mad Hatter, but not finding him. As the next gamer rushed past obliviously, Batman reached out and grabbed him by the collar of his coat.

"Where's the Mad Hatter?" he growled.

"Unhand me!" the man cried. His eyes were wide with fear, but Batman didn't seem to be the source. "I'm frightfully late!" Still the crime fighter retained his grip—if anything, he tightened it.

"Where is the Mad Hatter?" Batman repeated. He gave the man a shake.

"I beg you, sir, I do not know who that is. Let me go! There are arms to pull, numbers to see. Calculations must be performed!"

Batman let him go. With a gasp of relief the man scrambled to the nearest slot machine and pulled its arm. The wheels spun and returned a lemon, a cherry, and a number 7. The rabbit-eared woman following the patron dutifully recorded this, and then they were off to the next machine.

The casino floor had perhaps two hundred slot machines, and not all of them were being pulled in sequence. There was a pattern here, and Batman knew he would have to see it from above to understand it—if understanding it was worth the effort. Knowing Tetch, it would be some lunacy from Carroll's book. The whole place stank of fear.

Those who didn't believe fear had a smell had never been in its presence.

"There are numbers in the air here," the Mad Hatter said from nearby. Batman turned to see him in the dealer's position behind a blackjack table, his stringy straight hair falling out from beneath that ludicrously large top hat. The Dark Knight walked toward the table, and the Hatter dealt him two cards.

Batman looked at the cards. Ace of spades, ace of clubs.

He glanced back up at the Mad Hatter, who beamed at him.

"Mustn't act rashly," he said.

"Split," Batman said, flipping the aces over and lining them up next to each other.

"I do love an ace," the Mad Hatter said. "It means one, it means eleven. Those other cards, they're prisoners of their letters and numbers. Only the ace breaks free!"

From somewhere nearby, a raucous bell sounded loudly. Batman glanced over and saw a river of coins pouring out of the slot machine's payout tray.

"Jackpot!" crowed the Mad Hatter. The entire crew of gamblers and rabbit-eared scribes converged on that machine. The man who had won the jackpot fell to his knees and covered his face as the coins continued to fall around him. The scribes scribbled on their scrolls and the other players all drew knives from within their fashionable ensembles.

"A once-in-a-lifetime event!" the Mad Hatter bellowed as the slot pullers fell on their colleague. Before Batman could move a muscle, their bloody knives flashed in the lights from the machines. When their work was done, the Mad Hatter raised both arms.

"Now then!" he cried. "Mustn't be late!" The patrons and scribes ran in every direction, returning to the machines they had been approaching when the jackpot bell rang out.

"You're going to run out of slot pullers," Batman said grimly. He watched as the scribe who had been assigned to the doomed man took off her rabbit ears and approached the blackjack table. The Mad Hatter dealt her two cards.

She glanced at them.

"Hit."

He dealt her a third card, the seven of hearts.

She flipped over her other two cards. Eight of hearts, nine of hearts.

"Bust," the Mad Hatter said. He drew a knife from the inside pocket of his coat. The scribe tilted her head back, exposing her throat. "Batman," the Hatter continued, "the Riddler wanted me to teach him the secrets of controlling the human mind. You see I excel at this. The secret is simple. One must make the subject fear you more than he—or in this case she—fears death. Madness is quite useful in this regard."

Batman held himself in check, but if the Mad Hatter moved the knife, the fight was going to be on. He wasn't going to sit there while Tetch cut the throat of a brainwashed minion, just for fun.

"You know what I love about a casino?" the Hatter asked. "The randomness. Nothing is rational here. People try to beat the odds. It's silly, even stupid, but charming, because one sees human optimism and human desperation working together in intimate proximity. You know, the numbers we're creating here will lead me to my Alice."

"How?" Batman asked, to keep him talking.

"Because I, too, am a desperate optimist. As are you."

"I'm more of a realist," Batman said.

"That's an ugly word. You fight and fight and fight and never win, but you keep fighting. If that qualifies as realism, you're closer to madness than even I had hoped."

"You were telling me about mind control." Something

changed in the ambient sounds, but it was subtle, and didn't seem to be a cause for alarm.

"I do love that there are no clocks here," the Mad Hatter said, ignoring him. "That permits me to convince my comrades that they are always on the verge of tardiness; and lateness, *tsk tsk*, is most strictly prohibited. With no clocks," he continued, "I determine the time! It's always six o'clock! He gathered himself, and looked straight at Batman. "Tell me, has Robin enjoyed the tea and bread I set out for him?"

"You did that?" Batman responded. "If that's true, then you got here in record time. He said the tea was still hot when he came into the room."

"Did it, had it done—it's just a matter of verbiage. Words! We speak them. 'Callooh, callay, all mimsy were the borogoves, and the mome raths outgrabe.' Soon the numbers will reveal where my Alice has gone, and we will be together again." A dreamy smile spread over his face, and he leaned toward the scribe, who still waited with her throat held up for the blade.

That's it. Batman reached out, caught the Mad Hatter's wrist, and with his other hand slapped him in the face hard enough to knock his hat off. A look of shocked dismay took hold of his features.

"That was uncalled for, O Dark Knight," Hatter said. The look slipped and was replaced with a sad expression. He looked at his knife hand, imprisoned in Batman's grip. "May I put my hat back on?"

"Tell me about mind control, and the Riddler."

The Mad Hatter dropped the knife. It clunked hilt-first

onto the green felt of the blackjack table. With his free hand he reached down to the deck of cards and dealt Batman two, one for each face-up ace. Keeping his grip on the Mad Hatter's wrist, Batman flipped over the cards.

Eight of clubs, eight of spades.

He had the proverbial dead man's hand.

"Who could have predicted that?" the Mad Hatter said.

Abruptly Batman realized he wasn't hearing the sounds of the slot machines. He glanced over his shoulder and understood why. The gamers were all gathered around the blackjack table, and they all had their knives out.

As the first of them slashed at him, Batman pulled the Hatter's arm down, using his mass as a counterweight and launching himself into a twisting backward somersault over the table and into the dealer's enclosure. He landed with the Hatter between him and the knives. Tetch sprang at Batman, who spun into a judo takedown, driving his opponent to the floor.

The gamblers began to scramble over the table to get at him. He dropped the nearest with a straight right hand, doubled another over with a spinning kick, then felt the tug of a knife blade cutting through his cape and the sharp bright pain of a blade nicking the back of his shoulder.

One of the slot players grabbed him from behind. Batman countered with an elbow that blocked the slash of his knife and followed through to crunch into the side of his face. He glanced down and saw the Mad Hatter on hands and knees, picking up his knife again. At the same time another slot puller leapt from the table, knife high and aimed at Batman's face.

He stepped forward, ducking his head and grabbing a double fistful of the knife puller's shirt and cravat. Pivoting, he brought the man down on the Hatter's back with the force of his thrust and the slot puller's momentum combined. The air *whoofed* out of the Hatter's lungs and he rolled around on the floor gasping for breath as Batman stabbed a heel into the fallen gambler's head. He recovered just in time to dodge another knife thrust.

Four down, but there were plenty more where they'd come from. In this confined space, sheer numbers would overwhelm him sooner or later. They were all on the table now, spread evenly around its half-circle. Their eyes were completely devoid of consciousness, as if they weren't aware what they were doing. The contrast with the Hatter's manic whimsy was even more unsettling than overt bloodlust.

One of them jumped down into the dealer's enclosure. Batman dropped him as soon as his feet touched the floor, but in turning to do that, he exposed himself to others. A knife gouged at his ribs, slowed but not stopped by the protective material of his suit. He spun and kicked the wind out of his attacker, caught two others and smashed their heads together, then took another cut across the thigh as one of them flailed in mid-fall.

Eight down.

An idea occurred to him.

"That's eight, Tetch," Batman said. "Half of my hand. You're the ace." With one hand he fired a grappling hook up to the balcony. With the other he grabbed the Hatter around the waist. Still struggling to get his breath back, the villain didn't resist as Batman triggered the spooling mechanism on the grappling gun, and jumped up out of the enclosure.

He and the Mad Hatter swung up and across the floor to the balcony, where Batman braced his feet and heaved the Hatter up over the railing before vaulting after him.

"I do appreciate the symmetry of that," Tetch gasped. "Quick thinking."

Batman hit him hard, twice. His eyes rolled back in his head, and then slowly focused again. Glancing down at the floor, Batman saw the gamblers looking around. Their scribes waited patiently as they searched the casino floor for Batman, and when they didn't find him, they simply went back to what they had been doing.

It took some of them a while to recover from Batman's fists and feet, but soon the casino floor was jingling and clanging again with the sound of slot machines. Through the entire fight, the scribe assigned to the man who had won the jackpot hadn't moved. She still sat with her head tilted back and her eyes closed.

"Now that's dedication," the Hatter said, wheezing loudly. "That's the dedication I feel for my Alice. Are you my Alice, darling?" he called out.

"Yes," she said, and her voice barely carried over the thirty feet that separated them. "I'm your Alice. You've found me."

"You're not Alice!" he screamed in a sudden rage, his voice rising so high that it was almost a squeal. He strained against Batman's grip as if to jump off the balcony after her. Still she didn't move.

Batman pulled the Hatter back and bounced his head off the floor a few times to refocus him on the matter at hand.

"Mind control," he prompted.

"Oh, yes, mind control. Off with their heads! Or more properly, putting what's in my head in their heads, which amounts to the same things, wouldn't you say?" He was still wheezing.

"The Riddler told me where you would be," Batman said. "He sold you out, you and Mr. Freeze and Killer Croc. What's he trying to hide?"

"Well, I did him a little favor involving Rā's al Ghūl's journals, but that hardly seems worth killing me for," the Hatter responded. A jackpot bell rang on the casino floor. The Hatter jerked and started to yell out another call to murder. Batman punched him in the gut and he doubled over, spending the next minute or so gagging and hacking.

Looking out over the floor, Batman saw the slot pullers and scribes just standing around. They did nothing without the Mad Hatter's instructions. This was good—it meant that he could keep them alive simply by keeping the Hatter quiet.

He squatted next to his opponent, who didn't look as if he was quite ready to stand up yet. Batman didn't care—he hauled the Hatter to his feet.

"Rā's al Ghūl's journals," he growled. "Continue."

"Well, I had to get the information from somewhere," the Hatter said. "And I thought, who knew this kind of thing? Who had the secrets? Who had been the furthest down that particular... well, rabbit hole? (If you'll forgive the expression, and I know you will.) Why, it would be Rā's al Ghūl, with his marvelously named Lazarus Pits! All I had to do was track down the journals he left behind when you dismissed him from this mortal coil."

The Hatter paused.

"Or... did you? Surely not. But you were present at the event, and certainly complicit."

"Rā's killed himself while he was trying to kill me," Batman responded. "He died by the sword. I'm not sorry it happened, but I didn't do it."

"Distinction without a difference," the Hatter said airily. "In any event, I needed those journals. Thus I sojourned into the ruins of Arkham City, daring the remnants of TYGER and other threats more dire. Then I found a certain other party who informed me that what I sought could be had"—he paused and his expression registered the memory of a painful experience—"for a price."

"I'm not interested in the price," Batman said.

"Oh, I think you are. I was the one who coughed up the filthy lucre to convince Killer Croc to go to the dentist. Credit where credit is due, I always say. And once I had made that happen, I found the journals squirreled away in a little box. Incredible man, Rā's al Ghūl—if man he was." Tetch stopped to catch his breath, then continued.

"The Riddler wanted me to teach him how to control machines with his mind, and Rā's knew how to do it! I'm not even certain he knew what he had, but everything I needed was in his journals—brilliant techniques I could combine with my own. I built the Riddler his device, right in this very building. Components from computers, elements of high-res cameras, even spare parts from slot machines—a casino is a wonderland of surprises. When you put them together"—the Hatter's face got dreamy again—"magic happens."

Mind control over machines. Lucas Angelo, a software developer specializing in robotics and control systems. Rosalyn Mateosian, an electronics engineer. The pieces finally began to fall into place. The problem was, he didn't know the *reason*. He was caught up to the present, but had no idea what Nigma intended the future to look like. What machines? And when he established his mastery—if, in fact, he could do so—what was he going to accomplish with them?

Batman stood, and hauled the Mad Hatter bodily to his feet. As Tetch sought to gather himself, he shot Batman a strange look.

"When I asked whether or not you had dismissed Rā's from this mortal vale of tears," he said, "I wasn't questioning your motives, but the... shall we say, *finality*, of the act." The statement sent a chill through Batman.

"What are you getting at?" he demanded. "Are you saying that he's *alive*?"

"I am saying that in the end, a raven is like a writing desk. Nothing else matters." With that he launched into a torrent of gibberish, and no matter how Batman tried, he couldn't get anything more out of him.

RyderReport.com

Posted by JKB

Wednesday 2:38 p.m.

Vicki Vale is missing in Arkham City

Yes, you read that right. It's been widely reported already that she was going to meet the Riddler. Whether that's a) true; b) what she thought was true; or c) her cover story for whatever she was really doing, it doesn't matter. She went into the field chasing a story, and now she's missing and her cameraman, a solid pro and standup guy named Phil Chester, is dead. This is the kind of story we have to write all too often here on the *Ryder Report*.

What Jack said on his show applies here, too. Batman appears, and everything in Gotham City goes haywire. Is that an accident? We don't think so.

As we've been saying for years, this city would be better off without Batman, and we're not the only ones who think so. Rafael Del Toro, among others, feels the same way, and he's been around Gotham City even longer than Jack has.

And there's been a fourth murder, right on the hour like the first three. This time the victim was Theresa Gray, the manager of the mailroom and general factotum over at Gotham City Police HQ. She's the first victim who didn't have some kind of technology job, and her death shines a whole new light on

Batman's visit to Commissioner Gordon. Why was he there? Could it have been to take a look at something that showed up in the mail, this passing through Theresa Gray's domain? Did Deadshot then kill her to ensure her silence?

It's starting to make sense, isn't it?

If you can call it sense.

Continuing down that line of reasoning, it means Commissioner Gordon and Batman have known what this was all about from the beginning. They didn't tell you, and now people are dead. Is that any way to run a city? Is that any way to keep the people of this city safe?

You be the judges.

Now Vicki Vale is another victim of Batman's secrecy and Commissioner Gordon's complicity. She's in trouble, and all she was trying to do was her job—report the truth as she saw it. We've had our dust-ups with Vicki over the years, and still think she's a soft-headed liberal stooge who's never spent a day in the real world—but that doesn't mean we wish her ill.

She didn't deserve whatever has happened to her, any more than Phil Chester deserved what happened to him, and the blame for that lies squarely on Commissioner Gordon's shoulders. Batman's, too. Think about that the next time you feel like hailing either of them as heroes.

19

Robin was already moving when Harley Quinn's hand dropped to her belt, and the shot shattered the family portrait on the far wall instead of punching a hole through his face. He cartwheeled to his right, coming up with the bō ready.

She threw the gun away and drew another one.

"Ready to play?"

"You keep changing the rules," Robin said.

"That's the game, silly!" she said. She leveled the new gun, then made a comical show of squeezing one eye shut and sighting down the barrel. The gun was tiny. In her small hands, it looked like a toy. Even so, Robin would bet his life that it would fire a real bullet.

"And in this game, I always win," Quinn added.

She started to squeeze the trigger, when the back wall of the execution chamber caved in, and a huge humanoid figure burst through the rubble. A blinding flash lit the room, and Quinn was blasted off her feet by an energy bolt from a gun mounted on the robot's shoulder. As she sat up and shook her head, the figure lumbered into the room and placed itself midway between her and Robin.

Its eyes glowed a baleful green.

She looked up at it.

"Wow," she said, and she pointed comically. "Off with his head, too!" Then she dissolved into uncontrolled giggles. It was one of Wonder City's famed mechanical guardians, built by Rā's al Ghūl decades ago. Robin had seen them before, but never operational.

"I thought you wanted me to live long enough to see the Riddler's big show," he said to Quinn, his eyes still on the robotic newcomer.

"You dummy, that's what I *wanted* you to think," she answered with a laugh. "I don't care what the Riddler wants—he never gave a damn about Mista J. You'll see." She scrambled to her feet, having recovered from the robot's blast with surprising speed. "Time to go, I guess." She skipped to the edge of the hole in the wall. "I hope the Riddler doesn't kill you, sweetie," she said over her shoulder. "That would be soooo disappointing."

She blew him a kiss, and was gone.

The robot stayed where it was, frozen.

Was she on his side, or not? Robin shook his head. *Every time we run into her, I end up with a headache. Too much bull—*

"Ouch," Vicki Vale said. He turned and saw her hiding behind the couch—*chaise longue*, he corrected himself— looking at the inside of her arm. A trickle of blood ran down her wrist to drop from her thumb. "That's a sharp blade."

She'd cut the zip ties with the axe blade.

"When did you do that?" Robin asked.

"While you were chatting about mento moris, or

mementos mori… whatever," she said. "All that."

"Sorry," Robin said. "If you'd waited a second…"

"I'm not big on waiting," Vale said. "Especially not when someone's just tried to cut my head off. Now I need to get out of here and file this story." She stood up, bracing herself for a moment with her uninjured arm.

"I wouldn't go just yet," Robin said. He walked across the execution chamber and looked through the hole in the wall. A rough tunnel, almost looking like a natural cave, led away to what he thought was the north, sloping down into blackness. *A glimpse behind the Riddler's curtain,* Robin thought. *He's built in emergency measures to make sure nobody interferes with his game.* And he had control of at least one of the mechanical guardians.

"I didn't think those things really existed," Vale said. She walked up to the robot and looked it over. It was much taller than she was, taller in fact than any human.

"Well, they do," Robin said. "This one's been customized, I think. It doesn't look like the other ones I've seen." The mechanical guardians he'd encountered before were skeletal in design except for their torsos, which had to be larger to house their energy supplies. They reminded him of some robots he'd seen in an old *Superman* cartoon. Their heads were roughly the same shape as a human head.

Where human eyes would be, mechanical guardians had two glowing lenses. They had different built-in weapons, too, or at least this one did. Where the original guardians had been engraved with Victorian-style filigree, with a Jules Verne aesthetic, this one had question marks engraved on its armored exoskeleton.

"How many others have you seen?"

Robin shrugged. "A few, down in Wonder City."

"You've been to Wonder City?"

He turned to look at her as he realized he was being interviewed.

"Miss Vale, this isn't a good time…"

"Are you for real? *Every* time is a good time, when it comes to getting a story. That's what I do, kid. But we can talk about Wonder City some other time—let's get back to what you said about Batman losing someone he loves."

Ouch.

"You heard that, huh?"

She smiled. "I sure did."

"Well, you heard all you're going to hear," he said, making it sound final. "About that, anyway. You want to talk about the Riddler, we can do that—*if* we do it fast. I have to get out of here, and for all I know I just ate something really bad."

"Do you think you've been poisoned?" There was something more than interest in Vicki's voice.

Almost… glee, Robin thought. *That's sick.* Maybe it was the idea that she was onto a story of life and death, here in the ruins of Arkham City, that made her sound so hopeful.

"No, if the Riddler just wanted to kill me," he replied, "he's had more than his share of chances."

"How many more chances are you going to give him?" Vale asked. "Shouldn't you and Batman be taking a more active role here, instead of letting the Riddler lead you around by your noses?"

That stung.

"Look," he said, his jaw tight, "not too long ago, Batman

dug you out of a wrecked helicopter. Just now, I stopped Harley Quinn from giving the Riddler your head as a trophy. I think maybe you should allow us a little discretion."

"Discretion isn't something I do too well, doll," Vale said. "But I do appreciate what you did." She almost sounded as if she meant it.

"Appreciate it enough to not endanger more lives when you get out of here," Robin said. "Okay?" He looked straight at her, hoping she got the message.

She held his gaze for a long time.

Then she nodded. "Okay." She pulled her phone out of a pocket and snapped a few pictures, getting shots of the mechanical guardian and various angles around the two rooms, including the broken axe head buried in the wooden block. "So how are we getting out?"

"That's the thing," Robin said. "The way I get out of here is going to lead to a situation even more dangerous than this one. I can't be responsible for your safety."

"Don't patronize me," she said.

"I'm not patronizing you, I'm *telling* you. If you'd been in the last room where the Riddler sprang a trap on me, you'd be dead. So either you stay here, or you figure some other way out."

"Fine," Vale said. She walked into the parlor and under the hole in the ceiling, peering upward. "Where does that go?"

"That's how I came in," Robin said. "It won't be the way out—not for you."

"Then I guess that just leaves me with one option," she said, walking back into the execution chamber. She paused at the hole in the far wall. "Say, d'you think, um…?"

"Do I think Harley Quinn is still in there?" Robin said. "Probably not. The Riddler isn't happy with her for not finishing the job, and she knows it, so my guess is that she's making tracks for somewhere far away from him. But you saw her. There's no way to be sure *what* she's going to do."

"Yeah, you got that right," Vale said. She stood there for a long time while Robin resumed combing through the room for a clue. "Well, this is a hell of a story. It's worth some risk." But she didn't move. "What do you think will happen if I stay here?"

"I have no idea," Robin said truthfully.

"Okay," she said. "Well, thanks again for saving my life."

"You're welcome."

She tapped her phone's screen.

"How come I can't get any bars down here?" she said, mostly to herself. "Stupid." She tapped the screen and turned on the video flash to use as a torch. "Well, here goes," she said, and she disappeared into the passage.

Robin waited and listened. He didn't hear any screams or sounds of mayhem.

Vicki can take care of herself, he decided. It was his job to get back to the chessboard and find the Riddler.

Taking Them to Trask

Duane Trask, Gotham Globe Radio

"We're taking your calls. Lonnie in the Heights."

"Did you see what just happened? I saw Deadshot! He went right by my window, and he, like, pointed at me and did the finger-gun thing. Bang!"

"Lonnie, I hear the laughing in the background. You and your stoner pals can take a long walk off a short pier. Matilda, you're on *Taking them to Trask*."

"Duane, I think you have a very good perspective on what's going on here."

"Well, I'm glad to hear you say that, Matilda. Appreciate it. What's on your mind?"

"Where's Robin in all of this? Do you think something's happened to him? I don't know if I like Batman or not, but I do like that Robin kid."

"I'm sure he's fine, Matilda. He's very resourceful. Thanks for the call. Ivan's across the river, looking down at us from the Palisades. What's on your mind, Ivan?"

"There's something weird going on in the river."

"What do you mean?"

"Well, I look down at the same part of the river every day, from my office window. There's a part of it that

looks different now. The currents are all different and there's like a—I don't know the word. Like water's bubbling up there from down on the bottom."

"Is that right, Ivan? When did this happen?"

"A couple hours ago. I was eating lunch and, you know, looking out at the river and the city. Then all of a sudden, there's this like surge of bubbles and stuff. You should see it."

"We will. We'll take a look. Thanks for the call, Ivan.

"Huh. This morning Batman was seen at the Flood Control Facility, and now apparently the currents have shifted in the West River just downstream of Arkham City. Could Batman have done something to the outflow tunnels? They're everywhere along that part of the riverfront.

"Some of them might have changed the current—or hey, now I'm really going to speculate. When the old steel mill was running, it dumped a lot of water along the riverbed there. Wastewater from cooling operations, mostly. We're hearing rumors of activity in that area, and maybe explosions too. Ivan might just be onto something.

"We'll check it out and report back as soon as we know anything. Otto, you're on the air.

"Who was that last guy? Weird currents in the river? What's next? Someone's gonna claim that Batman's fighting UFOs?"

20

So the Riddler had plans in place for when Robin—or, as it happened, Harley Quinn—went off-script. That bit of information was key.

It meant Nigma didn't have absolute certainty in his own planning. For most people it would have been commendable caution, but for the Riddler it was almost like an admission of failure before the game had even begun. Or…

What if the whole thing was staged?

That made more sense to Robin than the "accidental" intrusion of Harley Quinn. She had staged the whole thing, in consultation with the Riddler. So if Quinn was the Red Queen, did that mean the king would be waiting back on the chessboard? And Vicki Vale hadn't just wandered into Arkham City. No, she'd been there on a tip.

Part of the Riddler's gambit was pure ego. He wanted publicity for what he was doing, and if Vale found her way back up to the surface, he would get it. That made it likely that she would make it out alive, no doubt along some long-forgotten passage that would lead her back to the surface.

Robin could try the same path, but he doubted the Riddler would let him get away with it. That would be too far off-script, and probably would get him killed on the spot. It might lead to Vale's death, as well.

So he turned back to the tea set. He hoped he could figure this out quickly. Sooner or later he would start to experience the effects of whatever Quinn had made him eat, and he wanted to be out of this room before that happened.

He counted the cups. There were twelve of them placed around the edge of the table. The teapot sat in the middle, and the long bread plate created a line between the teapot and one of the cups.

Then he remembered the Riddler's note.

"Time is of the essence!"

The tea set was arranged like a clock. What was it the Mad Hatter had said, in *Alice's Adventures in Wonderland*?

"It's always six o'clock now."

Then a bright idea came into his head. Robin went to the grandfather clock and opened the glass door that protected its face. Carefully he spun the minute hand around until the hands formed a single straight line. Six o'clock. He tensed, waiting to see…

Nothing happened.

Robin looked around to make sure he hadn't missed anything. But there had been no change. Everything looked exactly the same.

What was he not seeing?

Suddenly it struck him. *It was always six o'clock.* Always. Turning back to the clock, he stopped the pendulum swinging in its case. The minute hand had already ticked forward a tiny bit, so he shifted it back until the hands were at precisely six o'clock again.

This time there was a rattle from the ceiling, and a louder groaning of machinery. A short ladder dropped from the hole through which Robin had entered, although it didn't reach the floor. Gauging its height, Robin figured he could jump and catch the bottom rung easily enough.

Before he did, though, Robin once again considered making his exit through the hole in the wall, just as Vicki Vale had. Would that enable him to complete the puzzle without having to contend with door number seven? He made his way back into the execution room, and studied the opening.

With a grinding of gears, the guardian started to move again. Robin skipped back from the hole, ready to fight it if he had to. But the mechanical monster simply ignored him. It stomped back to where it had entered, turned around to face out into the room, and held its position.

That answers that question, Robin thought. *None shall pass.* The Riddler had to be watching his every move. When it looked like he was going to deviate from the plan, Nigma had used the robot to make his point. Whatever opportunity he might have had to throw a wrench in the Riddler's works, it was gone now.

Still, if Harley could go rogue…

"Hey, Riddler," he called out. "What, are you losing control, maybe just a little? Could it be that people aren't playing along the way you want them to?" With that, he waited to see what would happen.

A question mark lit up on the ceiling near the open hatch. That confirmed it. The Riddler wasn't just watching his progress as he made it through the death rooms. He was listening in, and making sure things went according to plan.

His comm pinged. Robin answered.

"Before we say anything," he said, "you should know that the Riddler is listening."

"Of course he is," Batman said. *"That's no surprise."*

"It's not meant to be," Robin said. "It's confirmation."

"You talked to him?"

"In a way," Robin said. "Harley Quinn dropped in, playing the Red Queen, with Vicki Vale on the chopping block. They're both gone now. The Riddler sent a mechanical guardian to stop Harley from messing with his script, but she got away scot-free."

"Interesting," Batman said. *"So he has contingency plans."*

"Either that, or he staged the whole thing," Robin said. "I don't think it's a coincidence that she was wearing a Red Queen costume. Do you?"

"Maybe not. How did he manage to take Vicki Vale as a hostage? She wouldn't have just wandered into the Riddler's labyrinth."

"The way she told it, she was tipped off that there was a story to be had—about you. She went looking where the tipster told her to go, and instead of a story she found Harley. Fun, right? Vale slipped out the way the robot came in. When I gave it a try, the metal thug made it clear that it wasn't an option. Be ready for Vale to deliver a story from the front lines, though," he added. "You're likely to figure prominently."

"Next time her helicopter crashes in the middle of a war zone, she can get herself out," Batman growled. *"I'm a little surprised the Riddler didn't have the guardian go after*

Quinn, though. He doesn't take it well when people interfere with his productions."

"Like I said, that makes me think the whole thing was staged. The Riddler's priority is keeping me on track," Robin said. "He put on this particular pageant so he could have Vale air a nice, dramatic story about him on TV.

"But that's not the issue at hand," he continued. "The question is, do I tell the Riddler where he can stuff his gambit, and take advantage of this other way out?"

"It sounds as if you'll have to go through the guardian to do that," Batman said. *"That's a tall order."*

"I can handle the guardian," Robin said, hoping he sounded convincing. "But what's the Riddler going to do if we bail on his game?"

"Are you asking me, or him?"

"I'm just playing my role," Robin answered. "If he didn't want me asking, he would have handled the situation differently."

The question mark started blinking.

"Do you think he can hear me?" Batman asked.

"Sometimes *I* can barely hear you," Robin answered. "But no, I've got you coming in through an earpiece. Unless he's cracked our encryption, he's relying entirely on my voice."

"Good move," Batman said. *"The timer's ticking down again, and I have a hunch about who's going to be next."*

"Who is it? How did you figure it out?"

"Oracle found a common element in each victim's recent history. They all exchanged phone calls with a number that led—through dead ends and misdirection—to a company called Conundrum Solutions. There were crates with that

name on them in the Ace Chemical factory, where Mr. Freeze was working."

"Clever," Robin said. "Conundrum Solutions."

"Good thing we weren't keeping that a secret," Batman said.

Crap!

"I wanted the Riddler to hear it," Robin responded. He looked around the room, wondering where the camera and microphone were.

"Right," Batman said, then he continued. *"Oracle found two more numbers that had multiple contacts with Conundrum during the relevant time frame. One of those numbers led to Theresa Gray, although we didn't know that until it was too late. She worked for Gotham City police, in the mailroom."*

"Uh-oh," said Robin. "Then the Riddler had a mole inside."

"Either that, or he coerced Gray into passing the package containing the USB drive through the system. Commissioner Gordon, as you can imagine, isn't handling it well."

"How many more loose ends does the Riddler plan to tie up? We're already at four."

"The fifth is one Pierre Ouellette, who owns a chemical supply company. Commissioner Gordon is hiding him at a safe house. He won't even tell me where it is, or I'd question Ouellette myself."

"A chemical supplier," Robin said. "That explains where the hydrogen and oxygen came from in the molecular puzzle room."

"Exactly. And that's the last number in the group," Batman said. *"The Riddler's almost done tying up his loose*

ends." Robin heard the Batmobile's engine start.

"So did you track down the Mad Hatter?"

"*I did, and I got some information from him,*" Batman said, "*though not as much as I'd hoped. He's designed a device that allows the Riddler to control the mechanical guardians remotely. The details weren't clear, but Tetch said it was a form of mind control. I'm not sure how accurate that characterization is, though, coming from him.*"

Over the exit, the question mark started blinking faster. The mechanical guardian's faceplate lit up again, and it raised its arms.

"Gotta go," Robin said. "I think the Riddler's getting antsy. If he's mind-controlling this guardian, then he's telling me it's time to get moving."

"*Keep me posted on door number seven,*" Batman said. "*And watch out for more of the robots,*" he added. Then he clicked off.

The mechanical guardian extended an arm.

At the end of it was a lens, starting to glow.

The question mark was blinking very fast.

"All right, I hear you," Robin said. He jumped up and caught the bottom rung of the ladder leading back up into the roof chute.

When he came through door number six, the chessboard was empty. No pawns, no king. The original three chessmen were gone. Door number seven was directly across the board.

This was the last thing Robin had expected.

Where was the king? He took a step forward to the next

square, ready for anything—but nothing happened. Nothing kept right on happening as he stepped on the second square, and the third, and right on across the board to number seven.

This was the endgame. Everything was coming full circle. His conversation with Batman reinforced it. The murder victims had a common link, and each puzzle they had solved was related to the USB drive and the material it contained.

He took a moment to study the room again, to see if he had missed something, but the other doors were shut. The chamber already seemed to have been forgotten. The Riddler had moved on. It was time for Robin to do so, as well.

Just as it was time to find the king, and discern the meaning of I AM LARVAL. He had a feeling the answer to both of those enigmas might just wait on the other side.

Bull's Eye
by **Rafael Del Toro**, GothamGazette.com

The body count is climbing, people are scared, parts of Arkham City appear to be exploding for unknown reasons... wait. Let me guess.

Batman's back, isn't he?

I've heard people say that Gotham City is sick, that it breeds criminals and psychopaths the way other cities breed tech startups and basketball players. I don't believe that. Nothing about Gotham City was predestined. We choose the kind of city we want to live in, and for some reason we've decided it should be a city overrun with lawlessness. We've chosen the one shining light of Batman to save us from all the things we've decided collectively we can't fix ourselves.

In other words, we created Batman because he makes things easier on us. If there's Batman, that means we don't have to do anything to make Gotham City a better place. If there's Batman, we have someone to blame when things go wrong—as in, "there's never a Batman around when you need him."

He's someone to cheer when cheering makes us feel better about our own apathy. And that's a problem.

It's not Batman's problem, it's our problem. No one's forcing us to have a city full of costumed villains and the occasional stalwart vigilante. We could have a normal city, with normal problems and normal issues. Instead we have Gotham City.

What are we going to do about it?

Today, apparently, nothing. Batman's chasing the Riddler and someone—possibly Deadshot—is blowing the heads off random people in the street. And all for what? If Batman wasn't there, what would the Riddler and Deadshot and Clayface and whoever else do? Who would they fight?

Sometimes I think that if Batman decided to move to Miami, the rest of the maniacs would follow him. Who wants to start a petition? We could call it the "Citizens' Call for a Normal Gotham City." Would anyone sign it? Who knows? We're not known for our sense of civic engagement.

Here's the thing. Everyone's always talking about how we need Batman. Okay. Let's go with that idea for a minute. We need Batman.

But why?

That's something we can only answer ourselves, and at least today, while we're all glued to our TVs and radios, waiting for the latest about the assassinations... today we're not going to answer that question.

Apparently we have better things to do.

21

He opened the door… and saw nothing.

Literally nothing. Just an empty space. Robin pulled out a flashlight and shone the beam through the doorway. He realized that he was looking into the interior of a vertical shaft, its walls painted matte black. It topped off at about twelve feet above the floor level of the chess room, but when he shone the light down, it was lost in the depths without showing a bottom.

About six feet below floor level were old steel frames, with a burned-out electrical box just above them. It appeared as if the frames had once supported a fan, which would make this a ventilation shaft, now capped.

How far down did it go?

The only way to find out was to start rappelling, so he affixed a line to one of the hinges on the door itself, and started to drop down. He had one hundred feet of line in the spool he was using. If the shaft went deeper than that, it would place him a long way below the water table. Nothing over here had been dug that deep when Arkham City—or, for that matter, Wonder City—had originally been built.

It took only about sixty feet of the line to get to the

bottom of the shaft. That wasn't as far as he'd anticipated, and his light should have revealed something from up above. Something in the paint must have absorbed the beam.

He clicked the flashlight on again as soon as he hit solid ground—damp concrete littered with rusty bits of metal from whatever fans and electrical relays had been ripped out during the renovations. A small metal door set low to the ground was the only way out. Robin opened it, pocketed his light, and crawled through the tight space, quickly coming out into a pitch-dark room that must have been huge, judging from the echoes made by the scrape of his boots on the floor as he stood.

He reached for his flashlight again, but as he put his hand on it the entire room lit up with a series of soft pops. He looked up and it dawned on him that he had come into Wonder City, and, even better…

…the Riddler's workshop.

Gaslamps glowed at twenty-foot intervals along the walls of the room, which was at least the size of the Batcave. The ceiling arched high overhead, made of brick and cast iron. Old signs and banners advertising Wonder City and its various attractions hung here and there. Some of the walls actually included old storefronts, and most of its floor space was taken up with machines and worktables.

Pieces of mechanical guardians lay in a heap near one table. There didn't appear to be any intact or active ones.

Embraced in a moment of awe, he walked through the room, seeing the genesis of all the Riddler's death rooms. Blueprints of the Sionis steel mill and the Flood Control Facility lay on a tabletop alongside a broken neon-tube question mark. Chemical diagrams and disassembled batteries were piled on another table, next to racks of chemistry equipment. Beakers and tubes, centrifuges, jars of chemicals, standing tanks of pure hydrogen and oxygen with the Conundrum Solutions logo overlapping the word FLAMMABLE stenciled on their sides. Further along, Robin came to an enclosed lab built behind a storefront.

LEANDRO'S LUNCH said the sign over the door.

Inside, the lab was sterile and white—in stark contrast to the aging steampunk motif of the great room. Gleaming stainless-steel racks held computers and instruments. A small sealed manufacturing chamber contained machinery for printing circuits, as well as other machines Robin didn't recognize.

He thought of the people the Riddler had murdered, or whose murders he had ordered. An electronics specialist, a nanotech researcher, a software engineer... their work was visible here, even if the results were not.

Back out in the main room, Robin recalled what he could from the last time he'd been in Wonder City. There were a number of ways in and out, or had been, at least. The Riddler might well have sealed or booby-trapped them.

There's got to be something I'm missing, Robin mused. *He didn't put me through all of those death traps just to let me wander back up to the surface.* There had to be another challenge here... somewhere.

He explored each of the storefronts in turn. Most of them were emptied out and falling into ruin, populated by the occasional rat and a wide variety of insect and arachnid life. One store held a small electric blast furnace and metallurgical equipment, while another was shrouded in shadows and completely empty except for a robotic suit standing in a gantry, held in place by a number of mechanical arms.

The suit stood approximately nine feet tall. Its torso hung in two pieces, front and back, next to each other. The limbs were disassembled and suspended in positions that made the whole thing look like an exploded-view diagram. Over it all hung the helmet, a steel dome with a transparent faceplate. The segments appeared to have been retooled from pieces of some mechanical guardians, embellished with the Riddler's customary touches.

A question mark-shaped control panel built into the floor near the gantry had only a single button—the period at the bottom of the question mark's reverse curve. It was blinking bright green.

Not exactly subtle, not that I should be surprised.

The sound of running water came from the darkened rear of the room. He walked past the gantry and saw that the floor ended abruptly after eight feet or so. Beyond that was running water, an underground river twelve feet wide, flowing out of a grate in the wall to his left. He couldn't tell how deep it was, or where it went after it passed under the wall to his right, but he did notice that there was no grate on the downstream side.

Outside, something exploded.

Robin ran out of the store and saw fire engulfing the furthest storefront on the opposite side of the room. Bricks rained down from the ceiling, and the banners nearest to the explosion were burning.

Another explosion, from the storefront facing the first blast, brought down more of the ceiling and started a fire on the near side of the room. A third detonation annihilated Leandro's Lunch and collapsed part of the roof. Along with bricks and iron beams, huge chunks of concrete and stone crashed down on the Riddler's workstations. The chemistry table was crushed by an iron beam, and hydrogen venting from a broken tank caught fire. The secondary detonation of the chemical tanks destroyed a shelf of computers and tools.

Another explosion, from just two storefronts to the right of where Robin was standing, staggered him. He dodged back inside as a piece of concrete the size of a car crashed to the floor and broke into pieces. Flying shards of it shattered the storefront windows.

"*Really* not subtle, Riddler," he said, hoping the lunatic could hear him. A fifth explosion blew apart the pile of discarded mechanical guardians and started a fire near the corner that led back to the ventilation shaft.

At that point his options had all but disappeared—with the exception of the most obvious. If Robin didn't climb into the suit, Wonder City was going to fall in on his head. There was no point hesitating and trying to figure out a way to work around it.

He turned and jogged up to the gantry. There were footprint-shaped marks on its floor. Robin pressed the blinking green button and stepped up onto the structure, turning around to place his feet exactly on the marks. He held his arms out in what seemed to be the correct configuration. With a mechanical whine, the machines activated. One arm swung the front torso piece into position, and then Robin was jostled a little as the back torso piece bumped into him. With that, he shrugged himself into position. There was a series of clicks and pings as the pieces locked together.

Next, his arms and legs were encased, to a chorus of continued locking noises. Another explosion brought down most of the roof outside, plunging the room into darkness. The only thing Robin could see was the array of lights on the mechanical arms and the steady glow of the button on the control panel. He felt gauntlets sliding into place over his hands, and when he flexed his fingers he heard the scrape of metal. Then he was lifted into the air and heavy boots snapped into place on his feet.

He looked up and had to suppress a moment of panic as the dark shape of the helmet descended. It slotted into a ring built around the neck of the torso pieces, turning thirty degrees and locking into place.

Outside, the fire had reached the storefront. That provided light by which he could see again, but it also meant that he would soon be roasted inside the suit, or crushed in the final collapse of the ceiling. This part of Wonder City was soon to be rubble.

He wondered if part of Arkham City above was falling into a giant sinkhole. If he lived through the next hour or so, maybe he would swing back by and check.

Air hissed inside the suit, and Robin's ears popped. It was pressurizing, and he heard dozens of little noises as seals and gaskets lined themselves up. The gantry set him down and almost immediately the floor started to shake. It sounded like a larger collapse was underway outside, but he couldn't see anything through the blocked windows.

He turned around. The suit moved slowly, deliberately. Robin raised its arms and saw that it had built-in energy weapons like the ones on the guardian that had threatened Harley Quinn.

The Riddler had armed him?

That didn't seem right.

He couldn't locate any control or trigger mechanisms.

Behind him, the storefront collapsed. A piece of the ceiling hit the suit on the shoulder, hard enough that it would have killed him if he hadn't been armored.

It was time to go.

Robin stepped to the edge of the water. He paused one last time, thinking furiously, trying to come up with a better solution.

The floor shook with another collapse.

"Here we go," Robin said. He stepped out over the water, and let himself fall.

RyderReport.com

Posted by JKB
Wednesday, 2:59 p.m.

Countdown… are we looking at a fifth murder? Or is Batman finally getting a handle on the situation?

He was spotted just a few minutes ago heading toward Burnley. Not a big crime area, it's more like the kind of place where a tech professional might live. Or someone who did design work, and maybe picked the wrong client.

Sound familiar?

Batman left after meeting with Commissioner Gordon outside the Gotham Casino. What might have transpired inside, we don't know, but the cops stayed behind after he departed. In a bizarre show of force, they stormed the casino with several SWAT units and the liberal use of tear gas. More on this as we get video from our field reporters.

One reporter on the scene at the casino tried to follow Batman, but didn't have the horsepower to keep up. Based on Internet reports, however, he's left the Batmobile and has disappeared over a rooftop. We're appealing for anyone who's in the Burnley area to look out your windows and, if you catch sight of Batman, take a photo and send it to us right away.

Pretty please?

Citizen journalism!

What's Batman up to?

Best photos get tickets to Jack's show!

Given the timing, he may be on the heels of the assassin who may or may not be Deadshot, depending on who you ask. Some reports are saying Deathstroke, and still others are claiming that it's a new villain on the scene looking to step in where the Joker left off.

A new villain. Just what Gotham City needs.

We'll continue to vet all these stories as they come in, and when we have one that meets the *Ryder Report's* standards of evidence, we'll get it right out to you. In the meantime…

Look out your windows and, if you catch sight of Batman, take a photo and send it to us right away.

Can you do that for us?

22

Commissioner Gordon and some of his officers were on standby, waiting for Batman to hand them whatever villainous flotsam he found, so when Batman called Gordon from the street in front of the casino, he didn't need to wait for long before they arrived.

"The Mad Hatter's inside, on the balcony," he said as Gordon climbed out of the lead car.

"Just standing there, or is there something else you want to add?"

"He won't resist you—he's too far gone," Batman said. "Also, watch out on the floor. Even though the Mad Hatter's not a threat right now, he's got a group of brainwashed flunkies brandishing knives."

"We'll take care of them," Gordon said. He motioned, and SWAT teams started to deploy from two personnel carriers that had parked across the street.

"Some of them will need medical attention," Batman noted as the preparations were being made. He worried that Gordon might go in with a heavier hand than was required, perhaps to prove that he had the situation under *his* control.

"I said we'll take care of them," Gordon said firmly, tossing him a look. "You just find the Riddler." He looked around. "Where's Robin?"

"He's still finding his way out. Where's Pierre Ouellette?"

Gordon took off his glasses and rubbed his nose.

"We talked about this," he said. "Ouellette is safe, and he's going to stay right where he is until—"

"Commissioner, with all due respect, do you think Pierre Ouellette is safe when you know there was a mole inside your force?" He regretted having to say that, but he couldn't see any other way forward. Before, Gordon had been protecting Ouellette and playing the odds. Now there were no odds. The man was Deadshot's next target, and Gordon was stopping Batman from confronting the assassin.

Gordon looked at Batman, his jaw tight and eyes burning. "Don't tell me how to do my job," he said.

Batman bit back a sharp reply as uniformed officers led by SWAT teams crashed through the casino's front door. There was a thud, and shortly following it the unmistakable tang of tear gas wafting through the broken entry.

The problem, Batman thought, *isn't that I'm telling Gordon how to do his job. It's that he's too prickly and too defensive to get out of my way.* That was ingrained cop behavior. They were taught to be suspicious when operating with other agencies—or individuals. If someone else closed the case and caught the perpetrators, it didn't look good in the press, and it didn't sit well when budget time came around.

"No, I won't tell you how to do what you do," he said as the stutter of automatic weapons fire echoed from inside. A news helicopter circled overhead, and at least two reporters were watching his conversation with Gordon. "What I *am* telling you is that we're less than ten minutes from the counter hitting zero again.

"You need to trust me."

Gordon deliberated for a long moment.

The timer ticked down.

He gave Batman an address.

That's the last favor we'll get from Gordon, at least for a while, Batman thought as he gunned the Batmobile away from the casino. *If it was a favor. It might have been an act of self-preservation.*

After all, if Batman went after Deadshot, and didn't get him, Gordon retained the moral high ground. He had shared important information, and it wasn't his fault if Batman came up short.

He couldn't blame Gordon for a maneuver like that—not really. He had a department to run and city politics with which to deal. Batman didn't have to factor such things into his decision-making processes.

He answered to the people of Gotham City.

00:04:07

He parked the Batmobile on a quiet side street in the Burnley neighborhood, not far from the new Gotham City police headquarters. He was a block from the address Gordon had given him. In this part of Gotham City, citizens went about their business unaffected by the plots of the Riddler and Gotham

City's other malevolent underworld figures... at least most of the time.

The streets were clean and the brownstones well kept. Most of them had small front gardens, and the cars parked on the street were nicer than in other parts of the city. These were the people who mistrusted Batman the most, because they were most isolated from the everyday degradations of crime and poverty. But he protected them all the same.

He slipped down an alley and climbed a fire escape running up the back of an old warehouse that was being converted into lofts. The safe house was located in the building next door, on the fifth floor facing the alley. Batman paused in the shadows, looking over the area, observing every detail. There was nothing out of order, but if Deadshot was involved, he might be set up in a sniper position blocks away. He scanned the rooftops that had a line of sight on the safe house's single window, but didn't see anything more unusual than rows of pigeons. That was good. If someone was on one of those rooftops, the pigeons wouldn't stick around.

"One minute," Oracle said in his ear.

Batman's intent had been to intercept Deadshot, or whoever the Riddler's assassin might be, but time was short, and he saw no one to intercept. So he took a different approach.

He waited, perched on the fire-escape railing.

Forty-five seconds.

Thirty.

Fifteen... Ten.

At five seconds he launched himself from the railing and crashed through the window into the safe house. It was a studio apartment. There was a small kitchen area with an island counter and a futon doubling as a bed. On the futon sat Pierre Ouellette, eyes wide and terrified, staring up at a figure who was standing over him.

With a pistol leveled at his head.

Deadshot hadn't changed since the last time Batman had seen him. Same red-lensed monocle, same pseudo-military clothing, same wrist-mounted guns, even the same stubble.

"Hey, the Riddler said you might drop by," he said.

"What's the matter, Deadshot?" Batman responded. "Don't trust your marksmanship anymore, so you have to work up close?"

"Please," Ouellette moaned. "Don't kill me. I didn't do anyth—"

Deadshot smacked him with the butt of his gun.

"You shut up." Looking at Batman, he said, "You want to joke with me? I still owe you, pal. You made me miss that reporter, whatsisname, Ryder. Now I have to listen to that guy yammering on the radio twenty-four seven, and if I wasn't nuts before, that would be enough to do the trick."

"Everyone's got excuses," Batman said. "Only the weak use them."

"Okay, Doc," Deadshot said.

"What's with the handgun? Why not the ones you've already got strapped to your arm?"

"Calling card," Deadshot said with a shrug. "Special ammo."

"Like the initials?"

"Hey, when you're freelancing, you need all the publicity you can get. Now who am I gonna kill here?" He swung the pistol from Ouellette to Batman and back. The motion was too smooth to leave an opening. "Maybe I should do you both."

"You've got a problem, then," Batman said. "If you shoot him, I'll take you down. But if you go after me first, I'll still take you down, and he's going to run."

"You'll take me down?" Deadshot grinned. "I like a challenge—but you're right, I gotta make sure this guy doesn't get away. Hmmm." He scratched at the side of his head with the muzzle of the gun. "Oh. I got it."

He pointed the gun down and shot Ouellette in the foot.

Ouellette's scream lasted a lot longer than the sound of the gunshot. It also lasted longer than it took Batman to leap across from the window to the futon and knock the pistol from Deadshot's hand. Ouellette rolled around on the ground, still screaming, as Deadshot smashed his left forearm into Batman's nose.

Both of Deadshot's forearms were sheathed in the steel housings for his wrist guns. Batman felt something crunch in his nose. Shooting pain caused his vision to go white for a moment, and his eyes watered. He went over backward, grappling with his opponent.

He had both of Deadshot's wrists locked in his hands to prevent him from utilizing the wrist guns. If he tried to use them, the resulting explosion would probably leave Deadshot with stumps. So he didn't fire.

Instead he lashed out with a head-butt. Batman turned just in time to avoid taking the blow on his already bleeding nose.

"I told you we weren't done," Deadshot snarled.

Deadshot ripped his left arm free. He pointed the wrist gun at Batman, who threw himself to the left. The weapon chattered, chewing a hole in the floor. Batman jackknifed forward, throwing Deadshot back. The wrist gun kept firing as he flailed, spraying the apartment's walls and ceiling.

Batman kept his grip on Deadshot's right wrist, using it as leverage to spin him around. He ducked his head under Deadshot's right arm and lifted him into the air, then slammed him down on the kitchen island hard enough to crack the granite counter top.

The wrist gun cut out, either because it had run out of ammunition or because the impact on the counter had interrupted Deadshot's fire control. Batman chopped a forearm into his throat and followed it up with three piledriver thrusts straight to his face. The last cracked the red monocle and bounced Deadshot's head on the granite hard enough that his visible eye rolled back in his head for a long moment before coming lazily back to focus on his assailant.

"You have two choices," Batman said. "We can talk, or I can keep hitting you."

"You made me miss again," Deadshot rasped.

Ouellette wasn't screaming anymore, but he was still moaning and clutching at his foot.

"At least you hit his foot," Batman said. "That ought to console you when you end up back in Blackgate."

"Whatever," Deadshot said. "I only stay there as long as I want to. Just like Arkham City, remember?"

"Tell me something," Batman said, ignoring the taunt. "Why did the Riddler set you off on a timed series of assassinations… just like the Joker did when he and TYGER were in charge here? Can't Nigma come up with his own ideas?"

"You're the world's greatest detective, aren't you? You figure it out—there's no deep, complicated reason here." His voice became clearer as he recovered from the effects of Batman's blows to the throat.

"Riddler's doing it because he wants to be the new Joker. He wants to run the show. Only way he can do that is to let everyone know that he can take on you and Robin, take on Gordon, and keep you all dancing to his tune. Like the Joker used to."

The expression on Deadshot's face was laced with real disappointment.

"I woulda thought you had that all figured out already." He shook his head. "You go off on a tangent, looking for deep, dark motives, when the simple truth is right there, staring you in the face."

He was right.

The answer had been right in front of them the entire time, and he'd refused to see it. The parallels had all been there from the beginning—the bomb in the Gotham Merchant's Bank vault, hunting Killer Croc, Mr. Freeze's research. The puzzle hadn't been difficult. He'd just refused to solve it.

He couldn't admit that the Riddler was making a play for the Joker's place in the underworld hierarchy, because to acknowledge that would mean admitting that the Joker was gone.

"I seen that look before," Deadshot said. "You thought the Riddler was just playing some sort of twisted game.

Think again, bud. He's shooting for the top, and that's what he's been trying to tell you this whole time. Man, wait'll word gets round!"

He started to laugh. Batman drew back and knocked him out with a single punch, pouring all of his anger and frustration—and, yes, embarrassment—into the blow.

Deadshot went down, and stayed down.

"*Now* we're done," Batman said.

He heard a whimper in the corner.

"You, uh… I thought you didn't do stuff like that," Ouellette said. Batman turned, and the man wouldn't look him in the eye.

"You thought wrong," he said.

Then he kicked open the window and was gone.

<click>

This is Vicki Vale. I'm still somewhere in the access tunnels, I think under the steel mill. Definitely in Arkham City. I haven't seen Phil. I haven't seen anyone since I got out of the room with Robin and Harley Quinn.

There are things moving in the darkness.

Maybe more of those robots?

<click>

Story notes. Robin was in a room, Victorian decorations, with a table set and pictures on the walls. He ate a piece of paper that had the words EAT ME written on it. No visible effect. He fought Harley Quinn to free me. I owe him one for that. I think she was really going to kill me.

Was that the Riddler's plan? I don't think so. He wouldn't have lured me down underneath Arkham City just to kill me. He wanted me to have a story, and that's what I have. If I can get out of here.

<click>

Damn, I wish my phone could get reception down here. Are there no towers anywhere in Arkham City? God.

Story notes. Harley Quinn and Robin were interrupted by a mechanical guardian. That's what Robin called it. A robot from Wonder City. He's been there. When I get out—if I get out—that's my first interview. Find Robin, find out about Wonder City, find out if the legends about it are true.

He stuck around to look for the Riddler, but he had to

solve some kind of puzzle in the room. Having to do with a clock?

I never did see the Riddler. Quinn had her own ideas. I don't think she's a Riddler fan. She's still hung up on the Joker—her "Puddin'"—plus she's as crazy as the day is long. I can still feel that axe blade biting into the wood block next to my head.

Note: I'm going to need a new haircut before I go on camera again. Harley gave me an asymmetrical look, and that's never really been my style.

Phil. I sure hope he's okay.

<click>

Looks like there's light ahead. Sunlight, I mean. Also I'm not seeing question marks anymore. I think that's the way out.

<click>

23

Batman notified Gordon that Pierre Ouellette was still alive, and that Deadshot was waiting for a ride to Blackgate.

He was furious with himself for losing control. His nose ached fiercely, and while the bleeding had stopped, he wouldn't be able to set the break until he'd returned to the cave.

On his way back to the Batmobile, he pinged Oracle.

"Are there any other names on the list? Any other numbers that had multiple contacts with Conundrum?"

"No," she said. *"I've found them all, and they're all accounted for. But I've lost contact with Robin. For a while I was able to find a pretty strong signal from his comm, but it cut out about twenty minutes ago. Also, here's another thing you should know. The timer app just deleted itself."*

There were two possible reasons. Either Ouellette had been the last name on the list, in which case the app's reason for existence had disappeared… or the Riddler had built a fail-safe into it, and deleted the app when Batman interrupted the latest hit.

He was inclined to believe the first possibility, and Oracle agreed.

"If there were more targets out there, the Riddler would have some kind of backup plan for dealing with the disruption," she said. *"Like the guardian robot he sent to interrupt Harley Quinn."*

"If that's what really happened," Batman said. "For all we know, the two of them staged that little drama."

"Yet the scene with Deadshot wasn't staged," Oracle said. *"He was going to kill Ouellette."*

Batman felt an almost audible *click* in his brain.

"He *thought* he was, yes. But what if the Riddler wanted me to stop him? That gets Deadshot out of the Riddler's way, cleaning up another loose end." *But why would Riddler leave Ouellette alive,* he wondered. "Pierre Ouellette possesses information the Riddler wants me to have."

"My dad is getting to the safe house now, with an ambulance," Oracle said. *"Better catch them before the EMTs drug up Ouellette, and he forgets whatever it is you need to know."*

Batman got there, but barely.

"Hold on," he said to an EMT who was loading Ouellette into the back of the ambulance. "Have you given him any painkillers?"

"No, they haven't," Ouellette groused. "And I wish to hell they would."

"Good," Batman said. He climbed into the back of the ambulance and gave the EMT a look.

"I'm going to need a minute here."

Without a word the EMT stepped back, and Batman shut the ambulance door.

"What's—what's going on?" Ouellette asked, his eyes wide and bloodshot. "I have a hole in my foot. I need to go to the hospital."

"Most people who cross paths with Deadshot get holes in worse places," Batman said. "But we can make this quick, as long as you give me some information. What did you do for the Riddler?"

"Uh-uh. No way," Ouellette said. "I already got shot once. What do you think he'll do if he finds out I talked to you?"

"He's going to assume that anyhow—if he has people watching, he knows I'm here," Batman said. "On the other hand, if you help me, I'll be able to find him. Then he won't be your problem anymore."

"If you find him, sure." Ouellette was panicking. "But you didn't find him in time to keep me from getting shot, did you?"

"I found you in time to prevent your being killed," Batman pointed out. "Face it, he's already decided you need to die. You think he's going to change his mind now? Your only chance is to tell me what you know."

Ouellette looked up from the gurney, terrified and confused. Despite the man's connection to the Riddler, Batman felt sorry for him, but he couldn't let Ouellette see that. He couldn't leave the ambulance without some answers.

"He, um… he had a big lab down in Wonder City," Ouellette said. "I didn't even know Wonder City was real, but he came and picked me up and took me down there. He had me work on this old robotic suit, rewire it so he could run it remotely."

"One of the mechanical guardians?"

"Yeah, I think that's what he called them. There were posters down there with pictures of them. Old stuff. I was surprised any of it still worked, but he—the Riddler— said he was getting some of them running again. He said it was for a show, like there was going to be a carnival down there or something. But he made me swear to keep it a secret.

"When he did that, he was scary—there was something in his eyes." Ouellette began to breathe heavily. "Look, Batman, I didn't know—"

"Spare me," Batman said. "You didn't care, is what you mean. As long as the check cleared." He opened the ambulance door. "People have already died because of what you did. More still might die. Think about that while you're whining about your foot."

Climbing out of the ambulance, he said to the EMT, "He's all yours."

The medical technician looked past him, as if he wanted to make sure Batman hadn't done something awful in there. Seeing only a morose and suffering Pierre Ouellette, he climbed in, closed the doors, and the ambulance drove away.

Commissioner Gordon was waiting.

"What was that all about?"

"I figured something out, Commissioner," Batman said. "But I'm not entirely sure what."

"If I wanted puzzles, I'd go get a newspaper," Gordon said.

"We've got puzzles whether we want them or not, Jim, but a little piece of one of them just fell into place. Ouellette helped the Riddler rewire and possibly program some of the old mechanical guardians, down in Wonder City," Batman said.

"Why? To build some kind of robot army? That's not the Riddler's style."

"Agreed," Batman said. "That's why I said I'm not sure."

Moving out of earshot, he called Oracle to find out whether she had managed to locate Robin. She hadn't.

Two police orderlies brought Deadshot out of the building, strapped down on a gurney. They had stripped off his wrist guns but left the monocle. As they passed, he turned his head toward Batman.

"Twice you've made me miss," he said. "Won't happen again."

It occurred to Batman that maybe he should have let Deadshot eliminate Jack Ryder. This would have accomplished two things—both of them positive. One, Deadshot wouldn't have a grudge and might have been happier to stay in Blackgate. Two, Jack Ryder wouldn't be polluting the airwaves of Gotham City with his toxic egomania.

Suddenly he felt something shift in his head, an almost physical sensation, and he realized he had been thinking like one of his foes—one of the people he had dedicated his life to stopping. He wasn't the kind of man who played enemies against each other, or who sacrificed lives to achieve goals. He *couldn't* be that. He stood for something more. But the train of thought had come so easily to him, had been so seductive… almost as if there was another consciousness in his head.

With a stirring of deep unease, Batman articulated the thought.

That was how the Joker would think.

Was that what it was like to internalize an enemy so deeply that when that enemy was gone, you kept him alive? Batman knew he didn't have the leisure to chase the Joker's ghost around the inside of his own head. He had to stay focused—but time and again, he had felt the Joker's presence. A psychiatrist might call it post-traumatic stress, but if that was the case, he'd had post-traumatic stress since he was a child.

His entire life he had been driven by the presence of the dead.

But right now Batman didn't have the time for psychiatry. Deadshot was still looking at him as the orderlies wheeled him to an armored ambulance for transport to Blackgate's secure hospital.

"Whatcha thinking about?" Deadshot said, taunting him again.

Out of the corner of his eye, Batman saw Gordon watching them. He waited until the prison ambulance was gone, then came over.

"What was that all about?" he asked.

"Deadshot had an insight," Batman said.

"That's all you're going to give me?" Gordon looked irritated. "I get a lecture about trust, I give you the address of this place… and you tell me 'Deadshot had an insight.'"

"I'm still figuring it out, Commissioner," Batman said.

"Well, figure fast," Gordon said. "I'm all out of ideas."

I'm missing something, Batman thought. Deadshot was right. The Riddler had walked him through the Joker's Greatest Hits… but what was the big finale? There were no puzzles left, no way for him to get in touch with Robin, or find another of the Riddler's associates.

Everything had gone quiet.

That, in Batman's experience, meant that everything was about to get very loud.

Taking Them to Trask
Duane Trask, Gotham Globe Radio

"We interrupt our regular programming to report that Vicki Vale is alive and well. Repeat, Vicki Vale is on her way out of Arkham City. She is unharmed, and we have her on the line. Vicki?"

"Duane! It's been quite a ride these past few hours, I can tell you."

"I bet it has. How about you fill us in?"

"Well, there I was, just an innocent reporter on her way to a little interview with none other than the notorious Riddler. I had a time and place, and I had a cameraman... oh. Phil. Has anyone seen Phil?"

"I have some bad news, Vicki. It's... well, it's terrible news. Phil, well... Phil didn't make it."

"Oh, no. I...

"Excuse me... I-I'm sorry."

"No, don't be. I hate to have to tell you that."

"I... Oh, Phil. Who...?"

"Police are still investigating that, Vicki. That's all we know. Listen, do you want to do this another time?"

"Just give me a second, Duane. Just... okay. Okay."

"Seriously, Vicki, if you—"

"Ask me a question, Duane."

"Okay then. You were going to a meeting with the Riddler. What happened next?"

"I was down in the subway, the line under Arkham City that was sealed off when Hugo Strange walled off the surface part. I looked up at one point and Phil was just... gone.

"I didn't know where he had gone, and I couldn't follow him because there were intersecting tunnels and I didn't know which one to take. Then I saw Harley Quinn."

"The Joker's associate? Meeting you on the Riddler's behalf?"

"I don't think so. She... well, she talked a lot. If you've ever seen footage of her, you know that weird act she does. Only she wasn't wearing her regular getup. She was dressed like the Red Queen. You know, the Queen of Hearts."

"Off with her head!"

"Not funny, Duane."

"Sorry. I'm sorry. Did she say that?"

"Yes. She did. And she had an axe, and she... well, she would have killed me, but Robin saved my life."

"Hold on, hold on. Robin was there?"

"He was. Still is, for all I know. He was working his way through a series of rooms—they're all puzzles, I guess, each one designed to be fatal. Harley Quinn found a way in. There was a Victorian theme in the one she dragged me to. She had my head on a block, was shouting, 'Off with her head!' The whole nine."

"And Robin saved you?"

"Yes. He did. Then he and Harley Quinn fought, and—I

have some pictures of that actually, just from my phone."

"We'd love to see those."

"Not a chance, Duane. At least not until Eye on Gotham *has them. You know how it is."*

"I sure do. Well, so Robin and Harley Quinn fought, and...?"

"A mechanical guardian broke through the wall and stopped the fight. Got right in between them—"

"Wait. A mechanical guardian? As in, from Wonder City? Are those even real?"

"This one was. It was remotely operated, or looked like it must be. Robin seemed to think the Riddler was running it. He was half convinced that the Riddler had set the whole thing up, to bring me in for publicity and show off what he's doing under Arkham City."

"Well, if that's the case, it's working. Sounds like a hell of a story."

"It was. I've been in a lot of strange spots covering Gotham City, but I've never before had a character from a playing card swing an axe at my head. Don't really want it to happen again, either."

"It's one for the memoirs. You might be interested to know that Commissioner Gordon just dragged the Mad Hatter out of Gotham Casino in manacles."

"That is interesting. Somehow Batman must have gotten in touch with Robin, and put two and two together."

"Maybe so. Let's all hope that's the case. We're up against the break here, Vicki. What's your plan, now that you're back above ground?"

"I'm going to find a ride and then I'm going to follow this story, Duane. Just like you would. Just like Phil would... would have..."

"Gotta go. Thanks for having me on."

"Thanks for dropping by, Vicki. Let's grab a drink sometime. I won't tell Jack."

"Sounds great. Talk soon."

"That was Vicki Vale, people. She was waylaid by Harley Quinn and apparently rescued by none other than Batman's wingman, Robin. She describes an underground labyrinth of passages below Arkham City, with lethal traps and patrols of the legendary—make that mythical—mechanical guardians of Wonder City! Do you believe it all? Or is Vicki doing what Vicki does best, putting herself at the center of the story?

"Oh, jeez. Did I say that out loud? Now she's never going to have that drink with me."

24

Robin was walking beneath the surface of the water, aided by the current. The underground river wound a sinuous course beneath the oldest parts of Gotham City. The mechanical guardian was airtight, and moved as easily underwater as it had in the open air—more easily, in fact, since the buoyancy gave the suit less of its own weight to carry.

As he walked, Robin saw bits of the city's history stuck in the silt on the floor of the tunnel. Old tools, pieces of machinery, and more recent additions like plastic bags and Styrofoam cups. He walked the way he imagined an astronaut on the moon might, bounding along with his arms out both for balance and to push off from the curving walls so he stayed in the center of the flow.

He lost track of how far he'd come, but his sense of time was still working. When he saw what looked like daylight ahead, he estimated it had been maybe a half-hour since he'd jumped into the water back in Wonder City. He slowed down and approached the opening. There the vista opened up in every direction.

Sure enough, it was the West River. Had to be. The bottom was littered with every kind of junk imaginable in a large metropolitan waterway—everything from construction debris to the sunken hulls of small boats to heavy cables laid from the island of Gotham City to the mainland. Most likely he was somewhere near the commuter train tunnels that ran under the riverbed, but it was hard to tell.

The stream's current pushed him forward and out of the mouth of the tunnel. Trying to avoid sinking too deeply into the silt, he picked his way along the bottom of the river, bearing to his left. If his sense of direction was intact, that was where Gotham City should be. Sooner or later he would see the pilings of the piers, and be able to find a way up and out onto the waterfront.

He tried to call Batman, but couldn't connect. Something in the suit must be compromising his comm link. Was that part of the Riddler's plan? If so, it was a change in tactics—until this point he had been happy to have Batman and Robin in constant communication.

But the jamming of his communications wasn't accidental. *Nothing* had been accidental so far—not even the appearance of Harley Quinn. The more he thought about it, the more convinced Robin became that the Riddler had staged the whole thing. It made sense for two reasons. One, to get Vicki Vale to give the Riddler the free publicity he craved, especially if he'd decided to be the new top dog in Gotham City crime.

Two, because it had focused Robin's attention on the mechanical guardians. If he hadn't seen the one in the tea room, Robin thought, he might not have taken any notice of the rebuilt suit in Wonder City.

In which case he would be dead.

The Riddler didn't want that.

At least not yet.

A dark shape loomed in the filthy water. Getting closer to it, Robin saw that it was a bridge pillar—largely stone, in the style of the early twentieth century. That put him about halfway down the island. He would want to move past it and to the left, coming over toward the old waterfront. There were still plenty of working piers down there, although most of Gotham City's freight traffic came and went from the east side of the island.

He climbed around a half-sunken caisson, probably abandoned when the bridge was being built, and on the other side of it found a forklift, a tangle of bent rebar, and a litter of corroded fifty-five-gallon drums, one of which had a skeleton inside of it.

Come to Gotham City for the history, he thought.

A few minutes later he found the pier pilings. The river here was dredged to thirty-five feet deep, give or take, in order to accommodate container ships. Looking up, Robin couldn't see the surface, but he could see light. He gripped one of the pilings and started climbing hand over hand. The suit was more than strong enough to lift its own weight.

Soon he spotted a ladder ending a few feet above his head, embedded in the wood, and grabbed onto its lowest rung. It snapped. He'd pulled too hard. So he climbed higher up the piling and gripped the outside of the ladder, which was made of heavier steel than the rungs. It held, and he used it to climb the rest of the way to the surface.

It was a bright, sunny afternoon in Gotham City.

Great, he thought. *Finally a sunny day, and I'm stuck inside.*

Robin blinked in the sunlight. He'd been either underground or underwater all day. As he clambered up the ladder, he felt the suit becoming heavier and clumsier around him as he left the water.

The pier was empty except for coils of rope and a pile of empty shipping containers lining the downstream side. Robin tried to call Batman again, but still couldn't get his comm link to work. He looked to his left and saw Arkham City, looking exactly as it had that morning. All the upheavals and explosions hadn't left a mark up here at ground level.

Turning more, he completed a 360-degree circle. The afternoon sun revealed something he hadn't seen when the suit was being assembled around him in the darkness of Wonder City. Lightly scored on the inside of the suit's faceplate was the word PUPA. Immediately Robin thought of the I AM LARVAL puzzle.

Had it really been only a few hours since they'd first seen it, back in the Batcave?

Robin tried to remember what the next stage was. Larva, pupa… it escaped him. Seemed like it was probably pretty important, if the Riddler had gone to all the trouble to put Robin in a cocoon made of a mechanical guardian.

What was that word…?

A truck pulled out onto the base of the pier. It was a city vehicle, with two men in the cab, probably coming to do some kind of work. They saw Robin—or rather, saw the mechanical guardian—and the truck came to a screeching halt. The driver rammed it into a three-point turn and got the hell out of there. As it turned back onto the waterfront access road, Robin saw the passenger talking on his phone.

For a moment this worried him, then he realized that Oracle would doubtless hear the results of that call, and contact Batman. Then presto! Their communications problem would be solved as soon as Bruce arrived on the scene.

Imago.

That was the word. That was it, the third and adult stage, after the insect had emerged from its cocoon, to assume its final form. So Robin had to get out of the suit somehow. That would complete the riddle's challenge.

And that, dear Robin, is where you will find the sternest challenge yet, the Riddler said. Robin tensed, and instinctively his eyes darted around. But he was alone on the pier.

Somehow, Robin knew the Riddler hadn't said it out loud. He'd spoken directly into Robin's head. For the first time since he'd entered the labyrinth, Robin was afraid.

"What's your game, Riddler?" he asked.

You are my game. Batman is my game. Gotham City is my game, and simultaneously the board on which I play. And when I play, I win. You survived the tests I set for you, but each was just a prelude. The story begins now; it's being written in—not on, but in—the little scrap of paper you ingested so agreeably back in the tea room.

"You didn't need to put me in a robot suit to poison me," Robin said. He started walking down the pier, the suit's weight booming through the timbers with each step.

Poison you? Riddler responded. *Where's the fun in that?*

Robin stopped...

But he hadn't meant to.

He tried to take another step, but couldn't. His legs wouldn't obey.

Not a poison, dear Robin. A tiny flood of machines, each building copies of itself along the nerve roots that emerge from your spine. It's the final move, and you have become my pawn. We've reached the final riddle Batman must solve!

Robin tried to say something, but he couldn't control his mouth any more than he could his legs. A wave of confusion—similar to what he felt when waking up from a violent dream—rippled through his mind. Was this really happening?

"How is a raven like a writing desk?" he said, but that wasn't what he had meant to say.

Now do you see? the Riddler said. *You are in my cocoon, Robin. You are my pupa. You do what I wish you to do. You are the key to the endgame of my elegant little construction, and all that remains is for Batman to choose whether to resign or battle through until the ordained checkmate.*

All of your questions addressed the solution, Robin, but you did not find it. You, in your mighty, slow-moving suit, are the king... and soon the king will be dead.

More desperately now, Robin tried to speak, but still couldn't. He fought to control his muscles, but couldn't. At a mental command from the Riddler, he took a step forward. Then another. He strode forward along the pier, toward the street and the city that lay beyond it. A low hum sounded throughout the guardian armor as its weapons powered up.

Let us see, the Riddler said, *whether Batman can solve this one.*

EYE ON GOTHAM NEWS

Filed by **Vicki Vale**

"We're just receiving a report that a mobile, walking suit of armor has appeared on a pier jutting out into the West River. This is Vicki Vale, and we are en route, as you can see from the aerial shot we're giving you now. We don't know whether this has anything to do with the series of sniper murders, or with the resurgent chaos throughout Gotham City, but it's a safe bet that with everything else we've seen happen in the last few hours, this is somehow related.

"I can confirm what Robin told me, that he and Batman were working through a series of separate, parallel puzzles, constructed by the Riddler specifically for them to solve. Whether this suit of armor is part of one of those puzzles, we'll just have to see. It—

"Hold on, Javier—can you take us a little lower?

"We've got visual confirmation of the figure, and it looks very much like it was built from parts of the mechanical guardians that once stood watch over Wonder City, the subterranean community that has lain nearly forgotten beneath Gotham City for decades.

"Now, I just saw a mechanical guardian up close when I was down in Arkham City not two hours ago, and yes, this looks like someone took a bunch of those constructs and decided to make them bigger. Also... this armored suit, it—as you can see, we're getting a little closer—in place of the robotic head, this newly appeared suit has a translucent bell jar for a helmet, and it appears to have a human occupant.

"There's too much sun on the visor of that helmet for us to see who might be inside. We're reaching out to Gotham City PD for comment, but as you can imagine they're stretched pretty thin at the moment. We can see—let's bring it around, Javy—we can see police cruisers and riot-response vehicles approaching from both directions along the West Waterfront Boulevard. There are also GCPD helicopters visible coming from their airfield on the other side of the city.

"The robot has stopped. It has stopped moving.

"It was walking down the pier, and now it is holding its position. We're going to take you back to the studio now for a recap of the day's events so far, but this new development makes it clear that the Riddler's plans are even more far-reaching—and potentially more dangerous—than was previously anticipated. And that's coming from someone who had an axe on her neck a couple of hours ago.

"I want to say quickly that I'm so grateful for all the well-wishers who have contacted the station or me directly on social media. I'm fine, and I only wish that Phil Chester was here, too.

"This is Vicki Vale, reporting to you live from the air over the West River waterfront."

25

Oracle alerted Batman that Robin had reappeared, although his signal still couldn't be located. She piped him a visual of the armored suit emerging from the river along one of the West River piers.

"I clipped this from GCPD security cameras," she said. *"That's Robin in there, but he's not responding to calls. You try."*

Batman did.

Nothing.

"Who are you talking to?" Gordon asked.

"Oracle," he said. "Robin is out of Arkham City. He's on the West River docks, in some kind of suit built from the mechanical guardians. I can't get in touch with him, though, and neither can Oracle."

"The situation here is under control," Gordon said. "You better go see what's happening with Robin."

Batman nodded and sprinted to the Batmobile. As he drove away, he activated the link to the Clock Tower. Oracle spread a new video frame on the inside of the windshield. Robin was walking down the pier toward the road that ran along the waterfront.

"Why isn't he answering?" Batman wondered aloud.

"I don't think he's receiving our transmissions," Oracle answered. *"Usually I can tell by monitoring a communications system where the interruption occurs, and in this case it looks like something in the suit is jamming Robin's comm link. I can't pick it up at all."*

Batman gunned the Batmobile west across the island. So this was the Riddler's next puzzle.

"Why doesn't he just get out of the suit?" Batman asked.

"My guess would be that he can't," she said.

"Mine, too," Batman said. Scenarios multiplied in his mind. If Robin was trapped in the suit, was he running short on air? Was there some kind of booby trap that wouldn't let him get out? How much control did he retain, if any at all?

Too many variables.

He arrived at the waterfront road and bounced across potholes to the base of the pier where he saw the guardian armor standing. Robin wasn't moving, and Batman jumped out of the Batmobile, then ran toward the armor, hoping he wasn't too late.

"Robin!" he called.

As he got close enough to observe the details, he saw that Robin looked barely conscious. His eyes were open but unfocused, his mouth hanging open. The suit's faceplate was clear and Batman didn't see any bluish tinges around Tim's mouth. Whatever was wrong with him, he appeared to be getting enough air.

"Batman!" the armor said. Robin didn't move inside it. The voice emanated from a speaker set in the base of the helmet.

Batman stopped.

"Riddler," he said.

"Yes! Edward Nigma here. I want to make sure you understand a few things before we proceed, since it's no fun giving someone a riddle without enough information to solve it. Anyone can spew out random gibberish. The master of the game proves his superiority by challenging his adversary, and giving that adversary every opportunity to fight back. Wouldn't you agree?"

"Let me talk to Robin," Batman demanded.

Inside the suit's helmet, Robin's eyes snapped into focus. He looked at Batman, and Batman saw that he was aware of what was happening to him.

"Batman!" he said—and then his mouth snapped shut. His eyes went wide. After a moment, it opened again, and he said, "I flee sky and earth alike, and all green things long for the touch of my tears."

A riddle.

"Clouds," Batman said.

"Very quick!" the Riddler said. "You see, Robin is alive and well. Yet your most difficult challenge is still ahead. You want to free Robin, of course you do, but I cannot let you open the suit, for I fear the very same batteries that power it will combine and explode if it is breached. There is one way—and only one way—to circumvent this mechanism. The answer lies in a riddle I have given you… and just to make things a little more interesting, I thought I would add another element. Robin?"

The guardian armor raised its left hand and spread the fingers. From its palm, a beam of energy lanced out, blasting apart the cabin of an empty GCPD patrol boat docked at the next pier. The boat started to burn fiercely as the Riddler continued.

"You see that young Robin is under my control," he said. *"He speaks in riddles, as I am fond of doing. His limbs move as I command, and the suit does what I tell it to do. It will continue to do so until you either solve my final riddle… or choose to sacrifice your comrade on the altar of public safety!*

"Shall we begin?"

The boat exploded as the fire reached its gas tanks. The pier caught fire as well, and Batman heard alarms going off.

"I've already contacted the fire department," Oracle said in his ear, *"but they're going to need some protection."*

"I'll tell your father," Batman replied, his voice low so the Riddler's sensors wouldn't catch what he said. "Start evacuating the area."

"That's a little above my pay grade," she said.

"Just start setting off alarms, at least in the major buildings—the ones you can access," Batman said. "Get people moving. When GCPD gets here, they'll start coordinating, but if we don't start this now, a lot of people are going to die."

Sirens sounded throughout the nearby area. Robin, in thrall to the Riddler, walked forward in the guardian armor. When he got to the base of the pier, he swept the road with the palm blasters, incinerating cars and setting fire to storefronts and warehouses. Luckily this part of Gotham City was sparsely populated. Gentrification hadn't reached the West River docks. But most likely Robin—and the Riddler—wouldn't stay here.

The armor stomped up to Batman.

He refused to move.

"Robin," he said. "Robin! You have to take control."

Robin stared at him though the faceplate. His eyes tracked back and forth—it was happening too evenly to be random motion. *A message,* Batman thought. *He looks like he's reading...*

He looked over his shoulder, but there was nothing there. Where else could Robin be seeing words? Or was the ocular motion a byproduct of the Riddler's control?

No. Robin wanted him to read something.

Thinking of the digital displays he had built into the Batmobile's windshield, Batman wondered if something might be inscribed on the inside of the faceplate. That would account for Robin's signal. He stepped to the right, and as the guardian armor stomped past him, Batman watched the faceplate carefully. He caught a brief luminescent image as the rays of the late afternoon sun struck the faceplate at a particular angle.

ᗄᑫՈᑫ

PUPA.

Throughout the day, as he had hunted the Riddler's associates and pieced together the different solutions, Batman had anticipated a grander riddle, an overarching theme to the scheme.

Now he had it.

IAMLARVAL had led to PUPA. The next stage of the life of a holometabolous insect was the imago, the fully mature adult form achieved when the insect emerged from its cocoon.

The letters in *imago* struck him, and another piece of the Riddler's grand conundrum fell into place.

Isaacson.

Mateosian.

Angelo.

Gray.

Ouellette.

IMAGO.

The Riddler had presented him with the answer, but not until it was too late. The lives of five people had merged into the final clue, and only one of them still lived.

To solve this last puzzle, Batman had to figure out a way to allow Robin to emerge from the deadly cocoon. Within the structure of the riddle, that would complete the cycle. Robin would achieve his imago form.

Yet the suit was set up to explode—the result of Victor Fries's efforts. The clue, seen in hindsight, had been on full display in the death room where Robin had moved the spheres. The Riddler had set up several of his puzzles, it seemed, so that they had dual meanings. They could be solved in the moment, but their role in his ultimate plan could only be understood after it was too late to do anything about it.

That in turn meant there was an element of the imago puzzle that Batman hadn't yet deciphered. In a gesture of irony, he wasn't meant to understand it until after he had witnessed Robin's death.

Batman snapped out a grappling hook and pulled himself up and across the waterfront road, his cape billowing in the updraft from fires below. When he was on the rooftop of an empty warehouse, he looked back. Robin had turned down the middle of the waterfront road. He destroyed a crane tower, then a transformer, then a small office shed.

Another element, indeed.

Sirens sounded and got closer. The police had set up a blockade shutting off the waterfront road both north and south of where Robin stood. Commissioner Gordon got out of one of the cars, a bullhorn in his hand.

"This is Commissioner Gordon of the Gotham City Police Department!" he boomed. "Robin, you need to stand down. We will use lethal force if necessary, but you know we don't want to do that." He paused and dropped his voice from an authoritative bark to a gentler level. "Come on, son. Whatever happened to you down there, you don't need to do this. Shut down the suit, and let's work this out."

A police helicopter hovered just behind the north blockade, a sniper poised in its open side door. Batman sprinted north, vaulting the gaps between rooftops until he was near enough to the blockade that he could jump off the roof and glide down with the assistance of his cape.

"Commissioner!" he called while still in the air.

He didn't get any further.

Robin raised both hands. The sniper in the helicopter got off one shot. It was a good one, hitting the faceplate just above dead center. If it had penetrated the armored glass, it would have hit Robin right between the eyes. But the guardian armor was engineered to handle heavier incoming fire than rifle bullets. The slug left a small conical divot on the faceplate, and ricocheted away into the air.

As the sound of the gunshot reached Batman, Robin activated the armor's palm beams. The helicopter's cockpit disintegrated into fragments of glass and steel. Two of its rotor blades snapped off and spun out over the river. The sniper fell out the open doorway, hanging by his safety harness as the helicopter spun down and smashed into a freight yard at the base of the pier just behind the blockade.

Officers ran to help, while others opened fire on the guardian armor. One of them, in a panic, aimed his gun at Batman as he swooped low toward the blockade. He spun and tucked into a somersault, hitting the pavement harder than he'd planned and tumbling into a controlled stand directly in front of the frightened cop.

"Don't shoot," he said calmly. The cop's gun was aimed right at his sternum.

After a moment he lowered it.

Batman glanced over at the guardian armor. It still held both hands out, but the cops had stopped shooting at it because their fire was making no difference.

"Commissioner," he said again, striding up to Gordon. "You have to get your officers back and manage an evacuation." Sirens were still sounding near and far, as Oracle commandeered emergency response systems.

"I do?" Gordon lowered the bullhorn. "Why exactly do I need to do that? What's going on here?"

"The Riddler showed his cards," Batman said. "He's trapped Robin in that suit and he's operating it remotely. Robin's not doing this, Commissioner."

"I'm not sure that matters," Gordon said.

"It does. The suit is a walking bomb. If we damage it before we solve the Riddler's final puzzle, it will explode, and Robin will be killed."

"Other people are already dead," Gordon said. "I've got additional helicopters on the way, and they're carrying more than snipers. I'm sorry, Batman, but we can't let this thing get any further—we can't let it reach a populated area."

The thudding of rotor blades reached Batman's ears. He looked to the southeast, in the direction of the new police headquarters, and saw three helicopters, spread a few hundred yards apart, coming into position. They hovered perhaps a quarter of a mile away, one over the river, one over the road, and one over the city.

Then there was another sound. Turning, Batman saw three more helicopters to the north, their positions mirroring the first to arrive. One hung just over Arkham City, one over the road, and one near the Wayne Industries building.

"Commissioner." A voice crackled over the radio clipped to Gordon's belt. *"We are in position. Awaiting orders."*

"Don't do it," Batman said.

Midday Gotham

with Jack Ryder
GNN CABLE NEWS NETWORK

WGTU Gotham City Radio

"This is Jack Ryder, on the scene of an incredible confrontation on the West River waterfront. It appears that Batman's partner, or sidekick, or whatever the correct term is—it appears Robin has been imprisoned in an armored suit being operated remotely by the Riddler.

"We've been following this story on the *Ryder Report* all day, and have pieced together what's going on. The Riddler drew Batman and Robin into a series of deadly traps, each keyed to a different villain. Batman has chased down Killer Croc, Mr. Freeze, the Mad Hatter, and Deadshot, that we know of so far. All of them, except for Killer Croc, are currently in Blackgate Penitentiary, so we've got him to thank for that, at least.

"But we also have Batman to thank for the scene unfolding here along the gritty industrial waterfront of the West River. Because it is here that the armored suit, with Robin as an apparently unwilling passenger, climbed out of the river and started strafing the area with weapons fire. We've got reports of numerous casualties, but they're conflicting at this point and we're going to wait for reliable numbers before we report them.

"What I *can* tell you is that the suit containing Robin is on the highway that parallels the West River. Police blockades are keeping traffic and pedestrians away. There has been an exchange of weapons fire, but Batman consulted with Commissioner Gordon and the police are now standing down, at least for the moment. We do not know what was said between Batman and Commissioner Gordon. That's often the case. They have a rapport that often excludes the citizens of this city, which is part of what got us into this situation in the first place.

"Anonymous sources have told us that the Riddler pulled off this escapade after leading Robin through an underground labyrinth below Arkham City, and finally trapping him in the suit. At the same time, Batman was investigating leads on the surface. At this point we do not know what the Riddler's ultimate goal is. He has made no public demands, and it seems that his sole aim is to attack Batman by striking at the younger, less experienced Robin.

"This may sound like a strange thing to say, but you have to admire his ambition. I'm not saying the Riddler's any kind of example for our kids to follow, but this is an astonishingly complex and audacious plan. He's been driving Batman's every action since the arrival of a mysterious package at Gotham City police headquarters this morning. Now comes the final flourish, the crescendo of the Riddler's murderous symphony.

"Batman is doing everything he can to save Robin's life, but it's been reported that Commissioner Gordon isn't going to wait for long.

"Riveting drama and the highest possible stakes here on the riverfront. We'll stay with this story right through until its end.

"Jack Ryder, *Midday Gotham*, reporting."

26

"Don't *what*?" Gordon asked. "Don't save my city? That's my job! Isn't it what you're supposed to be doing, too, Batman? Or has this gotten a little too personal for you?"

The armored figure had paused nearby on the highway, most likely because the Riddler was listening to their exchange. Batman suspected Robin could hear him, as well, but at the moment he was more interested in playing to the Riddler's sense of drama and superiority.

"I put Robin in this position, Gordon," he said. "I sent him down below Arkham City to investigate what the Riddler was planning. That was what the Riddler wanted all along. He set us up, and I didn't realize it until it was too late. Now Robin is trapped in that suit, and I put him there.

"If you destroy it, the Riddler wins."

"Wins?" Gordon replied. "Nobody wins this. It's not a game! We're talking about Gotham City on fire, Batman, or hadn't you noticed that?"

"Of course I have, but I'm close to solving the last riddle. Do you want the Riddler to walk away from this knowing he got exactly what he wanted? He'll start his next scheme the minute Robin dies, and we'll be right back at square one. For now, though, we have a chance of stopping him."

"Oh, we do?" Gordon countered. "If that's the case, then where is he right now?"

"Not far," Batman said. "After putting in so much time and effort, he'll want to see the grand finale."

"Well, you'll have to forgive me if I don't want to participate in a dog-and-pony show for a homicidal nut," Gordon said. "With the Joker gone, the Riddler's about the worst we've got, and he's proved it today. Yet you want me to play into his hands."

"Exactly. He's staking a claim," Batman said. "It all adds up. Everything he's done so far has been a message to me. He intends to replace the Joker. It's got to be me who stops him."

"Listen to yourself—you're not thinking clearly," Gordon replied, his voice almost a shout now. "You're too close to it—you've got to see the bigger picture. I care about Robin, too, but his is just one life. One. A precious life, a life that deserves to continue—yet how many people are going to die if that suit spends an hour shooting its way through Midtown? How many of those lives will you trade, just to keep Robin alive?"

"Only mine," Batman said.

"That's not an option."

"Yes it is. You hear the sirens. Oracle has begun the evacuation, and with the help of your men, we can clear the area. Buy me some time to solve the riddle." He paused to let it sink in. "Nigma always outsmarts himself in the end, Commissioner. In this case, he probably already has—I'm just not seeing it yet."

There, he thought. *I've thrown down the gauntlet.*

The guardian armor started to move again.

"Copters waiting for your order, Commissioner," an officer said. He was standing in the open door of Gordon's car, holding a dashboard handset. Static crackled faintly from the speaker.

Batman didn't say anything else. Gordon would have to make the decision. Five seconds passed.

Ten.

"If that suit gets within a hundred yards of any of those helicopters, they fire," the commissioner said finally. "You better know what you're doing."

With a nod, Batman spun and touched a button on his gauntlet that would bring the Batmobile under his control. Its engine roared to life and he locked his eyes on the guardian armor. It was moving toward Henry Avenue, which cut across central Gotham City from east to west.

Sensors in his cowl tracked the focal point of his vision and relayed it to the Batmobile's autopilot. The car surged forward and skidded into a drift, slamming into the guardian armor and knocking it half a block south. It slid on the pavement, then tumbled, snapping off a streetlight pole and coming to rest flat on its back in front of a taxi garage.

Batman keyed in another command and the Batmobile roared again, driving up and slowing as it approached the armor. Robin raised one arm, but too late. The vehicle struck it a glancing blow, knocking it aside and down before the Batmobile rolled over the armored suit, pinning it in place.

It was too bulky to move, and found no leverage.

He sprinted to catch up to the car and get a look at

the suit. There had to be a clue on it somewhere—a hint he hadn't yet seen. "PUPA" had revealed the overarching theme… but the imago solution wasn't yet within his grasp.

As Batman approached, Robin jammed the suit's free arm under the Batmobile's left-front wheel well. A blast of energy threw the vehicle over onto its side. Batman dodged out of its way, skirting the rear to get closer. Robin stood up and kicked the Batmobile, which rocked the rest of the way onto its roof, engine still running. Batman seized the opportunity to jump onto the suit's back. Judging from what he'd seen of its movements thus far, he didn't think it had the agility to throw him off, or the flexibility to reach back and get a grip on him.

Instead, the moment he put his full weight on the suit's back, it toppled backward.

The impact drove the breath from Batman's lungs. Black spots swam in his vision and he lost his grip as the suit got back to its feet and kept going. But as it did, he saw something in the design on the back of its torso armor: a clock face, surrounded by three concentric circles. Spaced around the outer circle were letters. He was still getting the air back in his lungs and clearing his eyesight, so he didn't immediately catch all the details, but he was certain this was the key for which he'd been searching.

"You saw that, right?" Oracle said.

"I did," Batman said. "Now I need to get a closer look."

This was the metapuzzle.

27

Robin's voice blared from the suit's loudspeaker as it stomped away from the waterfront and turned down Henry Avenue.

"You're facing two doors. Behind one is misery, behind the other is happiness. Twin brothers stand in front of the doors. One always lies and one always tells the truth. You may ask one question to learn which door leads to happiness.

"What is it?" he concluded.

Batman sprinted after the suit and shot out a zip line, wrapping it around the base of the suit's helmet and drawing himself close enough to get a look at the puzzle again. The suit was so strong that it hardly shifted as he pulled himself nearer.

It was a circular construction, in four concentric layers. Around the outside layer were letters, fourteen of them. The next two layers were blank. The inside circle was a clock face, with numbers, indicating ten minutes after five. The mounting shaft holding the hands of the clock was hollow, and the hole in the center of it was grooved. It didn't appear to be quite circular.

The suit tried to shake him off, but he held on. There were fourteen letters. AAAAPPIMULRVGO. They were raised, and looked as if they could be moved. Each "A" was bordered with a different shape—one each of a triangle, hexagon, octagon, and diamond. Each "P" was inside a square, and the rest of the letters—which didn't repeat, were circled. LARVA PUPA IMAGO, that was easy enough to figure out… but how was he supposed to arrange them? It was like the chemical puzzle Robin had faced below the Sionis mill.

In fact, Batman realized, it was *exactly* like that. He thought back to that puzzle, and mentally listed the active compounds in each battery type.

Lithium cobalt oxide. Four atoms.

Sulfuric acid. Seven atoms.

Lead oxide. Three atoms.

Fourteen atoms, fourteen letters. But how did they go together?

The guardian stopped trying to shake him off and instead worked its fingers into the zip line coiled around the base of its helmet. The cord was rated for a thousand pounds, but it snapped like cheap string when the gauntleted hands grasped it and pulled. One half of the line dangled from its right hand. Batman was holding the other half, and so was the guardian.

He flung out his left arm as if he was throwing a frisbee, and Batman was jerked off the suit back. He hit a plate-glass window which shattered on contact, and then he smashed down onto a desk, scattering papers and office supplies as he tumbled onto the floor. A framed picture of a young mother flanked by two children clattered down in front of him.

Through the broken window he heard the guardian

armor moving deeper into Gotham City. It fired again, and the sound of the explosions rolled down the street.

Batman jumped back through the window and resumed his pursuit. The sound of helicopter rotors filled the silence left in the aftermath of the explosions. Ahead of him and to his right, a delivery truck burned. On the other side of the street smoke poured from the destroyed facade of a clothing store. He spotted the helicopter swiveling into view several blocks ahead. It was still more than a hundred yards away—probably closer to three hundred—but Gordon was sending Batman a message.

He wasn't going to wait forever.

He activated his comm link.

"Commissioner," he said, "there's a puzzle built into the guardian armor. I can solve it, but I'm going to need some time."

"Time's in short supply, Batman," Gordon answered. *"I can't just stand here while that thing sets my city on fire."*

"It's my city, too, Commissioner." He broke the connection and went after the armor again.

Two revelations hit him at once.

Two doors, two brothers, one question. So the puzzle forced one of the brothers to eliminate both uncertainties at once.

He had it.

The other revelation had to do with the word puzzle. He'd been thinking about it the wrong way, trying to make the letters correspond to atoms—but they didn't. The puzzle had another step. It wasn't the letters that counted, but the symbols. There were eight oxygen atoms in the three compounds, therefore eight circles. There were two hydrogen atoms, and two letters inside a square. Then there were the four "A"s inside of their different shapes, each representing an atom that only appeared in the compounds once.

He had to get closer to the suit again.

The buildings were becoming taller, with fewer spaces between them. The streets still seemed to be deserted, which meant Oracle and the police had done their jobs. Yet the guardian was moving into more densely populated areas, and before long someone was going to get hurt.

There had to be a reason for the Riddler to be using Robin as a mouthpiece for seemingly random riddles. As he got close to the suit, it raised its palm weapons, and he tested his theory.

"Which door will your brother tell me leads to happiness?" he asked. The suit froze, and he leapt onto its back again. He held its collar ring with one hand and leaned slightly away, to give himself room to manipulate the elements of the puzzle. Three concentric rings, three chemical compounds. All of the letters were on the outside ring, so he would have to create the corresponding patterns by subtracting letters from the outside.

He had a feeling he'd only have one chance.

Batman slid the letters into different rings. Because sulfuric acid had the largest number of atoms, he left it on the outside, sliding four of the circled letters into the second ring, then three of the "A"s. He left both "P"s, which because of their matching shapes he figured corresponded to the two hydrogen atoms.

So the outside ring had PP A IMUL.

In this puzzle's structure, H_2SO_4.

The second ring now had seven letters: AAARVGO.

The next largest compound was lithium cobalt oxide. That would need two of the "A"s, for the individual lithium and cobalt atoms, and then two of the circled letters to represent the oxygen atoms. So he had to move one "A" and two circled letters to the inner ring.

That done, he looked at each of the three rings.

PP A IMUL

A A RV

A GO

A click sounded from within the puzzle. Testing the result, Batman again tried to move the letters. They wouldn't budge—they were now fixed in place. So he'd gotten that part right. And for the moment the figure remained still.

Maybe the Riddler wants to see if I can do it.

Next the clock face. He studied it more closely, searching for a clue about the position of the hands—but his grace period was up. The guardian armor unleashed a fresh barrage, destroying a row of cars in a corner parking lot and the entrance to a subway station on that same corner. Then it started walking toward the flames. Four of the cars were piled together by the force of the blast. Batman could feel the heat from across the street.

The guardian walked closer to them, and then stopped close enough to the fire that Batman couldn't breathe without searing his lungs. He held on as long as he could, then sprang off the suit into a backward somersault, landing out in the street far enough away that he wasn't being roasted alive.

With its assailant off its back, the suit lurched into

motion again. It turned and fired at Batman. He dodged the beam, which plowed up a deep gouge in the street. A shattered water pipe shot a fountain into the air, the roar and patter of the water merging with the sound of the fires and the thudding of helicopter rotors in a complete soundscape of disaster.

Gordon was right. They couldn't wait forever to stop the armor, no matter what the cost. But he had to keep trying.

EYE ON GOTHAM NEWS

Filed by **Vicki Vale**

"This is Vicki Vale, reporting to you live from the *Eye on Gotham* helicopter just to the southeast of where some kind of machine—call it a robot, or a suit of armor maybe—is walking down Henry Avenue and randomly destroying cars and storefronts as it walks. It appears as if Batman's partner Robin is somehow imprisoned in the suit.

"Emergency sirens are raising a deafening noise to the point that we can hear them over the sounds of the helicopter. It's moved away from the waterfront and onto the edge of Midtown. People are fleeing in every direction, though there appear to be far fewer than we might have anticipated. The machine, or robot, does not appear to be targeting them. It is, however, destroying property and resisting Batman's efforts to grapple with it.

"We've been informed that Gotham City Police Department special-tactics personnel have been given instructions to deploy heavy weapons. This may include shoulder-fired rockets—you may recall the *Eye on Gotham* investigative report when the GCPD purchased them a few years ago. It may also include even heavier weapons. A source on the ground tells us that Commissioner Gordon wants to destroy the machine at all costs.

"Can Batman get Robin out of the armored suit before

that occurs? Is Robin even still alive in there? We don't know. How long will Commissioner Gordon wait? We don't know that either. All we know is that Batman is engaging the machine and trying to slow its progress into the city.

"Commissioner Gordon already has assets in position, however, should he choose to take offensive action. There are helicopters in place, hovering over major intersections along the way from the west side into Burnley—and toward the new police headquarters, which may be the machine's target. I emphasize 'may be.' We simply don't know.

"We've got a parabolic microphone aimed at the machine, but the figure hasn't said anything except for a few sentences to Batman which sounded like riddles. We have heard Batman respond, and it appears that each time he does that, the machine stops for a short time.

"It appears as if the Riddler is trying to make the Gotham City police kill Robin, and Batman is doing everything in his power to prevent that. I can tell you from personal experience—*recent* personal experience—that Batman and Robin worked closely together to get Robin through the Riddler's underground traps. What a terrible thing it must be for Batman, or both of them really, to see all their efforts culminate in this scene.

"There are fires burning from the corner of Janson Square all the way back to the waterfront. It's a vista of incredible chaos and devastation—and in the middle of it all, Batman is still trying to deactivate the machine and save Robin from the Riddler's most deadly test yet.

"This is Vicki Vale, reporting for *Eye on Gotham*, in the air over Gotham City. More as we know it."

28

"What is most like a bee in May?" Robin's voice boomed through the speaker as the suit lumbered onward like a steampunk juggernaut.

That one rang a bell, but Batman couldn't place it at first. He dove out of the way of another energy blast that blew a sidewalk falafel cart to pieces, then scaled the facade of the nearest building. All of the buildings were skyscrapers now. From the rooftop he triggered a command on the Batmobile's remote control that fired the two small rockets mounted in the passenger side roof. They were designed to flip the car back upright in the event it rolled over. He was going to need the car again.

He had to slow the guardian armor, and he couldn't do it himself. A light on his gauntlet flashed green, notifying him that the car was ready to go again. At the same time, Oracle's voice came through the comm.

"Did you do that? The Batmobile's on its wheels again."

"That was me," Batman said.

"Good. For a second I was worried that the Riddler had gained control of the car."

"I don't think that's his game," Batman said. "He's not

even trying to kill me. He's trying to get Commissioner Gordon to do it, and take Robin out in the bargain. But he's also giving me time to solve the puzzle."

"A bit condescending, isn't it?"

"That's the Riddler. His one weakness is he always assumes he can outthink everyone else. He's made Robin into the king, hasn't he? Strong but slow-moving, and the key to the whole game. That's where the chess motif comes together with everything else."

The Riddler wanted him to solve the puzzle.

That was the only part of it that didn't make sense. Each trial had escalated, becoming more difficult, but the Riddler had held to his regular MO of giving just enough of a clue at each critical moment for Batman and Robin to advance to the next stage. Yet where was the moment Batman had been expecting—the moment when the Riddler decided to end the game and go for the kill?

It hadn't happened yet, and Batman didn't see how it could…

Unless the Riddler had decided to use the Gotham City Police Department as his cat's-paw, and savor the irony of Robin dying at the hands of his own allies. That was possible, but still it struck Batman as wrong, somehow. The Riddler liked to be in on the kill. All of their opponents did. The Joker certainly had. If the Riddler was angling to fill the space at the top of the food chain, wouldn't he do the same?

Batman raced after the guardian armor as Gordon bellowed in his ear.

"You're running out of time," he said. *"That thing is*

headed for police headquarters!"

"You don't know that."

"Should I wait until after the building's on fire? If you don't stop that suit before it turns the next corner, I'm going to do it."

Batman didn't reply. He focused on the most recent riddle, trying to figure out what it might have to do with the clock puzzle. The Riddler was teasing him with clues that didn't look like clues.

A clock…

The guardian armor reached the end of the block. Batman kept pace with it on rooftops. If Robin turned south, Gotham City police headquarters was five blocks in that direction.

Think!

He had it.

A bee in May. May-be. Maybe. What is most like maybe?

The answer was…

"Perhaps!" he shouted, and jumped.

The guardian armor froze when it registered the correct answer. Batman glided down and landed on its shoulders, knowing he would only have a moment to make the correct adjustment before one of two things happened. Either the Riddler would start the suit moving again, or Commissioner Gordon would incinerate them with airstrikes from the helicopters down the street.

He thought he had the solution. Assuming the Riddler was incorporating parts of the previous puzzles, that left the tea room and the slogan Robin had reported seeing in the first flood trap.

"One step forward, two steps back."

The clock was set at five-ten. So there were two different possibilities for moving it one step forward and two steps back. One result, moving the minute hand forward and the hour hand back, gave three-fifteen. The hands would be pointing in the same direction. This was an interesting possibility… but the other result, moving the hour hand forward one and the minute hand back two, gave six o'clock.

"It's always six o'clock in here."

Batman clicked the hour hand forward until it pointed straight down at the six. Then he clicked the minute hand backward twice. The hands snapped into place and stayed there.

He jumped off the back of the suit.

Yet the suit kept marching.

"Not quite, Batman," the Riddler crowed through the speakers. *"You've done very well so far, but you haven't yet discerned the final piece of the puzzle!"*

A helicopter loomed ahead, descending between the skyscrapers on either side and hovering less than fifty feet above the ground. It was maybe two blocks away, and Batman heard another above and behind him. He glanced over his shoulder and saw that it was staying higher, probably as backup.

"Batman," Gordon's voice crackled in his earpiece. *"We can't wait any longer."*

Smoke puffed from a launch tube built onto the bottom of the helicopter's fuselage, located between the landing skids. The missile burst from the launch tube in a halo of fire.

"No!" Batman shouted. He had expected this moment, even as he had hoped fervently it wouldn't happen.

Gordon's obligation was to the people of Gotham City—not individually, but as a whole. He was doing what he had to do, and he had given Batman all the time he thought he could spare. This played directly into the Riddler's plan, which was for Gordon to give Batman just enough rope to hang himself.

Or, as seemed more likely, incinerate himself.

He took three running steps to his right and dove, wrapping himself in his cape as he hit the ground and rolled. He felt the blast wave from the explosion a split second before he heard it, as if a giant hammer had pounded him into the street. He went deaf, and for a moment he couldn't breathe. Then he rolled one last time and threw his cape aside, dreading what he would see.

The last of the fireball from the missile's impact was still dissipating. Bits of asphalt pattered down, their sounds dull and muted against the tinkling from the rain of broken glass falling from windows that had been shattered by the blast. A cloud of smoke and dust roiled over a crater in the street.

"I... had... the... puzzle," Batman said slowly, keeping his voice low and even despite his anguish. One more element. Just one more. That was all he'd needed to figure out. He'd been so close...

"I'm sorry, Batman," Gordon said. *"There was nothing else we could do. Nothing else you could do."* He paused. *"Sometimes... we don't win every fight."*

Batman didn't answer. He had nothing to say to Gordon right then. His entire being was focused on finding the Riddler and making the man answer for Robin's death. He scanned the rooftops, and the windows of higher floors.

He would be near.

Smoke swirled away from the crater as the rotor wash from the helicopters swept down the wind tunnel created by the tall buildings along these blocks. Inside the crater, there was motion. Batman caught it out of the corner of his eye, thinking initially it was a piece of the street collapsing into the hole. But he was wrong.

It was the left hand of the guardian armor, clamping down on the edge of the crater. A moment later its head appeared, and then the entire armored suit, clambering out of the crater and onto the street.

The king wasn't done quite yet.

Taking Them to Trask

Duane Trask, Gotham Globe Radio

"We're extending the show beyond its regular midday hours because of the incredible scene unfolding along Henry Avenue between the West River and the Burnley section of town. I'm in the studio uptown, but we've got people calling in from along Henry Avenue, and their stories are incredible to hear.

"Emma, you're calling in from where?"

> *"I work in the Frump and Grind, right down Henry from the old bank building."*

"Frump and Grind?"

> *"It's a coffee shop and thrift store. I'm a barista, but I also do some design."*

"Thank you, Emma. What are you seeing?"

> *"The robot thing walked right by us here. It fired some kind of like laser thing into the phone store next door and everything blew up. We had to evacuate. Where's the fire department? The whole building's burning now."*

"I'm sure they'll be there as soon as it's safe for the firefighters to deploy."

> *"Well, it's not safe for us. There's a robot shooting lasers around, and Batman keeps fiddling around with its back, like he's trying to pull out a wire or something.*

There are helicopters hovering everywhere. We don't know where to go. We're out in a side street, trying to stay away from the robot.

"Can you ask someone to tell us where to go?"

"Emma, I'm going to put you on hold and my producer will see if he can help you. Donnie, can you help her? Good. Lloyd, you're on. Tell us where you are and what you see."

"I just saw a missile hit that big robot thing, man! There was a huge explosion. It shook a bunch of stuff off my shelves, but that's nothing compared to what it looks like closer in. Windows are all broken, there's a huge hole in the street."

"Is the suit destroyed? Can you see Robin? Is he alive?"

"The suit just climbed up out of the hole. The missile— well, I don't know if it didn't hit it or what, but the suit is still walking. It's still going."

"What about Robin?"

"I can't tell from here."

"Thanks for the call, Lloyd. We've got Eileen next. You're on with Duane Trask, Eileen. What do you see?"

"Batman's trying to do something on the back of the suit, like he's turning a combination or something. I saw him climbing on it, and working some kind of machine. It looks like a clock. The suit keeps talking to him, and Batman keeps answering.

"The last thing it said was 'What is most like a bee in May?' The suit said that one when it was right under my window. Then it kept going and then like your last caller said the missile hit it."

"'What is most like a bee in May?' Did I hear that right?"

"Yes. I don't know what Batman said as the answer."

"I don't know the answer either. But the suit survived the missile, Eileen, is that right?"

"Yes, it did. It's still walking."

"And you said the puzzle looks like a clock? Did I hear that right?"

"It sure does."

"Ladies and gentlemen, you'll recall that only two hours ago I spoke to a caller claiming to be the Riddler. He said before the end of the day, Batman would be trying to stop two clocks.

"We know the Gotham City police just hauled in Deadshot, and that Deadshot was in all probability responsible for the assassinations that started this morning. That's one clock. If there really is some kind of clock puzzle built into this armored suit, then I guess we have to conclude that our caller really was the Riddler.

"Mr. Nigma, if I was skeptical, I apologize, but I hope you understand. Call in anytime. My producer Donna will put you right through.

"Stay with us, Gotham City. Law enforcement is calling down airstrikes on the streets of this city. Batman is desperately trying to save the life of his comrade-in-arms, Robin... and somewhere, the Riddler must be watching. Is he done? Has he shown us his final move? Or is there yet one more masterstroke waiting to be revealed?

"We'll be right back."

29

A second chance, Batman thought. *This is where the Riddler outsmarted himself. He made the guardian armor too strong for a single missile to destroy it. Part of the credit—most of it, actually—goes to Rā's al Ghūl. Riddler isn't in his league. He knows it, too, and it'll make him desperate. That makes him as dangerous as anyone we've faced.*

The missile had done some damage, though. That much was obvious. The faceplate was cracked and one of the suit's legs dragged. Through the cracks, Batman saw that Robin's eyes were open and blood was dripping from his nose down over his mouth and chin.

The guardian armor gained its footing on the street.

Batman started to get his hearing back. He thought Gordon might have said something to him, but he didn't respond because Robin started voicing another riddle.

"A farmer is traveling with a fox, a chicken, and a bag of chicken feed," he shouted. Flecks of blood spattered the inside of the faceplate. *"He comes to a river and must cross it in a small boat that will only carry him and one other thing. If he leaves the fox with the chicken, the chicken will be the fox's dinner. If he leaves the chicken with the feed, the chicken*

will eat it. How does he get all three things across the river and on to market?"

Batman had heard a hundred variations on this puzzle. The trick was in realizing that you didn't have to bring the boat back empty every trip. Lateral thinking. You took the chicken over, then came back… brought the fox over, then brought the chicken back… brought the feed over and left it, then went back for the chicken. That way the chicken was never left with either the fox or the feed.

The long way was the only way.

This was a hint. There were more steps in the armor's puzzle. In his rush to take a direct course to the solution, he still was missing something. So what was it? He'd accounted for the word puzzle, the chemical puzzle, the flood puzzle, the tea room puzzle…

Of course. The puzzle that had forced them to work in parallel.

Killer Croc's tooth.

Which—like the hole in the mounting shaft in the clock face—just happened to be grooved, slightly irregular in cross section, and a little bit curved.

And which Batman still had in a compartment of his Utility Belt.

"Keep it. Make a Christmas ornament out of it or something," Killer Croc had said. Batman had a sudden deep certainty that Killer Croc had been in on the whole plan from the beginning. He had been coached to refuse the tooth. The Riddler, knowing Batman's attention to detail, must have guessed that he would keep it with him.

The Riddler had anticipated everything to near

perfection. When this was all over, Batman realized, he was going to have to reconsider his opinion of the man known as Edward Nigma. It wasn't a matter of comparing him to the Joker, but of acknowledging that he was stepping into his own class as a sociopathic mastermind.

The guardian raised both arms and activated the palm beams. One of them sputtered and strobed before the lens shattered and sparks flared in the gauntlet. The other beam lanced out, barely missing Batman and shearing away a row of flagpoles hanging from the facade of a hotel. Burning strips of cloth fluttered to the street.

Batman ran toward the armor, leaping over the crater and climbing up the malfunctioning arm. Wrapping one of his own arms around the bicep, he clung to the armor's back again, hoping his presence would keep Gordon from ordering another strike.

All he needed was a moment's hesitation.

"Cross with the chicken!" he shouted. "Come back for the fox. Cross with the fox, take the chicken back. Leave the chicken, cross with the feed. Come back for the chicken."

The guardian armor stopped. But unlike the other times, Robin immediately shouted out another riddle, this time in a sing-song voice almost like a nursery rhyme.

"As I was going to St. Ives
I met a man with seven wives.
The seven wives had seven sacks,
The seven sacks had seven cats..."

"You better clear out of there, Batman," Gordon said in his ear, blocking out Robin's recitation. *"We're going to finish this thing off."*

"This *thing* is Robin, Commissioner," Batman spat back. "And I just solved the puzzle."

"You've had all the time I can give you, and more. This city can't afford to lose you, Batman, but it also can't allow us to hesitate. Get out of there!"

"I'm not going to do that, Commissioner." The suit lurched under him, nearly throwing him off. It spun around as he heard the sound of a helicopter coming closer. It was the one he'd seen backing up the first, only now it was taking up a firing position.

"Don't do this, Gordon!" Batman shouted over the sound of the rotors. His own compromised hearing made it hard for him to tell how loud he was.

He'd also missed part of the rhyme.

"Say it again!" he screamed at the helmet. Robin looked at him but didn't speak. "You have to say it again!"

Nothing.

"I've got you covered," Oracle said. *"Listen up."* There was a click in Batman's ear and then he picked up the recorded sound of Robin saying the last three lines.

"The seven cats had seven kits.
Kits, cats, sacks, and wives,
How many were going to St. Ives?"

"That one's easy," Batman said.

"Fire!" Gordon roared.

The helicopter rocked as the missile blasted out of its launch tube. But this time Batman didn't jump off the guardian. He already had the Batmobile's remote control keyed in, and he stabbed a button as he ducked down behind the armor's torso, hoping he'd gotten the timing right.

Engine revved up to a scream, the Batmobile skidded out of a side street, taking the turn hard enough that it went up on two wheels. If it had been on four, the missile would have passed right over it on its shallow angle of descent toward the target: the guardian armor's center of mass. Up on its side, however, the Batmobile was nearly five feet tall.

The missile struck it squarely on the windshield.

The Batmobile was sufficiently armored to shrug off small arms and even portable weaponry and explosives. Rocket-propelled grenades might knock it over, but they wouldn't hurt it much. But the missiles fired by the Gotham City's Police Department were military-grade air-to-surface missiles designed to punch through the outer armor of tanks, armored personnel carriers, and small ships.

This particular missile punched through the armored windshield without any decrease in its velocity. The impact armed the two-stage trigger in its warhead, which detonated on the second impact—with the armored frame of the Batmobile's passenger seat.

Because the vehicle was up on two wheels, Batman missed the most spectacular part of the explosion. He did see all of the side windows blow out in gouts of fire, and other similar gouts blow out the windows angled down toward the pavement. They acted as rockets, and the pavement turned into a launch pad.

The Batmobile leapt up from the ground and started spinning end over end as its forward velocity turned into angular momentum. It pinwheeled across the street, shedding pieces of its interior and undercarriage and arcing over Batman and the guardian on a diagonal flight path across Henry Avenue. It hit the pillars supporting a shallow arched entry to a pedestrian arcade, crushing them.

Still trailing fire, the Batmobile rolled down the arcade, smashing aside empty vendor stalls. As it came to a rocking, groaning halt, the arcade roof caved in.

The reinforced chassis and armored passenger compartment had absorbed most of the missile's explosive force, but the noise was still loud enough to set Batman's ears ringing again. Enough of the blast wave reached the guardian that it nearly tipped over backward onto Batman. Having already felt its weight once that day, he was glad when it regained its balance.

It was about time to prototype a new Batmobile anyway.

The guardian armor raised one arm.

Another helicopter hove into view.

If Gordon was trying to warn Batman, he couldn't hear it.

He stood up. "So. How many were going to St. Ives?" He could barely hear himself, and thought the explosion might have shorted out his comm link, which meant no one else could hear him either. But he answered the riddle anyway.

He'd come too far not to do so.

"One."

As he said the word, he jumped straight up. At the peak of the jump, in that suspended moment before he began to fall again, he jammed the tooth into the circular opening and twisted it until its curve matched the inside of the asymmetrical plug.

There was a sharp electrical snap and a tiny blue arc from the socket numbed Batman's hand. The suit's outstretched arm dropped and the energy beam's lens went dark. It slumped, inert but still upright. A soft pop from the helmet was followed by a hiss as the collar ring unlocked and the air pressure inside the suit equalized to the outside.

He'd done it.

He'd solved the puzzle.

"Hold your fire!" he shouted. He didn't know if Gordon had heard him. A third helicopter replaced the one that had just fired its rocket, fresh rotor wash kicking up trash and dust from the street.

It didn't fire.

Batman leaped over the motionless armor's shoulders and held his arms up, interposing himself between the helicopter and Robin. It occurred to him in passing that this might not be the best idea, given how some Gotham City cops felt about him... but he did it anyway.

"Commissioner! Hold your fire!"

Dead air over his comm link.

The armor's helmet popped loose. Batman took a step back and turned to reach up and pull it off. He threw it away to bounce among the scattered remains of the Batmobile and the rubble of the arcade. Robin looked over at him.

"You there?" Batman asked.

"Yeah," Robin said. "I'm here—at least I think I am. I guess it's true what they say." He managed a weak grin. "You are what you eat."

Batman was about to ask him what he meant by that when they heard the Riddler's voice again.

Bull's Eye

by **Rafael Del Toro**, GothamGazette.com

It has come to this. Missile strikes in Gotham City.

Police firing heavy military-grade weaponry on our streets—
at those who are supposed to be protecting us when the police
can't.

An explosion big enough to freak out seismometers from
here to Florida, right under Arkham City.

The notorious assassin Deadshot hunting for the Riddler's
civilian contractors, to let them out of their contracts by means
of the proverbial Parabellum to the cerebellum.

A scramble and reshuffling in the criminal ranks of Gotham
City, just like the infighting and backstabbing that might have
occurred in fifteenth-century Venice. Only with weirder clothes
and no Medicis there to keep the worst of the mayhem in check.

Try that one on. Batman as Cosimo de' Medici. Bad—but not
quite as bad as the rest of the loons.

Missile strikes in Gotham City.

Missile strikes in Gotham City.

I read those words and I cannot parse them. They don't fit
in any world I want to live in, or in any city I want to live in. I
love Gotham City with all my heart, but I'm outta here. Enough.
Surely there's someplace that doesn't have a population of

vigilantes and cutthroat megalomaniacs. I hung on for a long time. There's a lot to love about this place, and even now I'm going to miss every single grimy and perilous block of it. But not everyone is cut out to live here. That's okay. I just wish I'd figured it out sooner.

I hear Central City is nice.

This will be my last column. *The Bull's Eye* has at last been gouged out by the sheer carnival batshit craziness of this town, the people in it, the bat-fights and the bat-worship and the batty relationship between the police and vigilantes who belong right alongside the self-identified criminal lunatics in whatever dungeon replaces Arkham Asylum after I'm gone.

In short: I quit.

Because Batman won't.

30

"Imago!" the Riddler called. "You must have solved it by now, or we wouldn't be speaking—would we, O most worthy adversaries?"

Batman looked up and across the street. There, standing on the roof of the same building where Batman had fought Deadshot, was the Riddler in his loose-fitting green frock coat—covered in question marks—and slacks, ludicrous bowler, green boots and glasses, his tie flapping in the wind.

"Batman! I must salute your accomplishment!" he continued. "As well as those of your doughty assistant, young Robin! These were stern tests, and you survived them all."

Before Batman could launch himself toward his opponent, Robin spoke.

"Wait. Help me get out of this thing."

"Riddler won't wait," Batman said. Robin banged the suit's gauntlets against its torso in frustration. The helicopter hovered, and for a moment he wished it would use its missile on that rooftop where the Riddler stood mocking them.

Shoot him! he thought.

Then the moment passed and he knew it for what it was—weakness. It was weakness to wish for someone else to take your responsibilities from you, and weakness to wish for someone else to kill when you had sworn not to.

Then Batman had an idea. The symmetry of the imago puzzle wasn't yet quite complete. Robin had not emerged from the cocoon of the guardian armor. The key was probably in the puzzle built into the armor. Quickly Batman went around to the back of the suit and twisted Killer Croc's tooth in the clock face.

With a series of clicks and pops, the suit fell apart. First its arms disconnected at the shoulder, and Robin shrugged them off. Then its torso separated into halves and fell away. The pelvic section snapped open and then the legs, each piece clanging on the street. Robin kicked the heavy boots off.

He fell to his knees, and for a moment Batman thought his injuries were more serious than they had appeared. Then he looked up, an expression of determination on his face, and he pulled himself to his feet. Wiped the blood from his face, staining his glove.

"Let's go!" he said, as if Batman had been delaying them.

Together they ran down the block and simultaneously cast grappling lines that pulled them to the top of the building where the Riddler waited.

"And the last piece of the puzzle falls into place," the Riddler said as they climbed.

"He's not running," Robin said.

"Maybe that's the last piece of the puzzle," Batman answered. They were just below the overhung roof rail. "One... Two..."

He didn't have to say three. They kicked off the wall and

used the tension in the grapple lines to swing up and over onto the rooftop.

The Riddler didn't move or speak.

A moment later they realized it wasn't Nigma at all. It was a dummy dressed in the Riddler's signature outfit. Bracketed onto the dummy's jaw was a small speaker, now emitting just a soft hiss of white noise.

Of the actual Riddler there was no sign. He had, however, left a note.

Batman,

I owe you my sincerest thanks. You've been a superb test of my next generation of… assets, shall we say? By now you will have learned that if I wanted you dead, you would be dead. But of course I don't want that, just as you, Batman, wouldn't really wish me out of commission.

The test of wills is the irresistible thing! And for you, the other irresistible thing is matching wits, solving the puzzle, isn't it, Batman? You know you feel it!

The future is going to be a little different around here without the Joker. He brought chaos and unpredictability. I have no interest in either. The great puzzle is only great if it has a solution. What I'm looking forward to, as the new sheriff in town, is seeing just how far I can push you.

Just how clever, how determined, how resolute are you going to be? We shall see. You will face a different adversary now that the Joker's not around anymore…

The old order is ashes, and the new is just getting started. You and I, Batman—and you too, Robin! I think you've probably survived this, and if you haven't, well, that's disappointing.

We had a grand time, didn't we? Let's do it again soon. As I was saying, we're going to be seeing each other quite often in the future... but when and where? Ah, one hates to answer a question when one can pose it instead.

So here's a question: If this was my initial gambit, then the opening position has only just been established. We now embark on the middle part of our game. What do you think I'll do next?

Until next time, I congratulate you on not resigning. You played a bad position and played it well! Let's call this one a draw.

Yours respectfully,
E. Nigma

"You think he's going to be able to do it?" Robin wondered.

"Take control?" Batman responded. "He might. This scheme is going to let every lunatic in Gotham City know that the Riddler used Mr. Freeze, Killer Croc, the Mad Hatter, Harley Quinn, and Deadshot for his own purposes. That's a powerful statement to a criminal mind used to having a warlord in charge."

"Then he won."

Batman shook his head. "No. I think he's just saving face. He wanted me to watch you die, and then figure out after the fact what I could have done to save you."

"He's a real charmer."

"Just like the rest of them," Batman said. "Misfits, misanthropes, weak people with powerful desires."

"He was the imago," Robin said. "This was all like a coming-out party for him. Too bad I didn't figure that out until he was inside my head already. That's when I saw the PUPA on the faceplate of the suit."

"Neither one of us figured it out in time," Batman said. "Is that what happened? Some kind of mind control?"

"Well, maybe I shouldn't say that," Robin said. "I could think, and move a little. Not enough to do any good. Mostly he was in charge."

"Is he still? I mean, could he do it again?"

"I don't know," Robin said. "He let me go when you solved the riddle. He said it was some kind of nanotechnology I ate along with a piece of paper in the tea room."

"You ate a piece of paper," Batman said.

Robin shrugged. "Hey, it said 'EAT ME.' What was I *supposed* to do?"

"Strange time to decide to start following instructions," Batman commented.

Robin looked out over the rooftops. Fire crews were battling the blazes the guardian armor had left.

"I did that," he said.

"No. The Riddler did."

"I know," Robin said. "But you know what I mean."

Batman nodded. "I put you in that spot by letting you go down into the labyrinth alone. You did well to survive."

"Thanks," Robin said. On Henry Avenue below them, they both watched Gotham City police cruisers approaching.

"Commissioner Gordon will be in one of those cars," Batman said.

"Yeah. You know I was fine down there, right?"

"Sure," Batman said.

Robin watched as Gordon got out of the lead cruiser. "We'll need a nanotechnology expert to see what's still in my bloodstream," he said.

Bloodstream, Batman thought. He was thinking of the Joker's blood, and all the blood shed during the past few months. What would come next? The Riddler thought he was fully emerged from his cocoon now. This series of riddles had been his announcement.

Now the real turbulence would begin. The other high-profile and powerful villains of Gotham City weren't likely to go along with the Riddler's proclamation. Some of them, like Solomon Grundy or Poison Ivy or the Calendar Man, wouldn't care. They did what they did no matter what anyone else had to say, driven by deep-seated desires only they could understand.

But others—the Penguin, the Mad Hatter, Mr. Freeze, Two-Face—they were ambitious. They wanted to be in charge, and built their own small empires into larger empires to prove to each other that they were in charge. Now the Riddler had called them all out.

Even though the physical emergence was Robin's, like Tim had said, the Riddler himself was the imago called out by the final puzzle. Throughout the day—and, Batman realized with astonishment, it had been only a single day— the Riddler had unfolded a series of puzzles with layers that interlocked and led inevitably to the claim that the Riddler was reborn as Gotham City's new criminal kingpin, emerging from the cocoon of the Joker's shadow.

That explained it all, every clue and puzzle and trap from

the moment the USB drive had shown up in the Gotham City Police Department headquarters. That was what had led him to the larval clue in the first place.

It was masterful, really, Batman thought. In the past, the Riddler had left puzzles. He had constructed lethal traps within confined rooms. But here he had developed a network of allies and contractors, gone into Arkham City and created a series of puzzles that not only had to be solved from multiple angles, but each contributed an element to a final master puzzle.

Shockingly, his goal had not been to kill Batman, or even Robin. Their deaths wouldn't have been unwelcome, exactly, but the Riddler wanted an adversary he considered to be worthy of him.

As the Joker had.

Something stirred in him.

I have to stop doing that, Batman thought. *The Joker is gone. Gotham City needs me present, and focused on the current threats. I don't have the leisure to indulge psychological weakness—and needing time to grapple with the absence of my most intimate and deadly rival is a weakness.*

Eliminate it, he told himself.

It was all well and good to think that. Batman knew he would have to keep working to habituate himself to the fact that the Joker was gone. The past needed to stay buried. Even so, something within him kept trying to add the Joker back into these scenarios. It was a bone-deep call back to a time he understood.

Now everything was going to reshuffle, and Batman needed to get to work understanding how alliances would shift and break and be remade among the underworld powers. The tension hadn't come to a head. It had just been ratcheted up a few notches. The real storm was still to come.

He had survived again, and he would be there to weather it. This was his city.

"Robin," he said. "You should head back to the Batcave and let Alfred take a look at you. See if those nano machines are still in there."

"If you're worried about that, you shouldn't let me go alone," Robin said. It sounded like concern, but it was actually a challenge. Robin was asking if Batman trusted him.

"If the Riddler has let go his control, he has his reasons," Batman said. "He's made his point. He wants to be the new man in charge of Gotham City's underworld, and after this I'm not sure who will challenge him. But I *am* sure that you should get a complete medical screening, so we don't have to worry about him turning you into a puppet again."

Robin flinched.

"Sorry," Batman said.

"Don't be," Robin said. "It's true."

"So get moving. I'd offer you a ride, but I used up my only Batmobile saving you from a missile strike."

Almost before he finished, Robin was gone across the rooftops, heading north toward the secret entrance to the Batcave. Batman flared his cape and dropped from the rooftop, alighting without sound on the sidewalk below.

"Commissioner," he said.

"You know I did what I had to do," Gordon said.

"I know you believe that."

Gordon looked away, up toward the rooftop.

"So... the Riddler?"

"Just a dummy," Batman said. "He was here, though. Somewhere nearby. He watched the whole thing and left us a message."

"What kind of a message?"

"The kind that lets us know he's already planning his next... challenge, I believe is his preferred term."

"Figures. Robin's okay?"

"He is."

Gordon sighed. "Good." After a pause, he lit a cigarette. "I guess we should start planning out what to do next, shouldn't we?"

"That's usually a good start."

"Times like this I'd like to burn Arkham City to the ground. Bulldoze the whole thing into the river and start over again."

Not a terrible idea, Batman thought. But Gotham City was what it was. There was a sickness in the city, maybe in all cities. That was why they needed people like Batman, and like Gordon. They needed people who would never give up.

"You have the Mad Hatter and Mr. Freeze in custody?"

Gordon nodded and flipped his cigarette butt into the missile crater.

"For now," he said. "Deadshot, too. We'll see how long it lasts."

Batman reached out and put a hand on Gordon's shoulder. "We have to keep going," he said. "Someone has to."

"Yeah."

One of the officers securing the area called out to Gordon. He turned to answer a question and felt Batman's hand lift from his shoulder. When he glanced back, Batman was gone.

EPILOGUE

They were talking about him. Everyone in Gotham City was talking about him. Vicki Vale, Jack Ryder, Del Toro, Trask… The Riddler flipped through the channels and saw file photos of himself on each and every one of them.

He tuned through different radio stations. Sports talkers ranted—and talked about the Riddler. Political ranters talked about the Riddler. The quiet cognoscenti on public radio murmured during their fund-raising breaks… talking about the Riddler. There were question marks in bright green on the front pages of every newspaper. He could hardly have asked for more… except for one thing.

Batman had spoken to no one. Neither had Robin.

This bothered the Riddler because he knew both of them had much to say. They wouldn't want to give him credit, even by way of backhanded compliments about the fiendish complications of the challenge rooms or their associated puzzles. He understood that. But surely they wanted to say something! Surely they had to acknowledge that he had driven them to the utmost limits of their strength, their focus, their resolve. He had brought them to the very edge of what they thought was possible, and then… he had let them survive.

Let them.

Batman would even now be thinking that he had solved every puzzle and bested his opponent, but the Riddler saw it differently. He had given Batman more than enough at each turn, drawing him along so Robin too would be drawn along so that he could make his grand gesture with the guardian armor. The whole thing had been a greeting card, a "how-do-you-do," a formal announcement that if the Joker was dead, long live the Riddler.

He knew it had been very close. His gambit had almost tested them too sternly. If Batman had wavered even a little in his decision to go after Killer Croc... or if Killer Croc had fought a little harder than the Riddler had asked... or if, and if, and if. So many things might have gone wrong. In retrospect he realized he was glad Batman had seen the final imago clock face puzzle. It would have been a terrible shame to have devoted all that time, all that energy, all those lives—and then have the whole pageant end before it had properly begun.

When he had left the message for Batman, the Riddler had been angry. He had been, essentially, faking it. Oh, so angry. He had wanted Robin to die, he had wanted to see Batman's favorite blasted into charred and bloody shreds by police missiles, and he had forced himself to write that message and set up the dummy just in case because he could... not... stand the idea of being caught unprepared.

It turned out to have been more than just prudent, it was the best decision he could have made. Why? Because he had, essentially, followed the old show-biz advice: Fake it 'til you make it.

It was much better to have both Batman and Robin survive. He knew that now. If either of them had died, the newspapers and radio stations and television airwaves of Gotham City, the blogs and social media and water-cooler conversations—all would have been about the dead hero. The martyr. He who had fallen to the nefarious bloody mastermind.

With both Batman and Robin alive, the nefarious bloody mastermind was the topic on everyone's lips, at everyone's fingertips.

It was marvelous.

Even if Gotham City police units were combing the wreckage in Wonder City. Even if Deadshot, the Mad Hatter, and Mr. Freeze had been removed from the board. Those were acceptable losses. In coming operations, he would have other partners. Already he had made overtures to some of them, and chosen new spaces that would be well suited to the next generation of puzzled.

Batman and Robin had learned the truth—that the Riddler wasn't a run-of-the-mill thug, or even a run-of-the-mill mastermind.

It was the idiots and savages who thought the world could be ruled through guns and violence. The real power was in words. He had proved it. Riddles, formed of words and forcing the mind to demand the utmost of itself. Riddles! They were the perfect control. You posed them, and then you watched as your opponent grew interested… then focused… then obsessive to the exclusion of all else.

Yes. This the Riddler had accomplished. Even if both Batman and Robin still walked the streets of Gotham City, he had served notice. In short, everything had worked out just as he had wanted. His gambit had paid off.

Because, as of now, everyone in Gotham City was talking about the Riddler as they had once talked about the Joker.

Imago.

It was a new day in Gotham City, a day defined not by a rictus smile but by a question mark. And the question was:

What would he do next?

ACKNOWLEDGMENTS

Thanks to Bob Kane and Bill Finger, for Batman; to Warner Bros. Interactive and Rocksteady, for the excellent Batman: Arkham games that gave this book its particular version of Gotham City; to Steve Saffel, Alice Nightingale, and Julia Lloyd at Titan, for wrangling a project with a lot of moving parts (one of which was me); to my children, Ian, Emma, and Avi, for their enthusiasm and suggestions about who Batman should fight; and to Lindsay, just, you know, because.